Praise for *Fated* by Aly

"Another captivating series from Alyson Noël. *Fated* did an excellent job setting up everything for the next books in the series. . . . I'm really looking forward to seeing where this series goes!"

—*The Story Siren*

"*Fated* reads very well and the descriptions set the scene perfectly. Noël takes the time to set the story up right so it never feels rushed or that any details were missing. . . . I'm glad there's not too long to wait for the sequel."

—*The Reading Date*

"If you're looking for a new series to get stuck into 'The Soul Seekers' is out of this world."

—*Dark Readers*

"I found myself unable to put this book down, completely captivated by the narration and the beautifully crafted world. It was a refreshing YA fantasy with new elements I've never seen before."

—*Love, Literature, Art, and Reason*

"A superb thriller. The key to this absorbing tale is the heroine who makes the Noël mythos seem genuine as she enters the underworld while wondering who she can trust. Filled with twists, this is a winning opening act."

—*Alternative Worlds*

"This book has it all—magick, spookiness, cute boys, a little romance, danger, fun and lighthearted moments, some mystery, and there's even good/evil twins (cute ones, too!). What more can you ask for? I am very intrigued by this new world that Alyson has created, and I cannot wait to read more about Daire and her friends in the future."

—*Once Upon a Twilight*

"Noël has surpassed all of my expectations with a new world filled with magick, trust, and love. . . . It just mesmerizes me how [she] can create a world filled with fast-paced, heartbreaking plots along with awesome characters and such a magical world."

—*Cover Analysis*

"I loved this book. All the characters were beautifully developed including some of the minor characters. . . . I for one had high expectations of this book because of *Evermore*, and *Fated* definitely met those standards."

—*Flamingnet*

"The world-building in *Fated* is fantastic. . . . The plot is amazing and the rich Native American history, along with the supernatural elements of the book, just made it even better. . . . *Fated* is a story of *pure* magic—breathtaking and wonderful, all at once."

—*Kindle and Me*

"*Fated* was absolutely original in its own way! From the vivid descriptions to the spiritual world the author, Alyson Noël, has cleverly created, I was so intrigued and stunned by this book that I can't wait to see where Noël takes this series to because she sure as hell has a winner right here!"

—*Tales of the Inner Book Fanatic*

"This novel is something different than anything I've encountered. *Fated* has a rich mythology, full of spirit animals, spirit journeys, fate, soul-seeking, and of course, good and evil."

—*Thirteen Days Later*

also by alyson noël

echo

alyson noël

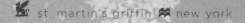 st. martin's griffin ☙ new york

This is a work of fiction. All of the characters, organizations, and events portrayed in this novel are either products of the author's imagination or are used fictitiously.

ECHO. Copyright © 2012 by Alyson Noël, LLC. All rights reserved. Printed in the United States of America. For information, address St. Martin's Press, 175 Fifth Avenue, New York, N.Y. 10010.

www.stmartins.com

Design by Anna Gorovoy

ISBN 978-0-312-66487-9 (hardcover)
ISBN 978-0-312-57566-3 (trade paperback)
ISBN 978-1-250-01578-5 (e-book)

First Edition: November 2012

10   9   8   7   6   5   4   3   2   1

Animal Spirit Guides

Bear

Bear represents strength, introspection, and knowledge. Bear teaches us to look within to awaken our inherent potential. Extremely strong, Bear will react fiercely if its lair is threatened, reminding us to protect our loved ones. Able to live on stored body fat during its winter sleep, the spirit of the Bear shows us how to draw on internal resources for our survival and to remain balanced during change. Active day and night, Bear reflects both the power of the sun and the intuition of the moon, cautioning us to temper our strength with thoughtful reflection.

Hummingbird

Hummingbird represents agility, happiness, and wonder. Hummingbird teaches us to be awake to the present moment and to be flexible and agile with the twists and turns of life. Very playful, Hummingbird reminds us that life is richer if we enjoy what we do and find goodness in any situation. The most skilled flier in the avian world, the spirit of the Hummingbird symbolizes accomplishing what appears impossible. Being the only bird to fly backward, Hummingbird encourages us to explore and extract sweetness from the past without dwelling in it.

Bat

Bat represents transition, rebirth, and initiation. Bat teaches us to face our fears and embrace change. With its ability to navigate perfectly in the dark, Bat instructs us to trust our instincts and discern the hidden meaning of words spoken as well as those left unsaid. As the guardian of the night, the spirit of the Bat encourages us to face down the fears that dwell in the dark corners of our mind and trust our inner guidance. As the only winged mammal, Bat reflects the ability to move to great heights and embrace new beginnings after tumultuous change.

Opossum

Opossum represents appearance, strategy, and flexibility. Opossum teaches us to make use of appearances and to see when others are projecting false impressions. A skilled thespian, Opossum is a master at creating an image that will allow it to achieve its desired outcome. Able to appear dead at will, the spirit of the Opossum reminds us that things are not always as they appear and that there may be hidden meanings. As a marsupial carrying its young in a pouch, Opossum encourages us to look into our own bag of tricks and find our unseen talents and hidden wisdom.

Otter

Otter represents joy, laughter, and sharing. Otter teaches us to let go of our need to control and to seek out our inner child so we can enjoy life and all it offers. Naturally curious, Otter reminds us that everything in the world is interesting if looked at from the right perspective. Fast and agile in the water, the spirit of the Otter shows us how to maneuver through the problems and emotional upheavals of life with ease and fluidity. One of few animals to use tools, Otter encourages us to strike a balance between unadulterated play and skillful provision.

Back of every creation, supporting it like an arch, is faith. Enthusiasm is nothing: it comes and goes. But if one believes, then miracles occur.

—Henry Miller

prophecy

one

Daire

Horse carries us across an expansive terrain with Raven riding high on his neck. His steps measured. Sure. The sound of his hooves meeting the earth resulting in a satisfying *shuffle and crunch* that always makes me feel as though we're getting somewhere. Making progress. Despite the fact that we've been hunting for weeks with no sign of the enemy.

That's what I call them—the enemy. Sometimes I switch it with *intruders* or even *interlopers*. And when it's been an especially long day of hunting that has me feeling punchy, I refer to them as *fiends*.

Though I never call them by their real name.

I never refer to them as Richters.

They may be undead Richters, but they're still Richters, and Paloma warned me to never inform Dace of his dark origins. Claimed there's no need for him to know his existence stems from magick of the blackest kind. And even though being the keeper of such a horrible truth makes me feel dishonest at best and disloyal at worst, I can't help but think that my grandmother's right.

If anyone should tell him, it's Chepi, his mother. But so far she's kept silent.

I loosen my hold on Dace's waist and sigh as I look all around. Taking in a spread of gleaming tall grass—the blades bending and flattening under Horse's forged path—the grove of tall trees that mark the perimeter, providing shelter to birds, monkeys, and the occasional nut-seeking squirrel. My gaze cutting through the fading afternoon light—searching, always searching. But as always, there's no sign of corruption, no sign of their presence.

Maybe the Bone Keeper found them?

I clasp the thought tightly, liking the feel of it. Not wanting to release it no matter how improbable. While I've no doubt the skull-faced, serpent-skirt-wearing, star-eating queen of the Lowerworld is more than capable of capturing them, if not obliterating them, I also know it won't be that easy.

Having made this mess, it's mine to fix.

"It still seems odd." I press my lips to the nape of Dace's neck, the words muffled by his long glossy sheet of dark hair. "You know, this perpetual cycle of night and day. It seems too normal, too ordinary for such an extraordinary place."

I study the late-afternoon shadow that appears to be stalking us. An unlikely, elongated silhouette of a raven with a spindly stem of a neck, and two ridiculously tall people sitting astride a horse with legs so stretched and skinny they hardly look able to support us—the exaggerated shape heralding a night soon to fall.

Though the truth is, what qualifies as *night* in the Lowerworld isn't much more than a trifling fade, falling far short of the heavy, black, star-dusted New Mexico sky I've grown used to. Though, I'm glad for its arrival all the same. Glad to have this day reaching its end.

I rest my chin on Dace's shoulder, picking up where I left off. "Not to mention there's no sign of a sun—so how's it even possible? How can it rise and set when it doesn't exist?"

Dace laughs in response, the sound throaty, deep, and so alluring I inch my body closer until it's pressed hard against his.

Determined to conform to every valley and curve of his back, wanting him to be as aware of me as I am of him.

"Oh, there's a sun." He cricks his neck until he's looking at me. "Leftfoot's seen it." His icy-blue eyes capture mine, reflecting my long dark hair, bright green eyes, and pale skin until I look away, dizzy with the sight of it.

"And you believe him?" I frown, unable to keep the skepticism from creeping into my voice. Convinced it's yet another of the old medicine man's fantastical tales he told Dace as a kid.

"Of course." Dace shrugs. "And if we're lucky, maybe someday we'll see it too."

I rub my lips together and slip a hand under the hem of his sweater. My fingers are chilly, his flesh is warm, and yet he doesn't so much as flinch. Rather he welcomes my touch by urging my palm flat against him.

"The only thing I want to see now is . . ." I try to push my mind back to the job we've set out to do, but it's not long before the thought fades along with my words.

The lure of Dace is too strong, and he must sense my mood because the next thing I know, he's turning Horse around. Nudging him back over the wide, grassy slope, heading toward a favored destination of ours.

I tighten my hold on his waist, tuck my knees into the crook of his. Struggling against the barrage of guilt that always overwhelms me after a long, fruitless hunt. I promised Paloma I'd find them—evict them. Swore I'd run those Richters right out of the Lowerworld before they had a chance to do any damage that would impact the Middle- and Upperworlds too.

I thought it would be easy.

Thought that in a wondrous land of lush foliage and loving spirit animals, those undead freaks would stand out in the very worst way.

Convinced that with Dace and me working in tandem, we'd easily defeat them.

But now I'm no longer sure.

"Not to worry," Dace says, his voice as confident as his words. "Together we'll find them." Then, meeting my skeptical look, he adds, "Haven't you heard? Love conquers all."

Love.

My breath stills, my eyes widen, while any attempt at reply stalls in a throat gone suddenly dry.

He drags on Horse's reins, stopping just shy of the Enchanted Spring, where he helps me to my feet and folds my hands in his. Misreading my silence, he says, "Too soon?"

I clear my throat, longing to tell him that it's not at all too soon. That I knew it the first night he appeared in my dreams—felt it the day I ran into him at the Rabbit Hole—the stream of unconditional love that flowed between us.

Wishing I could just say it—confess how it both terrifies and excites me. How being loved, truly loved, by him is the most exhilarating thing that's ever happened to me.

Longing to explain how whenever I'm with him, it's as though I'm filled with helium—my feet don't quite touch the earth.

We're destined.

Fated.

But now, after weeks of being his girlfriend, this is the very first time the *L* word was mentioned.

Dace cocks his head, shooting me a look so dreamy, I'm sure he's going to say it—those three not-so little words—and I ready myself to utter them too.

But he just turns on his heel and heads for the bubbling hot spring with the fine mist of steam dancing along the surface. Leaving me disappointed that the moment was lost—yet secure in its truth all the same.

We rid ourselves of our clothes until Dace is stripped down to his navy blue trunks, and I'm shivering in the plain black bikini I wear underneath. Merging into the water with Dace just behind me, my heart racing in anticipation as I head for the wide bank of rocks, knowing the hunt is now over—the fun will begin.

I smile shyly. Captured by the sight of his strong, square shoulders, gleaming brown skin, the promise of his hands hanging open and loose by his sides. Wondering if I'll ever get used to this—used to him. So many kisses have passed between us, and yet whenever he's near, whenever we're alone, it feels like the first.

He moves in beside me, the water rising to his chest as our lips press and merge and our breath becomes one. My fingers seeking the sharp angle of his jaw, tracing the shadow of stubble that prickles my skin, as he toys with the strings of my bikini top. Taking great care to avoid the buckskin pouch that hangs from my neck, knowing it holds the source of my power, or one of them anyway—that its contents may only be viewed by Paloma and me.

"Daire . . ." My name is a whisper soon chased by the path of kisses he trails along my neck, over my shoulder, and down farther still, as I close my eyes and inhale a sharp breath. Torn between the lure of his touch, and the memory of a horrible dream that took place in this very spring—in a moment much like this one.

A dream where his brother raided our paradise—stealing Dace's soul along with his life, while all I could do was look on.

"What is it?" Sensing a shift in my mood, he lifts his gaze to meet mine. But I just shake my head and pull him back to me, seeing no reason to share. No reason to wreck the moment by mentioning Cade.

His breath quickens as his lips meet mine once again. And when he lifts me onto his lap, I have the vague sensation of something slimy and foreign passing over my foot.

I lean into the kiss, determined to ignore it, whatever it was. It's a hot spring—an *enchanted* hot spring, but still a hot spring.

It's probably just a leaf or even a fallen flower bud from the canopy of vines that swoop overhead.

I focus on the feel of his lips molding hard to my flesh as I squirm tightly against him. Entwining my legs with his when another slimy object skims past my hip before surfacing beside me with an audible *plop* that's soon followed by another.

And another.

Until the chorus of objects popping to the surface forces us apart. Forces us to blink free of the fog of each other, only to gape in horror as the spring fills with swollen, lifeless, gaping-mouthed fish—their vacant eye sockets staring accusingly.

Before I can so much as scream, Dace swoops me into his arms and hauls me out of the spring. Clasping me tightly to his chest as the two of us stare, breathless and horrified, at a truth that cannot be denied.

The enemy is still out there—alive and well and corrupting the Lowerworld.

And if we don't find them soon, they'll corrupt the Otherworlds too.

two

"Did you tell her?" Dace gestures toward Paloma's blue gate as I slip inside his old beater truck and settle beside him.

"Not yet." I gnaw the inside of my cheek and steer my gaze from his. Hearing his softly muttered *hmmm* as he pulls away from the curb. Recognizing it as Dace-speak for: *I'm not sure I agree with your methods, but I'm sure you have your reasons.*

Dace doesn't judge.

He's so nice, kind, and accepting, he wouldn't even consider it. He's the literal definition of *good*.

The result of a split soul—his is the pure half—the opposite of his twin's. While mine is of the more usual variety—straddling the varying shades of light and dark, swaying toward one or the other depending on the circumstance.

"I was going to," I say, my voice pitching too high to convince, but it's not like it stops me. "But by the time you dropped me off, she was with a client—she's starting to see them again—and by the time she was finished, I was already asleep."

"And this morning?" He looks at me, lips quirking at the side, knowing Paloma's an outspoken advocate for proper nutrition.

Starting each day with a healthy breakfast is pretty much the heart and soul of her manifesto. The only way I could've avoided the subject—avoided her—is by skipping it entirely. Which I did, by staying in my room until the very last minute, then making a mad dash for the door the instant I sensed Dace drive up. Pausing just long enough for her to press one of her freshly baked, organic, blue-corn muffins into my hand as I made for his truck.

There's no graceful way out. I'm guilty as charged. "I got a late start." Sneaking another peek at him, I add, "But, honestly, I guess I just wasn't ready."

He nods, grips the wheel tighter, navigating a series of deeply rutted dirt roads as I stare out the window. Noting how the old adobe homes lining the perimeter no longer sag like they used to. How the cars parked in the yards seem a little less rusted—and the chickens that roam those yards appear a little less emaciated. All of it thanks to Dace and my small triumph in the Lowerworld, when we convinced the Bone Keeper to release all those poor souls the Richters had stolen.

Yet despite our success, the town still doesn't come close to living up to its name of Enchantment. Though it is a little less dismal than it was when I first arrived, and I consider that progress.

"If you want, we can tell her together." Dace looks at me. "I'm scheduled to work after school, but I'm willing to go in late if it'll help."

I shake my head, too choked up by his offer to speak. Dace relies on every penny he earns working at the Rabbit Hole. After paying rent on the tiny apartment he keeps in town, gas and insurance for his two beat-up cars, and the small amount he sends to help Chepi, there's not much left over. There's no way I'll let him take a hit in pay for something I should've done on my own.

"I'll handle it," I say. "Really. Today. After school. Before I head back to the Lowerworld, I'll tell her. Though I've a pretty good feeling she already knows. Paloma knows everything. It's more than an *abuela*'s sixth sense—she's beyond perceptive. I'm sure my silence speaks louder than any words could."

"Still," he says. "Those fish . . ." His voice fades, as his gaze grows cloudy and troubled, his lips pale and grim. "I think I should mention it to Leftfoot. Chepi too. Maybe they can help?"

At the mention of his mother, it's my turn to go grim. Having spent Dace's entire childhood shielding him from the more mystical side of life—only to watch me come to town and drag him headfirst into all the trouble and weirdness this place has to offer, she's not exactly my biggest fan.

Yet, according to Paloma, it was our destiny to meet, just as it's our destiny to work together to keep the Richters contained, and the Lower-, Middle-, and Upperworlds balanced. And once in motion, destiny cannot be stopped.

I'm just about to ask if he might reconsider telling Chepi, when he turns into the school parking lot and brakes beside Auden's ancient wood-paneled station wagon. Lowering the window enough to allow a gust of cold air to rush in, we watch Auden guide Xotichl out of the passenger seat and lead her toward us, her red-tipped cane weaving before her.

"Xotichl claims it'll snow by Christmas, but I say no way." Auden pushes his tousled golden-brown hair from his eyes and grins. "In fact, we're taking bets—you in?"

"You're seriously betting against Xotichl?" I ask, my voice as incredulous as the expression I wear on my face. She may be blind, but she's the most perceptive person I've ever met—next to Paloma, that is.

Auden shrugs, slips an arm around Xotichl's shoulders, and plants a kiss on her cheek. "I should probably know better—betting against her never comes to any good—but I'm pretty convinced she's wrong on this one. It hasn't snowed in Enchantment in years. Not since I was a kid. And there's no sign of that changing anytime soon."

"It certainly feels cold enough to snow." I watch my breath

billowing before me as I pull my gloves from my backpack and slip them onto my hands. Thinking it's time to trade in my usual olive-green army jacket—recently left a bit shredded in places, thanks to an unfortunate encounter with a certain undead Richter—for something a little more weather-resistant. "I thought it snowed pretty much everywhere in these parts?"

"It does," Auden says. "But not here. Not anymore."

"That used to be true, but this year is different," Xotichl says, a sly smile lighting her beautiful, heart-shaped face as her blue/gray eyes flit in the general direction of mine.

"You sensing snow energy?" My arms circle my waist, bracing against the cold as I slip free of the truck and move to join them.

"I'm sensing something." Xotichl's voice is soft and lilting, clearly enjoying her secret.

"So?" Auden looks at me.

I glance between them, not missing a beat, as I say, "Sorry, Auden, but I'm pretty much always going to bet on Xotichl."

Auden shoots me a rueful look and turns to Dace. "And you?"

Dace grasps my hand in solidarity, his icy-blue eyes meeting mine. "And I'm pretty much always going to bet on Daire."

Auden sighs, turning in the direction of Lita, Jacy, and Crickett, who call to us from across the lot. "Still can't stop thinking of them as the Cruel Crew. Guess I need to update our Facebook status to 'friends.'" He shakes his head and grins. "What do you think, should I even bother asking them?"

"Only if you can handle the rejection." Xotichl laughs, as we widen our circle to admit them.

"What's so funny? What'd I miss?" Lita flips her hair over her shoulder, allowing it to fall in gorgeous dark waves down her back, as her eyes—still heavily made-up, though much improved since Jennika's professional makeover—move anxiously among us. She hates to be left out of anything, no matter how trivial.

"A white Christmas. Is it possible? Yay or nay?" Auden gets right to the point.

"Yay. Definitely, voting for yay." Lita claps her gloved hands for emphasis as the others nod their agreement. "It's gonna require a freaking miracle though. Last time it snowed, I was like, six. Then again, it is the season for miracles, right?"

She bounces on the tips of her toes and buries her mitten-covered hands under her armpits in an attempt to ward off the cold. The trill of the bell prompting Auden to kiss Xotichl goodbye so he can head off to rehearse with his band, as the rest of us make for the building, where I pause at my locker long enough to drop off some books and lighten my load.

Lita lingers beside me, watching in annoyed silence as Dace gives me a brief peck on the cheek and promises to find me at break before heading to class. Waiting until he's well out of earshot before she thrusts her hand toward me, and says, "Quick. Take it. Before you make us both late."

I stare at the folded piece of paper pinched between two of her fingers. About to remind her that she's here of her own volition—that her tardiness is completely on her—but squelching it just as quickly. Being friends with Lita means not only learning to ignore half of what she says, but never forgetting that deep down inside, her heart is mostly good.

"Secret Santa," she says, watching as I unfold the note and squint in confusion. Her voice competing with the sound of her boot tapping hard and fast against the tile floor. "Yesterday, when we drew names at lunch, I got Dace. And I figured you'd want to trade since you guys are together and all. Besides, it's way too weird for me to buy him a gift after breaking up with his twin."

I nod in agreement, knowing it'll be a lot easier to come up with something Dace will like that fits within our set twenty-dollar limit, than it would be for the name I'd originally drawn. Then seeing her expectant face, I say, "Though I'm not sure that works—I drew you."

Lita's eyes brighten. Clearly taken with the idea of shopping for herself, she turns on her heel, saying, "No worries. I'll work it out."

She dashes down the hall, the sound of her boots meeting the floor nearly drowning me out when I call, "Hey, Lita—"

She pauses, a look of impatience fixed on her face.

"Speaking of—have you seen or talked to Cade?"

She rolls her eyes, smiling smugly as she says, "Are you kidding? He's gone underground. Totally fallen off the radar. Probably licking his wounds and tending to his poor, broken heart. Had I known how amazing this would feel—how easy it would be to break him—I would've done it years ago!"

She chases the words with a laugh. The sound so light, happy, and self-satisfied, I wish I could buy into it that easily. Wish I could trust in her theory that Cade is simply suffering the unexpected ego blow of being rejected by a pretty girl for the very first time. Then she turns on her heel and flees down the hall, her hair fanning behind her as she steps into class. Leaving me standing before my locker when the second bell rings, officially marking me tardy.

I gaze all around, taking in the quiet, empty hall as I heave my bag onto my shoulder and head back the same way I came. Speeding past the guard's outraged warnings as I tuck into the frigid morning chill and make my way back to Paloma's.

three

Paloma moves about her warm cozy kitchen, pulling her tattered, sky-blue cardigan snugly around one of the crisply ironed housedresses she favors, not the least bit surprised by my sudden return.

With her large brown eyes shining and bright, and her long dark braid with its smattering of silver curving down her back, she seems as normal as ever. Though a closer look reveals movements that are slower—less nimble, more labored. Especially compared to the unmistakable aura of determination and strength she projected the night I first appeared on her doorstep just a few months earlier. Not long after my breakdown in that Moroccan square.

Back when I was haunted by terrifying hallucinations of glowing people and crows—staring down a future in a padded white room.

Paloma saved me. Rescued me from that horrible fate. Only to startle me with a truth so strange I did my best to escape it.

Though, as it turns out, she knew what the doctors didn't.

I wasn't crazy.

Wasn't haunted by delusions.

The crows—the glowing ones—they're all real. I was hardly

the first to undergo the experience. Every Seeker gets the calling—it was simply my turn.

It's the Santos family legacy. The birthright passed from parent to firstborn child for too many generations to count. For the first sixteen years it lies dormant—but once it emerges, the whole world is flipped upside down. And while it's tempting to run, it's better to accept that destiny is not always a choice. For those who try to deny it—it never ends well.

My father, Django, is the perfect example.

His tragic, premature death made Paloma even more determined to save me.

As the last in line, I'm the only one who stands a chance at stopping the Richters. But with my training cut short due to Paloma's recent illness, I'm hardly up for the task.

I watch as she rises onto her toes, her arm straining to retrieve two mugs from the cupboard overhead. Her limbs appearing stilted, stiff. As though the joints need to be oiled and greased in order to move easily again. The sight serving as a bitter reminder of her recent soul loss that claimed all of her magick and nearly her life—one of the many reasons I need to find Cade and his undead ancestors before things continue to deteriorate.

I close my eyes and take a deep breath. Filling my head with competing scents of spiced herbal tea, the sugar-free ginger cookies left to cool on the stovetop, and the smoky allure of the vertically stacked mesquite logs burning in the corner kiva fireplace. Their melodic crackle and pop providing an ironically soothing soundtrack for the bad news to come.

"*Nieta.*" She places a steaming mug of tea before me and claims the opposite seat.

I warm my hands on either side of the mug and blow a few times before venturing a first sip. Then I look at my grandmother and say, "Still no sign of them."

She nods, doing her best to keep her expression stoic, unchanged.

"Actually, that's not entirely true . . ." My voice drifts along with my gaze. Assuring myself I can do this. I have to do this. At the very least, I owe her the truth. I clear my throat and start again. "What I mean is, while we haven't been able to find them, there are definitely signs of their presence . . ." I describe the deluge of dead fish we found in the Enchanted Spring (strategically omitting the bit about why we were there in the first place), but other than fussing with the sleeves of her sweater, she continues to sit quietly, giving nothing away. "And there's absolutely no sign of Cade. He's been absent from school—the Rabbit Hole too. No one's seen him, and I'm no longer sure what to do, where to look."

My eyes search Paloma's, seeking guidance, answers, something. But she merely nods in reply, urging me to finish my tea and enjoy one of her delicious ginger cookies before she pushes away from the table and leads me to my room, where she perches at the edge of my bed and instructs me to open the beautiful, hand-painted trunk she left for me the night she fell ill.

I unlatch the lock and peer at the contents. My heart racing in anticipation of whatever bit of magick she's willing to share. It's been weeks since she taught me to crawl with the lizards and soar with the birds—merging my energy with theirs until I'd claimed their experience for my own. And the truth is, I've missed our lessons. Missed our talks and the time we spent together.

Other than cooking my meals and looking after me (despite my protests that there's really no need, that thanks to my mom and my nomadic existence, I've been looking after myself since I was a kid), the last few weeks she's spent mostly resting. And despite Leftfoot's assurances that she'd soon recover, up until now, I had no good reason to believe him.

Paloma's willingness to resume my training as a Seeker is the first solid sign that she might really be on the mend. And while there's no doubt things will never return to the way they once were, there's no reason we can't move forward from where we are now.

"The blanket." She gestures toward the intricate handwoven blanket folded tightly at the bottom. "Spread it out before you, and place each object upon it."

I do as she says. Pairing the black-and-white hand-painted rawhide rattle with the drum bearing a picture of a purple-eyed raven. Then I start a new row reserved for the feathers. Each of them bearing a tag identifying their individual uses—the swan feather for transformative powers, a raven feather for magickal powers, and an eagle feather for sending prayers. And just below that, I place the pendulum with the small chunk of amethyst attached to its end. The trunk now emptied of everything but the crisp, white note from Paloma, her careful script promising to one day show me the magick that lives inside all of these tools—a day I was beginning to fear wouldn't come.

I lift the long black feather and wave it before me. Thinking it looks a lot like the one I wear in my pouch—only bigger—much bigger.

"As your spirit animal, Raven is always prepared to guide you. Have you called on him, *nieta*?"

"All the time." I shrug, my voice as glum as my face. "But lately it seems like he does way more *following* than *guiding*. He just sits on Horse's neck, like he's merely in it for the ride, while Dace and I wander around, pretty much aimlessly."

"And Horse?" Her spine straightens as her eyes narrow on mine.

"Same thing. If Dace didn't push him, he'd spend all his time grazing. It's like, the more we need them, the lazier they get, until they just barely cooperate. It seems to get worse every day."

Paloma's face pales, as her eyes flash in alarm. The effect lasting only a moment before she's back to her usual calm, serene self—determined to hide the worries that plague her.

But now that I've seen it, I've no intention of letting it pass.

If Paloma's ready to resume my training, then she needs to be honest and stop with the secret keeping. If it's true what she says, that as a Seeker I'm the only hope left, then sheltering me from the facts will only end up endangering everyone else.

"Paloma," I say in a voice filled with urgency. "I need you to be straight with me. I need you to tell me the truth no matter how ugly. When you told me that a Seeker must learn to see in the dark, relying on what she knows in her heart—I assumed you were speaking metaphorically. But lately I'm starting to feel like Dace and I really are just floundering around in the dark, and it would help us a lot if you could shed a little light. Truly, *abuela*, I'm ready. There's no need to protect me."

She lifts her chin and takes a deep breath. Her delicate fingers smoothing the creases of her crisp cotton dress. "From what you say, it seems Raven has been corrupted. Horse too. And while they're not yet working against you, they're not quite working for you either. All of which means we'll have to rely on other sources for knowledge and guidance until we can evict those Richters from the Lowerworld and return the balance to normal." She sighs softly, shaking her head as she adds, "I was afraid this might happen. And trust me, *nieta*, the dead fish are just the beginning. If we don't stop them soon, it won't be long before the effects are felt in the Middle- and Upperworlds too. Each world is dependent upon the other. When one is corrupted, the others fall into chaos, which is precisely what Cade wants. When the spirit animals are no longer able to guide and protect us, it will allow him free rein to rule as he pleases."

My fingers instinctively reach for the soft buckskin pouch I wear at my neck. Seeking the shape of the small stone raven, and the black raven feather that marked the beginning and end of my vision quest. Objects I once considered sacred, the main source of my power, but now I'm no longer sure. Like my guide, Raven, have they been corrupted too?

"Should I not wear this anymore?" I ask, surprised by the panic that creeps into my voice. I've grown so accustomed to wearing the pouch that I can't bear the thought of being without it.

Paloma motions toward the blanket. "Why don't we consult the pendulum?" She joins me on the floor. The two of us sitting side by side with our legs crossed, knees nearly touching, as I dangle the pendulum by the tip of my finger until it stills on its own. "The pendulum serves as a very powerful divination tool. But don't be fooled, *nieta*. While it's easy to think of it as magick, the answers it provides come from a place deep inside you."

I squint, not sure I understood.

"The pendulum simply tunes in to your own higher consciousness and retrieves the answers you already know but that you may not have immediate access to."

"So, you're saying it sees through the dark to find what I already know in my heart?"

"Exactly." She meets my grin with one of her own, the soft laugh that follows instantly brightening the room. "Oftentimes, we get so bogged down in choices and indecision that we can no longer access the truth that lives within us. That's where the pendulum comes in. It helps you break through the clutter to get to the heart of the matter."

"So, how do we start?" I stare at the crystal, eager to get going on the long list of questions crowding my head.

"First, I want you to close your eyes and imagine yourself surrounded by light."

I stay as I am, lips screwed to the side, doubting the validity of that.

"Whenever you engage in any sort of divining activity, even if you are merely divining the answers within you, you need to protect yourself."

"Protect myself from what exactly?" I frown, unsure where she's going with this.

"From dark entities. Lower spirit forms." She locks eyes with me. "You may not see them, but they're always lurking, ever-present. They can be found in every dimension of the Middle-world, and they thrive off the energy of others. Which is why you must always take great care to guard against them, and never allow them the chance to latch onto you. They are tricksters. They are capable of causing great harm and will use any opening you give them. So let's not give them one, okay?"

That's all I need to snap my eyes shut and envision myself surrounded by a brilliant white nimbus of light.

"Good." Her voice is soft, pleased. "Now we need to determine which direction indicates a *no* answer, and which way indicates a *yes*. So, we'll start by posing a few simple questions, ones in which we already know the answer, and see how it responds."

I lower my gaze, staring intently at the small amethyst stone that's carved into a point at its tip. Trying to keep my voice serious, I say, "Is my name Daire Lyons-Santos?" Watching in amazement as the pendulum begins to sway on its own. At first moving in a slow back-and-forth motion, though it's not long before it begins to form a clockwise circle, despite the fact that my fingers haven't moved.

"I think it's safe to assume that clockwise means yes." I glance at Paloma who nods in agreement.

"The pendulum should slow on its own, and once it does, you may bring it to a complete stop before venturing a question that you know will result in a *no* response."

I focus on the pendulum. So caught up in the excitement of training with Paloma again—of accessing the magick that lies at my fingertips—I decide to ask it a question that will not only result in a resounding *no* but that already has me laughing when I say, "Pendulum, tell me—am I in love with Cade Richter?"

I press my lips together, trying to keep from grinning, but it's no use. It's too ridiculous to contemplate. Besides, Paloma told me to ask a question that will result in an unequivocal *no*, and the question of me loving Cade definitely fits.

I stare at the pendulum, my mirth quickly turning to confusion when it starts to swing clockwise again. First looping slowly, then swiftly picking up the pace, until that amethyst stone is whirling at a dizzying speed.

Desperate to stop it, I grasp it hard in my palm. Squeezing so hard, its sharp, pointy tip slices the pad of my finger, eliciting a thin stream of blood. "Clearly it's not working," I say, my voice lacking the confidence of my words. "Either that, or it has no sense of humor and it's out to teach me a lesson—"

My rant interrupted by Paloma saying, "The pendulum has only one purpose—to reveal the truth that lives inside you. That is all, *nieta*."

I frown, not one bit amused.

"You must never forget that Dace and Cade are a split soul, which makes them two halves of a whole." Her voice is as gentle as the hand she's placed on my knee.

"Yeah, two *very different* halves," I snap, the words as sharp and bitter as I currently feel. "Dace is good—Cade is evil. Dace I . . ." I pause, not quite ready to admit to the *L* word just yet, even though Paloma's the one who told me we were destined for each other. Starting again when I say, "Dace I care deeply about— Cade I hate."

I drop the pendulum onto the blanket, and wipe my finger down the leg of my jeans, leaving a light trail of red. Then I reach for the row of feathers, choosing the eagle, the one for sending prayers, eager to move on with the lesson.

"So, how does this work?" I wave it before me. Wanting to move past the pendulum debacle and staring in dismay when Paloma takes it from me and forces the pendulum back in my hand.

"You must try again, *nieta*. Ask another question this time— one that will definitely result in a *no*.

"I already did! What's the point?" I cry, instantly regretting the harsh tone—but, seriously, what is she getting at? "Trust me when I say that me loving Cade is about as ridiculous as it gets.

It's revolting. Grotesque. Completely unfathomable. It's what nightmares are made of. It's my own personal version of hell. It's the definition of *no!*"

I shake my head and scowl. Muttering a stream of angry words under my breath as Paloma sits patiently beside me, waiting for me to get back to the task. But there's no way. I'm too tightly wound. Too inflamed by her reaction—choosing to believe some stupid pendulum over what I know to be true.

We sit like that for a while—Paloma in silence, me an angry, fuming wreck. And then it hits me—she's holding something back.

"What are you not telling me?" I eye her with suspicion. "What's going on here—what's this really about?"

I rise to my feet, knees shaking so badly I fight to regain my balance. "Tell me!" I insist, the words hissed between clenched teeth. "Just say it, whatever it is. Because I promise you, whatever I'm thinking is way worse than the truth could ever reveal itself to be."

She reaches for my hand, grasping it tightly in hers and pulling me back down beside her. "No, *nieta*," she says, her voice so troubled it only makes me feel worse. "If I've learned nothing else, it's that here in Enchantment, the truth is often far worse than anything the mind is able to conjure."

four

I try it again.

And again.

And even a few more times after that—and the result never differs.

Every time I ask the pendulum a question that should result in an undeniable *no*, it responds as it should by spinning in a counterclockwise direction. And yet every time I repeat the one about me loving Cade, it spins the opposite way.

The ritual leaving me so red-faced and frustrated, I can't help but blurt, "Paloma—what the heck?" I scowl, having no idea what this could possibly mean, why the pendulum insists on torturing me.

And then I remember something the Bone Keeper said.

Something about Dace being the Echo.

Which mirrored Cade's taunt the last time I saw him:

You've been working for me since the day you started having those dreams about my brother . . . you know, the Echo?

An echo is a repetition.

A reflection.

A figure from Greek mythology who pined for Narcissus until all that was left was her voice.

How could that possibly relate to Dace?

I search Paloma's face, in need of some answers.

"They are connected, *nieta*. It is all that I know. As for how deep that connection goes is for you to discover. But clearly it is deep enough for the pendulum to confuse the two."

"It's not possible!" I say. "They're *nothing* alike!"

But Paloma just nods and places her hand over mine. "My client will be here soon," she says. "Let's move on to the feathers while there's still time."

When Paloma's client arrives, I start to head out. But when I pass a window on my way and get a glimpse of a dark and ominous sky, I make a quick U-turn and head for my room where I stand before my closet, weighing my options.

As much as I love the old army jacket I always wear—given to me by the wardrobe stylist on a hit movie Jennika worked on a few years ago—it's no match for a New Mexico winter. I need something heavier, thicker, something that might actually defend against the harsh wintry chill.

I stare at my meager belongings, consisting of jeans, tank tops, slouchy boots, and not much else. The warmest thing I own being the black V-neck sweater I picked up in a duty-free store in the Charles de Gaulle Airport on my way to Morocco, so I'd have something cozy to wear on the plane.

If nothing else, living life out of a suitcase has taught me to keep my belongings pared to a minimum. Books, clothes, shoes, jewelry—anything that no longer serves me is either given away or left behind. And since my last stop was LA, I'm a little deficient when it comes to winter wear.

I drum my fingers against my hip, screw my mouth to the side, and stare as though I'm expecting something new to appear.

Wondering if I could maybe borrow something from Paloma until I can get to a decent clothing store, though doubting she has anything that would work. No matter how low the temperature dips, I've yet to see her wear anything heavier than a cotton housedress and cardigan.

I shift my gaze higher and scrutinize the still unexplored brown cardboard box on the closet's top shelf. While I've lived in this room for the past several months, I still have a hard time thinking of it as mine. I guess I'm not used to claiming a space, any space.

Ever since I was a kid, all of my homes have been temporary at best. And despite Paloma giving me free rein to do whatever it takes to make it my own, the only signs of my existence are the few items of clothing occupying the closet, the small stash of socks and underwear in the tall chest of drawers, and the laptop I've set up on the old wooden desk—all of which can easily fit into a duffle bag when it's time to move on.

This room is still very much Django's, and that's how I like it. Makes me feel close to my father in a way I've never experienced until now.

There's a picture of him in a pretty silver frame that sits on the dresser—taken when he was sixteen, same age as me. And his initials are carved into the desk in the space next to my computer— the jagged D.S. half the size of my hand. Even the dream catcher that hangs above the windowsill belongs to him, so I guess I always assumed the contents in the box on the top shelf belonged to him too. And up until now, I didn't feel I had the right to go snooping.

Although my five-foot-six-inch frame isn't exactly what I'd call short, the shelf is still just a little too high for me to grab hold of the box without risking it crashing onto my head. I consider dragging the elaborately painted trunk that holds my Seeker tools over to the closet so I can climb on top and retrieve the box, but then I think better.

Deciding to use some of the magick I've been practicing, the telekinesis I've been working to hone, I focus hard on the box. Employing Paloma's advice to *think from the end*, claiming it's magick's second most important ingredient, coming just after *intent*.

"The universe will work out the details," she'd said. *"The most important thing you can do is to state your intention, then envision the result as though it's already done."*

So instead of imaging the box lifting from the shelf and drifting lightly to the floor as I used to, I imagine it already secured at my feet. Only to watch as it launches itself from the shelf and crashes hard to the ground. Guess I still have a few telekinetic kinks to work out.

I glance toward the door, hoping Paloma didn't hear the commotion and won't choose to investigate. Then I drop beside the old box and open the flaps. Instantly overcome by a whiff of dust, must, and a deeper earthier aroma of spice, mesquite, and a few other unnamed scents I've come to associate with this place.

I riffle through the contents. Skimming past an old hand-knit sweater I reject at first sight, an old flannel shirt worn nearly to death, a pile of yellowing T-shirts that used to be white . . . until I come across a black down jacket that might be a bit on the big side but will definitely serve the purpose I need.

About to close the box back up and return it to its place, I notice a pile of papers lining the bottom and decide to go through those too. Finding an old report card of Django's, with A's in Spanish and PE, a B+ in English, and C's in both history and science, I rock back on my heels and smooth my fingers across the crinkled page. Shuttering my eyes as I try to picture how he was back then—a good-looking guy with a nose like mine—an average student headed for a-not-so average destiny he just couldn't face.

I set the report card aside and dig a little deeper. Feeling oddly guilty for prying but equally eager for anything I can get, I read everything. More report cards, class schedules, a folded-up note from a girl named Maria, who was obviously into him if the string of small hearts lining the edges are anything to go by. Eventually coming to the note he left for Paloma the day he ran away, having no idea his journey would be both tragic and short. That not long after arriving in California, he'd fall hard for my mom and impregnate her, only to end up decapitated on a busy LA freeway well before she could break the news.

I take a deep breath, unable to keep my hands from shaking when I read:

Mama,

By the time you read this, I will be well on my way, and though you'll be tempted to come after me, I'm begging you to please let me be.

I'm sorry for any disappointment and pain that I've caused. It was never my intention to hurt you. I am lucky to have such a kind, loving, and supportive mother, and I hope you'll understand that my leaving has nothing to do with you as a person.

This place is closing in on me. I can't take it anymore. I need to get far away—go to a place where nobody knows me.

Where the visions can't find me.

You speak of destiny and fate—but I believe in free will. The destiny I choose is one that happens in a place far from here.

I'll be in touch when I settle.

Love,
Your Django

I read the note again.

And then again.

And after reading it so many times I've lost count, I fold it up neatly, slip it back toward the bottom, and return the box to its place.

Then I drag on my dad's old down jacket and explore all the pockets. Inching to the edge of each seam, stopping when I discover something small and smooth, with a surprising amount of heft to it.

I uncurl my fingers, revealing a small stone replica of a bear that's etched in the same style as the raven I wear in my pouch. The one that was mystically carved following my very first visit to the Lowerworld, when I traveled on a soul journey aided by Paloma's tea. And I can't help but wonder if this is how Bear came to him too.

I always assumed that Django, haunted by the horrific visions that mark the start of every Seeker's calling, left long before Paloma could share the ritual with him—but now I'm no longer sure.

Still, I'm happy to have a token from my dad, no matter how small. So I add it to my collection of talismans, remembering what Paloma said just after the pendulum confirmed that I should continue wearing the pouch: *You shouldn't abandon the spirit animals when it wasn't their choice to abandon you.*

I make my way to the yard, forging a path past the various gardens. One for the herbs Paloma uses in her work as a healer, one for the organic fruits and vegetables she uses to prepare all our meals. Pausing to survey the plot of land reserved for her hybrid experiments—where strange, misshapen plants sprout from the earth, perpetually in bloom no matter the season—before continuing past the fountain and the small stone bench, ultimately stopping at Kachina's stall.

When I spot my adopted cat napping in the corner, I take

great care to quiet my approach. Still, the second he senses my presence, his head pops up, his ears perk high, he springs to his feet, and he's off like a shot—hopping the nearby fence and disappearing into the neighbor's yard.

"Looks like Cat still hates me." I nuzzle Kachina's whiskers, running my palm over her perfectly striped brown and white mane as she nickers softly in greeting. "Think you could put in a good word for me? Remind him that I'm the one who feeds him—I'm the one who rescued him?"

Kachina nudges her nose against my side, prodding me toward the door of the stall—a sure sign she wants me to bust her loose so we can go for a ride. And while I like the idea as much as she does, I can't help but think about all the other things I should be doing instead.

Like heading back to school so my tardy doesn't turn into a truancy.

Or, more important—heading back to the Lowerworld so I can get an early start on Richter hunting.

Before I can decide either way, my phone vibrates with a text from Dace that reads:

Missed you at break—you okay?

I hesitate. Torn between an overwhelming need to see him, and knowing that if I even so much as hint that I'm thinking of going hunting, he'll not just skip school but probably work too, in order to help, and I can't let him do that. If he has any hope of going to college, he needs to maintain his GPA just as much as he needs to boost his paycheck.

So I type the reply:

No worries. All is well. I'm with Paloma. Drop by tonight after work?

I chew my bottom lip as I wait for his reply. Feeling guilty about the lie—a white lie but still a lie—while assuring myself it had to be done.

As soon as he answers, agreeing to meet up with me later, I toss a bridle onto Kachina, hop onto her back, and nudge her out of the stall. Leading her onto the rutted dirt road, with one destination in mind.

five

Paloma once told me that Enchantment is a place of many vortexes. She said it contains a number of portals that allow access to
the Otherworlds and that someday soon I'd learn to distinguish
them all.

But despite her claims, so far I've only found three. One in the
cave where I endured my vision quest, one on the reservation
where Dace was raised, and one inside the lowest level of the
Rabbit Hole.

With the Rabbit Hole vortex not only on enemy territory, but
also well guarded by demons, and the cave many miles away, I
steer Kachina toward the reservation instead. It's not often I get a
free pass to skip school, so I may as well make the most of it and
choose the closer portal.

We make our way along a series of dirt roads, Kachina keeping
to a pace that's slow and steady until we reach an open meadow. I
lean into her neck and give her free rein. Enjoying the feel of her
racing beneath me, the wind lashing hard at my cheeks, wishing I
could always feel as light, and free, and unburdened as this.

When we reach native land, Kachina slackens her gait. Picking her way toward the grove of twisted juniper trees—their

branches grossly distorted from the constant whirl of energy that marks the entrance to invisible worlds—as I scan the area for signs of the elders, Leftfoot or Chay—both of whom I wouldn't mind seeing—and Chepi—whom I hope to avoid. But the reservation is quiet today, so I slide off her back, run a hand over her forelock, and say, "Don't bother waiting, I'll either call if I need you or find my way back." She snorts, nostrils flaring as she shoots me a dubious look. Prompting me to give her a light pat on the rump and repeat my instructions. "Trust me," I tell her. "You do not want to follow. The journey's unpleasant. Now go!"

She whinnies in reply and swiftly trots away, as I take a good look around to ensure no one's watching, step between the trees, and slip deep into the earth.

I speed through the dirt. Traveling through the earth's core with my palms pressed hard to my face in an effort to guard against the snarl of tree roots, worms, and all the other slick and slimy things that thrive in the dark. Unlike my first few journeys to the Lowerworld, I no longer fight it. Having finally learned that the less I resist, the quicker I'll be delivered to wherever I'm destined to be.

Once I'm free of the tunnel, I skid to a stop. My heels wedged into the ground as I slowly lower my hands and adjust to the light. Not the least bit surprised to find I've landed on a vast white-sand beach (it's quickly becoming one of my more consistent deposit spots) and that Raven is not here to meet me. Apparently, Paloma was right when she said he's no longer working for me. But the question remains: Is he working against me?

I wipe the dirt from my clothes and make for the shore. On the lookout for spinning dolphins, breaching whales, and all the other creatures I've grown used to seeing. But while the sea appears as calm and inviting as ever—or at least it does from a distance—there's no sign of activity, no sign of life. Even the usual schools of small silver fish are nowhere to be seen. The water is darker, murkier, and when I dip a finger inside, it comes out coated with a greasy film of dark sludgy ick.

I wipe the gunk on my jeans, watching in horror when that same finger swells and flares into a bright angry red. The water's polluted—grossly so. Leaving no doubt it's the same contamina tion that's responsible for killing those fish we found in the hot spring, and that it's Cade Richter's doing.

All it takes is a quick glance all around to leave me feeling small, overwhelmed, and so ill matched against the task at hand, even I'm betting against me.

Without Raven's guidance, without Dace beside me, I've no idea where to begin. The Lowerworld is an immense place of many dimensions and no conceivable end. It's a haystack-meet-needle situation.

I grab hold of my soft buckskin pouch and wrap my fingers around it. Hoping the pendulum was right, that I really should continue to wear it in good faith—I send a silent plea for help. Appealing to the elements, my ancestral spirits—whoever and whatever might be willing to guide me. Then I tuck the pouch back in place and start walking with no real direction in mind, but determined to cover as much ground as I can.

Though I don't actually see any undead Richters, their presence can be sensed in the lack of chirping birds, the absence of animals at play. Even Wind, my guiding element, usually so willing to serve, is felt only by its lack—resulting in the grim weighted silence that surrounds me. While the terrain grows increasingly bleak with each passing step.

The lawns normally so luxurious and verdant are now a muddied patchwork of browns. The grove of tall trees normally cloaked with a thick blanket of leaves are reduced to mere skeletons of their former selves. Their trunks scorched and hollowed, the remaining foliage parched and split at the edges. It's the opposite of everything I've come to expect.

I consider a trip to the Bone Keeper, but nix the idea just as quickly. She may hold a certain insight into Dace and my destiny, she may know just exactly what the Echo is, but she's also made it clear she'd much rather mock than help. Besides, I doubt she'd be the least bit disturbed by the way this place has transformed. Bones are her game, and death is the vehicle that brings them to her.

I continue walking, journeying for what feels like forever. Well past the point when my feet are blistered and sore, my legs shaky and fatigued.

Continuing until I'm sure I can't take it anymore—and then I go on some more.

Stopping only when I come across a large, smooth boulder, where I plop myself down and bury my face in my hands. Wondering what to do next. Wondering how I'll ever succeed when all I seem to do is wander in circles with no hint of progress.

So immersed in despair, I nearly miss the *swoosh* of wings flapping overhead.

Raven.

My Raven.

His purple eyes wildly glimmering as he flies a perfect circle above me.

I frown, unsure if I should trust him. There's a good chance he's working for the enemy . . . then again, I did ask for help, and maybe he's simply answering the call?

He lands right beside me, purple eyes glimmering as he drops a flower bud onto my lap and gives it an insistent nudge with the curved tip of his beak.

I grab it by the stem, examining the satiny petals, trying to remember where I've seen this particular bloom, when Raven lowers his head and pecks hard at my leg.

I scowl. Push him away with my knee. Watching as he spans his wings wide and lifts into flight—circling insistently over my head until I heave a deep breath and give in. Convincing myself that even if he is leading me into some kind of trap, it's still better than wandering aimlessly. If I end up in the Richters' lair, at least it'll give me something to do—something to work with. Anything is better than this.

The thought vanishing the instant I realize he's led me to the Enchanted Hot Spring where Dace stands at its edge. Poking deep into the water with a long sharp branch he's plucked from the canopy of blooming vines that swoop overhead.

Vines that bear the same type of flower Raven dropped in my lap.

"Why aren't you at work?" I ask, taking a moment to appreciate the long lean line of his back.

He turns, eyeing me slowly when he replies, "Why'd you ditch school?"

My eyes dart toward Raven, now comfortably perched on Horse's neck, then I head for the place where Dace stands. "Guess this seemed more important." I reach for his hand, lace my fingers with his.

"Ditto." He grins, his icy-blue gaze fixed on mine. Though it's only a moment later when he's frowning at the spring once again.

"More fish?" I ask. "Or, God forbid, something worse?"

He shakes his head and prods the stick into the water once more. Swishing it around a few times before he tosses it aside and says, "Not worse, just weird. From what I can tell, it's perfectly clear."

"But that's a good thing, right?" I crane my neck to get a better look. Confirming that the water is indeed back to the way I first encountered it—bubbling, enticing, and free of dead, bloated fish. But one look at Dace tells me he remains unconvinced.

"There's no doubt they've gone—but where did they go?" he asks.

I screw my mouth to the side and stare hard at the spring. Noticing for the first time how everything about this place appears brighter, lusher, than all the other times we were here. The vines are springier—their blooms fatter. Even the water seems extra sparkly. The bubbles skimming the surface resembling delicate crystal orbs that float 'til they pop and then reform again.

"It's like it's been restored." I blink, stare, blink again— unwilling to trust what I see. Glancing at Raven and wondering if he's maybe not nearly as corrupted as I thought.

Is there a small part of him that's still on my side?

Is he trying to show me that things are not as bad as I think?

"It's like it never happened—like it was never contaminated. Unlike the rest of this place."

Dace looks at me, alerted by the edge in my tone. "I came straight here. Horse led me. I haven't had a chance to explore. Is it bad?"

I nod. Hoping my look can convey what words can't. I'm exhausted. My feet hurt. My finger is still a bright angry red, only now it's swollen to twice its normal size. I study the spring once again, longing to take a quick dip. Surely a short break will rejuvenate me enough to go hunting again?

I kneel beside the water, about to immerse my finger, when Dace stoops beside me, grasps my hand, and says, "What happened?"

"Nothing." I jerk free of his grip. "Really. It was just a small cut, but then I dipped it into the ocean and it came out like this. The sea is polluted. It's awful. You gotta see it to believe it. But if this place truly is enchanted, if it truly is exempt from all the other contamination around here, if it really can heal itself, well, then it should also be able to heal me too, right?"

Dace meets my gaze, not the least bit convinced.

"Look," I say, unwilling to argue. "I'll either keep a finger or lose a finger. But either way, I have to try."

Then before he can stop me, I plunge my hand in. And the relief I experience is so overwhelming, it's not long before the rest of me plunges in too.

six

I submerge myself underwater—wonderful, warm, silky, soft water. Holding my breath for as long as I can, intensely aware of my cells being rejuvenated, revived. The knots in my shoulders unraveling, while the seeping blisters on my feet shrivel and close, leaving the skin smooth and healed, bearing no trace of injury.

My transformation complete, I spring to the surface—resurrected, reborn. Finding Dace right beside me, his icy-blue eyes glittering, his smile beckoning bright as a beacon, guiding me into his arms.

He covers my mouth with his—our lips merging, colliding, tasting, exploring—while our tongues swirl and dance—finding and losing each other again and again. Our bodies melting, conforming, as his hands seek my flesh, causing ripples of pleasure wherever they pass. Drawing away ever so slightly, he presses his forehead flush against mine. His gaze blunted by a yearning matched by my own.

I hasten my breath and press toward him, eager to claim his kiss once again. But Dace holds me firmly in place, voice thick

with meaning, as he says, "Daire—I love you." His lids narrowing, jaw tensing, as he studies my face, waits for me to respond.

Those same features softening in relief when I say, "And I love
you." Surprised by the way the words just rolled off my tongue. It
was so much easier than I imagined. The big, sturdy wall I've
spent a lifetime building, in an effort to shield myself from moments like this, came crashing down with one little push.

Though it's only a second later when my heart fills with
panic—feeling vulnerable, exposed. Unused to baring itself after
a lifetime spent frozen in ice, placed under quarantine, and neatly
tucked away in a corner no one could reach.

If I know one thing for sure, it's that nothing lasts forever. Re-
lationships end, good-byes must be said, and that's the part I've
never been any good at. It's always been easier just to skip out of
town, board the next flight, and never look back.

I take a deep breath. Fight to steady myself. Forced to acknowledge that the words have been spoken, the walls have crumbled,
and there's no way to reverse it—no way to return to that safe,
lonely place I called home.

But when I meet his gaze once again, seeing the way it brims
with reverence and love, my heart swells until the panic's edged
out. Replaced by the pure joyful giddiness of breaking free of my
cage.

I say the words again.

And then again.

And then a few more times after that.

My lips moving along the edge of his jaw, slipping down to
the hollow of his neck, where I seal the words in his flesh.

Each declaration leaving me increasingly strengthened. Finally
understanding what they mean when they say that love heals—
empowers—that love conquers all.

I shift until I'm sitting astride him. Running my palms up a
chest slick as silk, I cup my hands to his shoulders. My gaze deep-

ening, my intentions laid bare. The declaration was just the beginning—the act will now follow.

"Are you sure?" he asks, reading the look on my face.

I nod. I've never felt surer. Of anything. Ever.

He runs a finger down my cheek, his touch tender and sweet, as he moves to kiss me again. His lips falling lightly upon mine, when something odd and slick skims past my shin and plops to the surface beside me.

I gasp. Already bolting from the spring, scolding myself that I should've known better—that it was too good to be true—when Dace stops me and pulls me back to his lap. Displaying the object now cupped in his hand—an overripe bloom that must've fallen from the canopy of vines overhead.

He smiles softly, lifts me out of the water, and deposits me on a soft patch of grass where he lies down beside me. Studying me with a look so conflicted—so full of longing, wonder, and nervous anticipation—I can't help but draw him to me, eager to assure him that this is exactly where we're both meant to be.

His lips find mine, but just as the kiss grows deeper, more heated, he pulls away, saying, "I hope you don't think this is weird, but—I've only done this one other time."

"Anyone I know?" I avert my gaze, biting back a small stab of jealousy.

Please don't let it be Lita. Or Jacy. Or Crickett. Or Xotichl. Or anyone else I've befriended . . .

"No," he murmurs, gaze far away. "No one I know anymore."

I weave my fingers into the soft silken strands of his long, glossy hair, trying to temper my relief. I say, "Well, that's still one more time than me." My eyes meet his, fielding his curious look when I add, "Despite what you may have heard about my wild Hollywood past." I know what he's thinking: That someone who's lived the kind of life I have, who's hooked up with someone as presumably hot as Vane Wick, must've been here at least once, and I'm quick to refute it. "Seriously, I never quite got to this point. Guess I was waiting for you."

He angles closer, not saying a word. His face clouded with emotion as he traces a finger along the strap of my buckskin pouch, circling the place where it rests just over my heart.

Leaving me so dizzy with his touch, I can't help but whisper, "Though I have seen enough movies to know this is how it starts . . ."

My fingers inch lower, peeling his briefs from his hips, as he rids me of my underthings. Absorbed by the sheer glorious sight of him, I allow my hands to roam the curve of his shoulders, the taut muscles of his chest, the lean valley of his abdomen. My skin sliding deliciously against his when he pulls me tightly to him, trails his lips over my flesh, and eases his body into mine.

I gasp—stunned by a sharp stab of pain that's soon eased by his hips pressing and circling, as his heart pulses wildly. And it's not long before I lose myself in sensation. In the feel of him—the magick of him—the euphoria of him.

All of him.

Surrendering to the wave of splendor rolling through me—leaving me untethered—released. Floating free of my body. Soaring beside him.

Two souls ascending at dizzying speed—swirling through constellations—skimming across a bright pool of stars.

The words unspoken but true all the same: This is the moment that joins us—unites as—for all of eternity.

His gaze never once leaving mine, he cradles my face in his hands and guides me back toward the earth where he draws me into his arms and nestles his body around me. His face buried in my hair, he breathes deeply, slowly, seeking rhythm with mine, as I fight to hang on to the moment. Desperate to fend off all thoughts of the real world but not coming close to succeeding, I say, "I refuse to feel guilty."

Dace lifts himself onto his elbow and stares down at me, unsure of my meaning.

"For this." I roll over to face him, flattening my palm against his taut bare chest, aware of his heart beating against it. "I refuse to feel guilty for us—for pausing the hunt to be with you." My gaze burns on his, wanting so badly for the words to be true. But with so much chaos occurring around us, it's a pretty tough sale. Still, I go on to add, "I've been down here for hours. I was an exhausted wreck when Raven led me to you. And look, the spring really did heal me." I wiggle my finger as proof, smiling when he latches onto it, curls his around it.

"Daire, you don't have to make excuses," he says. "Love is the highest energy of all. It needs no forgiveness, no apology."

"I like when you say it." I grin. "In fact, I was wondering when you'd get around to it."

He laughs, tossing his head back and exposing a glorious column of neck. "That's a pretty big declaration to put out there, you know. Guess I wanted to be sure there was a chance it might be reciprocated."

I study him closely. Amused he couldn't see what I thought was so clear. "Did you seriously doubt me?" I slide my leg across his, reveling in the deliciousness of his skin.

He smiles softly, focusing his gaze on the vines overhead. He summons a glorious red bloom to his fingers and tucks it into my hair. "You can be a little guarded sometimes—a little tough to read." He shrugs.

"Oh yeah?" I grin. "Then tell me, Dace Whitefeather, how would you read *this*?" I pull him back to me.

He replies with a kiss.

seven

"I'm glad this place was spared." I pull my sweater back over my head, as Dace pulls on his jeans. "It really is enchanted, able to heal itself—just like it healed me."

I look to Dace for confirmation, but he's no longer listening, his attention's been claimed.

"What is it?" I start toward him, halting when he turns, presses a finger to his lips, then continues creeping ahead.

I snatch my jacket from the ground, shrug it onto my shoulders, and rush to catch up. Nearly smacking into his back when he stops without warning, only to peer past his shoulder and find a familiar coyote with gleaming red eyes and Dace's twin brother Cade standing beside it.

So this is where he's been all this time.

His ultimate plan—despite a few hitches—has been a success.

Those undead Richters—initially fueled on the pure love and goodness of Paloma's soul, which allowed them to breach the Lowerworld—a world long denied them—have managed to wreak just enough havoc, just enough damage and corruption, to allow Cade the admittance he sought all along.

Clearly reminded of the last time we met when he ripped a hole in my jeans and I reciprocated by slamming my foot in his snout, Coyote lowers his head, flattens his ears, and springs into attack. His burning red gaze fixed on mine, he comes at me in a blur of glistening fangs and razor-sharp claws. Jaw gaping wide as though starved for my flesh, about to claim a piece, when Dace shoves before me, offering himself in my place.

I shriek in horror, regain my footing, and try to intervene, only to have Dace drive his shoulder into mine and push me away once again. Somehow managing to stand his ground, as Coyote descends on him in a snarling rage. Clamping hard on Dace's arm, he tears at his flesh, savagely biting him again and again, until Cade calls him off by grabbing the beast by the neck and dragging him back to his side. Leaving Dace's arm a mess of bite marks and blood I try to attend to, but his pride won't allow it.

Sparing an impassive glance at Dace's wound, Cade says, "A noble display, brother. Very noble indeed. And yet also incredibly, absurdly naïve." He makes a face of disdain, then turns to me with an icy-blue gaze fixed on the bloom still tucked in my hair. "Trust me when I say you couldn't protect her if you tried. Only I can do that."

"What the hell are you doing here? What do you want?" Dace presses his mangled sleeve hard against the wound in a vain attempt to stanch the flow of blood. Confused by his brother's sudden appearance, the strange tone he's adopting, the invasive look that he gives me. So uninformed, so out of the loop, I can't help but curse Chepi. Leftfoot too. They should've told him. Heck, *I* should've told him. But now it's too late. Leaving no choice but to see where Cade leads.

"I think a better question is—what are *you* doing here? Aren't you scheduled to work?" Cade tilts his head, staring hard at his brother, as my gaze veers between them.

They share the same strong brow, the same high cheekbones, square chin, and generous well-shaped mouth. Yet their demeanors are so different it's easy to forget they're identical twins. Dace is tense and confused, while Cade remains confident, poised, all too aware he's in charge.

"Not to worry." Cade waves it away. "I'll find a way to cover. It's the least I can do after what you've done for me. In fact, I should thank you—though I probably won't. Expressing appreciation isn't really my thing."

Dace narrows his gaze, keeping a wary eye on Coyote, as he clutches hard at his arm with blood-slickened fingers.

"You have no idea what's going on here, do you?" Cade smirks. Spikes a hand through tousled black hair that's an exact match to Dace's in both texture and color, though Cade keeps his shorter. "Guess Chepi never got around to telling you. And it looks like your girlfriend didn't bother to fill you in either. Speaking of— hello, Daire." He flashes me an insincere smile—the kind that used to melt the hearts of all the girls at Milagro, or at least until they got their souls back. Holding the look for so long, I fight not to squirm under the weight of it. "You're looking quite . . . *radiant*. Guess it's safe to assume you two enjoyed your little retreat?"

At the sound of his words, my entire body goes tense. Veering close to full-blown panic when he gestures toward the place just behind us.

"You know, your little oasis. Your *Enchanted* Spring. Same one you used to dream about, right?" He flicks his tongue across his front teeth, leering at me. "I staged it especially for you. Doubled the amount of bubbles and flowers, made the lawn just a little bit *springier*—which I thought made for a nice romantic touch. Judging by the flush at your cheeks, you thought so too."

My breath stills. My hands grow clammy and cold. And when I reach for Dace, I find he's experiencing the same physical reactions as me.

"What's going on? What is this?" Dace looks between us, his expression pained and confused, while I remain silent. Knowing only part of the story. His brother holds the key.

"You want the short version or the long version?" Cade fishes in the pocket of his brown suede jacket, retrieving a silver-and-turquoise lighter along with a cigarette he shakes free of its pack.

"I want the truth," Dace says, his jaw so clenched he's forced to grind out the words.

"You sure you can handle it?" Cade lifts a brow, flicks the lighter's metal wheel with the pad of his thumb. The resulting flame illuminating his blank empty eyes in a way that chills me to the core. "After all, the women in your life didn't seem to think so."

Dace curses under his breath, advances on his brother, ready to end this before it begins.

The sight of it prompting Cade to laugh, as he says, "Relax, brother. No need for big shows of false intimidation. Truly." Seeing Dace take another step forward, he rolls his eyes and adds, "Trust me and do as I say. I'm only trying to save you from yourself. Whether you like it or not, you and I are connected in ways you cannot imagine, and it's time you learned the truth."

Dace pauses, stopping halfway between his twin and me. It's enough to allow Cade to continue.

"See, we're not just twins, brother—we're a split soul. Identical on the surface and yet very different inside. They tell me yours is the good and pure half." He makes a face of exaggerated gagging distaste. "While mine is pure only in its darkness—evil to the bone. Though it's really of no interest to me." He shrugs to illustrate his indifference. "*Evil* is just an unimaginative label used by pathetic losers who never accomplish anything interesting in their dull wretched lives. They cling to their false beliefs— use it to shore themselves up. Convincing themselves they'll someday be rewarded for living a useless life of no conceivable consequence—while I'm doomed to an afterlife spent burning in hell." He slips his cigarette between parted lips and takes a long drag, exhaling as he says, "Tell me, brother, do I look worried to you?"

Dace remains silent, still. His expression guarded, though notably lacking the shock I would've expected.

"Truth is, they can't bear to see the truth. Can't bear to face the fact that their lives are worthless, and their suffering pointless. So they exalt themselves with false promises—while wagging a finger at me. Idiots." He laughs as though greatly amused by the folly. "Make no mistake, it is *I* who will inherit the earth. It's my destiny. It's what I was specifically designed to do. You see, our father, Leandro, is a powerful sorcerer who set out to make a perfect heir, which he did." He runs a flattering hand over himself, the tip of his cigarette sparking and flaring as it works its way down. "On the Day of the Dead, when the veil between the living and deceased is lifted, he called upon some of our long-dead ancestors to work a little black magick on our mother. You and I are the result of their handiwork. Only Leandro didn't plan for you. His goal was simply to split the soul in two—nurturing the dark half while extinguishing the light. But something went wrong, and he accidentally made you as well. For years we considered you a deviant aberration—an embarrassment to the Richter El Coyote clan. We thought you were worthless, of little value or use. Hell, it wasn't long ago when I begged Leandro to let me kill you." His gaze turns inward, as he muses at the memory. Returning to Dace when he says, "He was just about to give in, when I stumbled across some interesting information hinting that you are far more useful than we ever imagined. Turns out, you have a purpose far greater than embarrassing us . . ."

He pauses dramatically, relishing the way he's claimed our attention. And I can hardly believe that it's here—the answer I've been seeking—or at least one of them anyway.

Cade drags on his cigarette, squinting as he exhales a series of perfectly round smoke rings he pauses to admire. Purposely delaying the reveal, if only to prove he's in charge. "As it turns out, you were born to help us achieve our destiny. It's the reason you survived. You see, you . . . my brother . . . are the Echo."

I cast a nervous glance toward Dace, seeing him shudder, as a jolt of anxiety shoots through my limbs. Needing to hear what comes next but dreading the reveal all the same.

"You are the Echo of me—and I am the Echo of you. We share the kind of connection I am only just beginning to understand. While I'm far too dark to personally experience this supposedly wondrous emotion you refer to as *love*—as it turns out, the love you hold for Daire and the love she holds for you allows me a sort of all-access pass. The Seeker loves you, and you love the Seeker." He spreads his arms wide and bows low before us. Rising with a flourish, he says, "I couldn't have asked for anything better! And now, thanks to a little smoke and mirrors on my part, a little tweak in your perception, you've not only seen fit to declare your love—but also to share it."

"You were *watching*?" Dace rushes him in outrage, failing to stop even when Coyote lunges for him yet again. His razor-sharp fangs veering for Dace's other arm, intending to maul it as well, when Cade catches him in midflight and hauls him back to his side.

"Don't flatter yourself." Cade balks, makes a face of outraged distaste. "Trust me when I say I couldn't bear the sight of it. The very thought of your tender moment makes me ill. Though make no mistake." His face hardens, turning his eyes to mere slits. "I'm always aware. I know *everything* about you, brother. It'd be smart of you to never forget that."

"You're crazy!" Dace roars, oblivious to the continuous trail of blood that streams to his wrist, over his fingers, before mixing with the dirt at his feet. "You're a freak!"

He lunges again, but Cade shakes his head and shoves his palm square in the middle of Dace's chest. Holding him off with only one hand in a show of unexpected brute strength that sets me on edge. With a final drag of his cigarette, he flicks it to his feet and gives Dace a backward shove, saying, "No, brother, you're wrong. I'm well beyond labels. I transcend anything your small mind can conceive. I'm simply superior—to you and everyone else—as I've already explained."

Dace stares hard at his brother, as Coyote stares hard at him, ready to attack at the first sign from Cade.

"Though that's not to say I'm not glad you enjoyed your little lovefest." Cade grins in a way that comes off looking creepy, obscene. "In my own way, I guess you could say I enjoyed it too. There's just so much positivity and love in the air it's as though I'm completely *transformed!*"

His eyes level on mine. Those icy-blue irises banded by gold appearing nearly identical to his twin's. Though unlike Dace's kaleidoscope gaze that reflects everything in its vicinity—Cade's eyes are empty. Nonreflective. A fathomless abyss absorbing the essence of all that it sees.

And now they're absorbing me.

Tugging on my soul.

Siphoning my energy.

Determined to drain me, while hinting at something far too horrible to speak.

His gaze deepens, features lifting in triumph, as he says, "Oh yes, Santos, I'm afraid it's all true. While you think you can refuse to work with me—while you think you can refuse the generous offer I've made you—what you fail to realize is that you've been working for me all along. Since well before you arrived in Enchantment. Dace and I are two halves of a whole. Connected. Intertwined. Which means the love you feel for him—in thought, deed, even in your dreams—it all serves to strengthen me. I'm the beneficiary of every kind and loving emotion you have toward each other. Same goes for the sexy thoughts too."

The pendulum!

Paloma was right. They're connected so deeply, the pendulum sees them as one. My subconscious mind already accepting the horrible truth my heart fought to refuse.

"There's no avoiding it," Cade taunts. "No way to undo what's already done. You two are destined. Fated. And now, the prophecy has begun. In other words"—his gaze slants to his brother—"the snowball's headed for hell and there's no way to stop it."

Dace's features sharpen with rage. Despite his wounded arm, despite all he just learned, he refuses to fold. Refuses to be cowed by his freak of a brother. "I always knew you were crazy—but now you've reached a whole new level," he says. "You stay away from us. And don't even think about going near Daire!"

He reaches for me with his good arm, tries to pull me away, but I'm frozen in place. Sickened by everything Cade just revealed, but even more disturbed by the words that repeat in my head:

Thanks to a little smoke and mirrors on my part, a little tweak in your perception . . .

Reminded of what Paloma told me about El Coyote's ability to change people's perception. Remembering how Cade and Leandro toyed with mine during my first visit to the Rabbit Hole—making it seem as though the ceiling was dropping, the walls caving in. How they stood back and watched—father and son—enjoying my breakdown, my split with reality.

Though once I discovered the true physical difference between Dace and Cade, realized how their eyes are nothing alike—something Paloma claims no one else has been able to discern—I was sure I was immune to his tricks. Sure he couldn't mess with me. Yet there's no denying the tug I felt just a moment ago when he fixed his gaze right on mine.

The way he yanked hard on my soul.

I drop Dace's hand and bolt for the spring, gasping in horror when I see that what I once thought was healed, returned to its former enchanted glory, was anything but.

"Not quite the paradise you took it for, is it?" Cade's laugh creeps up from behind. Teasing. Taunting. As I gape at the canopy of blooms I once viewed as vibrant, budding with life—now turned to a snarl of blackened dead vines infested with rats, left to droop over a horrible, putrid, rotting cesspool of a spring that smells just like death.

Even the lawn of green velvet where Dace and I shared our love is nothing more than a burned-out rug swarming with insects.

And the wounds I thought healed are now back—my finger once again throbbing, swollen, and red—my feet covered in seeping blisters that stick to my shoes.

Dace lets loose a long stream of curses and yanks hard on my hand. Urging me to leave, to run, to get out while we can. But I can't go just yet. There's something still left to see.

I whirl around, horrified by the monstrous sight that confronts me.

My stifled cry of anguish cause Dace to turn. His eyes widen in disbelief when he sees the Cade from my nightmares. The one with gleaming red eyes, an open gash of a mouth, and the swarm of two-headed, soul-stealing snakes shooting out from the place where his tongue ought to be.

But unlike the Cade from my dreams, this one swiftly expands as though molded and stretched by unseen hands. His flesh adopting a strange scaly texture, emitting an odd reddish glow—as his torso lengthens, his limbs bulk up and widen with thick corded muscles—while his clothes, no longer able to contain him, shred and disintegrate, falling like feathers to his enormous clawed feet. Leaving him massive and naked and looming before us, with his faithful coyote inflating right along with him—two sets of eyes glowering an identical red.

Without a word, Dace drags me toward Horse. His good arm circling my waist, about to heave me onto his back when Horse gallops away and Raven soars with him. Leaving us with no choice but to race through a dying land that grows bleaker with each passing step.

Our exodus mocked by Cade's taunting voice, calling, "Run, brother! Run all you want. But you'll never escape me. I'm your Echo—always with you—always watching."

eight

"How long have you known?" Dace paces his small functional kitchen. Taking two steps to the old stove, one from there to the ancient white fridge, three more to the stained porcelain sink, and then one and a half to the stove again, where he pauses, rubs a weary hand over his eyes, and shoots me a look so conflicted, I hesitate to meet it.

I drop onto a chair next to the carved wooden table that's nearly identical to the one in Leftfoot's adobe, wishing Dace would come join me. But realizing he won't even consider it until I provide some of the answers he seeks, I take a fortifying breath and say, "Paloma told me about the circumstance of your birth— about Leandro altering Chepi's perception long enough to seduce her."

"*Seduce* her?" Dace whirls on me, his face a mask of outrage. "He *raped* her. Chepi was a sixteen-year-old virgin that day. She wasn't looking for trouble."

I shrink under his gaze, then force myself to straighten again, determined to explain. "I didn't mean it like that—like it was some romantic tryst. What I meant to say is that he *lured* her. He lured her with witchcraft and black magick. The Richters know how to change people's perception—they've been doing it for centuries. It's how they rule this town and nearly everyone in it. It's how Cade made us think the spring was still enchanted when it had already been corrupted. Leandro fed into her dreams, allowed her to see what she most wanted to see, and then, once she was completely enthralled . . ." I leave the sentence unfinished, seeing no reason to illustrate.

Dace waves it away, batting the empty space before him, his eyes fatigued and red-rimmed in a way I've never seen them. "I'm the product of violence." He shakes his head, his gaze cold and empty. "There's no getting around it. I never should've been born."

"Don't say that!" I grip the table hard, fighting the urge to leap over the counter that separates us and hug him tightly to me. Right now he's an island—a population of one. He wouldn't welcome the intrusion.

"Do you know how much easier her life would've been without me?" His voice is flat and dull. "Every time she looks at me she's reminded of the worst day of her life."

"I don't believe that," I say. "And you shouldn't either."

He dismisses my meaningful look, saying, "Really, Daire? Just how am I supposed to see it?" Practically spitting the words.

I sit quietly, refusing to rise to the bait. I just stare at my hands, noting the way my finger grows more swollen and red with each passing second.

"And, while we're on the subject, how am I supposed to feel knowing you knew all of this and couldn't bother to tell me?"

I tip my chin until my gaze meets his. Aware that the word *sorry* doesn't quite cut it, but it's all that I've got. "I wish I'd told you, believe me, I do. I wish you never had to find out this way." I shake my head and sigh. "Thing is, Paloma made me promise not to tell you. She said you're a truly good and pure soul, and that it wasn't my place. In this case, I'm sorry I listened to her instead of my heart."

"A good and pure soul?" He scowls. "I'm an abomination! The result of an act so evil—"

"You're *not!*" I cry, refusing to let him venture along that path. "That's your brother, not you." I shift my gaze to his arm, staring at the place where Coyote attacked. Wishing he'd let me do something to tend to it, but when I tried, he waved me away, reached for a dish towel and wrapped it around the wound.

"He's a monster." He unwraps the blood-soaked dish towel and drops it into the sink, before replacing it with a clean one. And though the words came out like a statement, his gaze holds a question.

"He is." I nod to confirm it.

"And yet, we're an Echo of each other."

I sit silently, kneading the worn linoleum floor with the toe of my shoe, having no idea how to respond.

His voice bleak and hollow, he says, "We can't see each other anymore."

The words come out of nowhere.

Slamming me sideways.

Knocking me senseless.

"*What?*" I stare blankly. Aware of the floor shifting under my feet, threatening to drop out from under me, swallow me whole.

"I'm sorry, Daire, but we have no choice. I have to protect you, and the only way I can do that is by refusing to see you."

His words leave me mute. Unable to do anything more than gape.

"I'm not completely in the dark here, you know." He swipes a hand through his hair, scrunches his brow, as his gaze drifts from mine. "I've heard whispers through the years. Seen the way the elders, Leftfoot especially, looked at me when they thought I was too busy to notice. I was a quiet kid. A loner, a reader, a thinker— all of which made it easy to go unnoticed. I became very good at eavesdropping, collecting random bits and pieces through the years that never made any sense until now. I always knew I was

different, I just didn't know *how* different. I also had this pro-
found understanding that I was headed for an unusual destiny,
and while I still don't know exactly what that is—it's all starting
to come together. The puzzle I've been sorting for years is now
that much closer to completion."

I look at him, so bereft I have no idea what to say.

"You're the Seeker," he says.

I close my eyes, wishing I could rewind my life. I never
would've come here. I never would've let it get to this point. And
because of it, I would've ended up just like my dad—dead before
my time. So, in an effort to avoid that, I decided to claim my destiny, only to find myself nothing more than a cog in its wheel.
Steered by circumstance, with no say of my own.

So lost in my thoughts I nearly miss it when Dace says, "And
Cade is Coyote—a member of the El Coyote clan, which all Richters are."

My shoulders sag. I wish I could disappear, vanish straight
into the ether.

"And I'm the Echo of Coyote."

I rub my lips together, growing increasingly uncomfortable,
having no idea where he's going with this but sensing it's about
to get worse.

He takes a deep breath, scratches hard at his chin. His voice a
chilled whisper, he says, "This won't end well." His eyes light on
mine. "Someone is destined to die. I've had dreams—dreams I
now recognize as prophecy. We can't all survive. And while I
can't stop loving you, Daire—while it's far too late for that—I can
stop . . ." He grinds his jaw, speaking the words with great effort.
"I can stop *feeding* our love. Now that I know it strengthens *him,*
I'm left with no choice. It's like he said, he's the beneficiary of every loving thought that I have for you. And there's no denying
that the more time I spend with you, the more my love for you
grows. But now, knowing what we know, we can't afford to

continue—can't afford to be together. We have to make the sacrifice. Put some distance between us. We're left with no choice."

"No," I say, the word so shaky I repeat it with all the force I
can muster. "*No!* No way. I won't have it. Your brother's a creep—
a freak! He's a power-hungry, black-hearted beast, bent on world
domination, and I refuse to roll over and let him win. I refuse to
play by his rules. Besides, how can we be sure that it's true?
Maybe that's not what the Echo is. Maybe it means something
else entirely." I cry, but the words ring desperate and untrue even
to my ears.

"Did you not *see* him?" Dace cries, his voice as incredulous as
his face. "That was no illusion—that was all too real!"

I sigh, reluctantly admitting, "It wasn't the first time. I've seen
it before."

"Me too . . ." Dace's voice fades as he stares at the peeling yellow paint, his mind traveling to a faraway place. "And that didn't
end well either, or at least not for us. Though he seemed quite
pleased . . ." I shoot him a quizzical look, but he just shakes his
head, and folds his keys in his palm. "Come on. It's getting late.
I'll drive you home."

I follow him outside to his old beater truck, climbing in beside
him as he cranks up the heat to ward off the chill. But the hot air
blowing from the vent bears no effect. My body's as numb as my
heart, and a rise in temperature is not going to change that.

He navigates the dirt roads in silence, until he stops before
Paloma's blue gate and turns to me to say, "This doesn't change
the way I feel about you. Nothing could ever do that."

I swallow hard. Turn my back on the words. Reaching for
the door handle with burning eyes and a throat gone too tight
to reply.

"If you want, I'll drive you to school tomorrow, but you might
want to try to arrange something else after that. No need to
make this any harder than it is."

I push the door open and slip free of his truck. Aware of the weight of his gaze, following me as I carefully pick my way past the blue gate. Then the moment it slams shut behind me, I race through Paloma's front door, where I collapse into her arms in a big sobbing heap.

nine

"*Nieta?*" Paloma clasps me tightly to her chest and coos into my hair. "*Nieta*, what has happened?"

I pull away, furiously erasing the tears with the backs of my hands. Crying is something I rarely allow, and crying in front of others is something I can barely tolerate from myself. I try to speak, but the words sputter and stall in my throat, as if I'm reluctant to give them any more weight, any more power to hurt me than they already have.

Paloma studies my face. Brushing a soft, papery hand across my brow, her eyes shining with compassion, she sighs softly and says, "And so it begins."

I squint, having no idea what that means. Paloma's always had an uncanny way of reading my emotions, but this time feels different. It feels like a setup. Like she was camped by the door, waiting for me to burst in.

"I'm so sorry, *nieta*. I feared this would happen." Her voice rings sincere, but the words leave me disturbed.

She hands me a tissue I use to dab at my face, until the tissue grows so soggy and useless I crumple it in my fist. "Feared what would happen?" I try to get a read on her, but as usual, her expression is inscrutable. "I haven't told you anything yet."

She stares into my eyes, and not missing a beat, she replies, "The life of a Seeker is difficult." Her hand reaches for me, but seeing the way I recoil at her touch, she quickly drops it to her side. "And romance always comes with a price."

"So you knew?" I cross my arms in defiance, thinking it would've been nice if she'd thought to share that with me. But then again, maybe she did and I just didn't listen.

She's definitely dropped a few hints along the way. Including the night just after her soul was returned, when she told me that Dace and I were fated. I was completely exalted by the news, while her own reaction was anything but.

I return to her, a cold chill pocking my skin when she says, "No, *nieta*, I didn't know for sure. I merely suspected what the pendulum, along with your appearance just now, have confirmed."

"But I haven't confirmed anything. I haven't said a single word about what happened today. So how could you know? Are you spying on me too?"

"Too?" She lifts a brow.

But instead of explaining, I clamp my lips shut, refusing to say anything more. The vow lasting only a handful of seconds, before I look at her and plead, "Paloma, please, I need to know what you know—and I need to know it now."

She nods sagely, about to speak when Xotichl pokes her head out from the archway that marks the entrance to Paloma's office, saying, "Maybe I should leave?" Her gaze seems to dart between Paloma and me as though she can see us.

Great. Now I'm crying in front of my friends. Could this possibly get any worse?

Knowing Xotichl needs Paloma's help just as much as Paloma needs the money her clients bring in, I shake my head and turn toward my room, saying, "No. You should definitely stay." Though I don't even make it to the hall before Paloma's noticed my finger and pulled me back to her.

"*Nieta*, how did you get this?" She inspects the wound that just a few hours ago was barely noticeable, but now, after a trip to a grossly corrupted Lowerworld is a hot flaming mess. Then she takes me by the elbow and steers me up the ramp that leads to her office, where she deposits me onto a chair at the square wooden table next to Xotichl, before busying herself at the counter with her potions and herbs.

I peer at Xotichl's black long-sleeved T-shirt, the word EPITAPH, the name of Auden's band, scrawled in a blaze of silver across the front, and her dark skinny jeans that are tucked into dark suede boots. With her hair gathered into a loose ponytail that allows her finely honed features to take center stage, I'm struck once again by her quiet brand of prettiness. Her soft blue/gray eyes staring straight ahead, she reaches for my shoulder, and says, "I felt your distress the moment you arrived. I'm so sorry for whatever's happened. If you want my help, just say the word."

I smile faintly, so unused to having friends, people to confide in, people willing to help, I'm unsure how to respond. So other than a quick, mumbled thanks, I sit silently beside her. Feet crossed at the ankles and tucked under my chair, as Paloma grinds a handful of carefully selected herbs with her mortar and pestle. Humming one of her healing songs under her breath, she forms the mixture into a thick green poultice she applies to my finger, then wraps a strip of gauze over the concoction, telling me to hold it in place until she says when.

I do as instructed. Waiting for her to join us at the table before I ask, "So how did you know? Or, better yet, *what* do you know?"

Paloma pauses long enough to warm her fingers against the base of her mug. "I'm afraid it's all part of the prophecy," she says. "I read it in the codex."

I inhale sharply. Vaguely aware of Xotichl stirring beside me, placing her hand on my arm, providing a welcome comfort I didn't expect.

"Please know, *nieta*, that a prophecy is a tricky thing. It's never as black and white as it seems. The language is often confusing, written in code. Allowing for more than one interpretation. It was only when I saw you and Dace together—saw the stream of energy that binds you—that I began to suspect. Then after a little digging, I learned that your birthdays fall on the same day. Did you know that?"

I shake my head, scowling when I say, "Guess I forgot to check his ID."

My caustic remark causing Xotichl to pat my arm in an attempt to calm me, and Paloma to flash me a look that tells me that while she forgives my mood, she's not about to answer my question until I get ahold of myself.

"So, what does it mean?" I ask, making a concerted effort to soften my tone. "What exactly is it you're getting at?"

"While the prophecy hints at the Echo effect, its definition is not entirely clear. I took it to mean that the twins are connected—deeply so." She looks to me for confirmation, and when she gets it, she adds, "Though, I must warn you, *nieta*, the prophecy also states that one of you will die."

Xotichl gasps, squeezing my arm so hard it jolts me awake from my dumbfounded state. I lean back in my seat. Allowing the words to roll around in my head, before I heave a deep breath and say, "Fine. Then Cade dies. I'll kill Cade. Then it'll be over and done and we can all move on. And I doubt anyone but Leandro will miss him. And I seriously doubt Dace will mind, since they're not exactly close." I stare at Paloma, my decision now made. But she returns the look with an expression of compassion tainted by pain.

"No one is here by accident, *nieta*. The universe does not make mistakes. Everyone has a purpose, and that includes Cade.

Which means we don't just go around killing people. You can't be so cavalier when another human life is concerned—" She's about to continue, but her words are cut short by my own.

"Cade isn't human. He's a demonic freak." I fight to steady myself, to contain the bubble of anger rising inside me. "Besides, I'd be doing the whole world a favor. Things have changed since your day. It's beyond hostile out there. And while some of that may be my fault for sparing your soul, which allowed them access to the Lowerworld, the fact is, if some prior Seeker had had the foresight to kill them all a long time ago, I wouldn't be sitting here now feeling like my heart has been crushed while the only future I can look forward to is a dark, lonely, bleak one where I'm expected to fight a battle I've been set up to lose." I narrow my gaze, eager to see how she'll respond. But Paloma remains true to herself. Steady. On course. Refusing to veer from the message no matter how much I bait her.

"And if some prior Seeker had done as you wish, then Dace never would've been born. He may have come in another form, yes, but he wouldn't have been your fated one. It is written. Nothing here is an accident."

I sit with the words, unable to deny them no matter how much I despise them.

"*Nieta*, make no mistake, a Seeker's job is to restore and heal—to keep the balance between the worlds—and to never stray from the light. We can only contain evil. We cannot eradicate it. As long as humans exist, evil will too. It's up to us to lessen its effects."

I pick at the gauze on my finger, unwilling to fold quite so easily. "Yeah, well, maybe that no longer holds true. Maybe it's time for a new generation of Seeker—one who works in new ways. The balance is clearly out of whack, and I can honestly say, after this last trip to the Lowerworld, that it's getting worse every day. The enemy is not one you're used to fighting, *abuela*. He's bigger, stronger, more . . . demonic." I pause, remembering the way

Cade rose up before us—how he and his creepy coyote tripled in size. "You're used to dealing with humans—bad humans, dark humans, but still humans. But Cade is *not* human. He's a psychopathic, demonic freak—the result of magick of the darkest kind. Driven by a pathetic need to impress Leandro by achieving world domination. Oh, and he can also turn into a scaly-skinned, snake-tongued monster at will. I know, because I've seen it, and let me tell you, it is *not* pretty. So, with that in mind, I hardly think pounding a drum and waving an eagle feather will do anything to stop him."

"Then what about Dace, his twin—is he human?" Paloma asks, her gaze on mine, her voice quiet and even.

"Of course he is!" I frown. Annoyed by the question. "He's good, and kind, and—"

"And yet, he's also the result of the dark magick you speak of."

I squirm under her gaze, not liking what she's getting at, even though I'm not entirely sure what that is.

"So you're saying that Dace is the human half of an inhuman twin? How can that be?" She waits for me to respond, but for once, I have nothing to say. My silence prompting her to add, "The world's greatest atrocities were committed by humans, *nieta*. Dark, deranged, misguided, egomaniacal humans—and yet humans all the same."

I continue to rub my thumb over the gauze, enjoying the cooling sensation the poultice provides. At the moment, it's the only thing I feel good about. "Listen, if he turns into a demon, then he's a demon." I nod. Hoping that'll put an end to the argument. But one look at Paloma, and a quick peek at Xotichl, tells me I've failed to convince.

"It's not quite that simple . . ." Xotichl pauses, tilting her head toward mine. "I'm sorry, Daire, but I have to side with Paloma on this one. Cade's energy patterns are not at all like that of the demons that guard the Rabbit Hole vortex."

"Maybe he's a different kind of demon," I say, barely giving her time to finish. "Maybe there's more than one breed."

Xotichl shakes her head. Toying with the hem of her sleeve, she drags it over her knuckles and down toward her fingertips. "A demon's energy is like electrical interference. It's frenetic and strange, with a vibration that's hard to contain. Cade's energy isn't like that. It's definitely human—darker than most, no doubt. It's extremely heavy and dense. But human all the same."

"But maybe you've only encountered him in human form," I say, realizing I've lost the argument the moment it's out. "Okay, yeah, I get it. *Human* form, which means he's human. Still, he's not a *normal* human, not even close." I sigh in surrender. Xotichl's blind sight is a formidable tool. It bears no bias—it merely states it like it is. Kind of like the pendulum.

"Are either one of you familiar with the legends of the Navajo skinwalkers?" Paloma asks, her eyes darting between us.

Xotichl squirms in her chair, reluctantly admitting she is, while I merely shrug. Having come across the word once or twice, but unable to grasp a clear idea of just exactly what it means.

"They are *brujos* and *brujas*." When she sees my blank look, she goes on to explain. "Evil witches and sorcerers, dark magicians who are able to take on the appearance of other forms."

"Like shape-shifters?" I ask, remembering the night I spied on Cade via the cockroach. How he stripped off his clothes before his run with Coyote, which struck me as odd (not to mention disturbing). But before I could see anything more, he slammed his boot into me—er, the cockroach—severing our bond. But now, I can't help but wonder if Cade was preparing to turn into a coyote? I sneak a peek at Xotichl, perplexed by the way she fidgets in her seat, as though she'd love nothing more than a change of subject.

"Similar, but not exactly." Paloma's fingers trace the rim of her cup. "They utilize animal hides, also known as magick skin. Draping themselves with the skin of the animal they seek to become allows them to complete the transformation and adopt many of the animal's characteristics, including the ability to travel great distances rather quickly. They're able to read minds, to climb inside a person's head and persuade them to cause great harm to others as well as themselves. It is said that a skinwalker can absorb themselves into one's body simply by locking eyes with their prey. They're often associated with Coyote. Though whether or not Cade is an actual skinwalker I can't say for sure. What I can say is that from what you've told me, he, and probably other members of his clan, share the unique ability to transform. And we already know they excel at mind control to the point where they're able to alter perception. But the fact that he seems able to retain his human consciousness and ego-bound desires while he's in this altered state, tells me he's more of a halfling."

I stare hard at my finger, reminded of the moment Cade and I locked eyes at the Enchanted Spring–turned cesspool. How I felt him tug on my soul—siphon my energy. The thought makes me shiver.

"Only in Cade's case, he merely transforms into the physical manifestation of the true nature of his soul." Reading my confusion, she adds, "His soul is dark—when he transforms, he's merely exhibiting what lurks inside."

"Like turning himself inside out!" Xotichl grins, instantly grasping what I was still struggling with.

"So, does that mean Dace can turn into a rainbow, or an angel, or a dazzling white stallion with wings?" I ask, regretting the words the instant Xotichl cringes and Paloma shoots me a look.

"I've no doubt that Dace has the power to transform into something very powerful and good. Though I'm not sure he's discovered that yet," Paloma says.

I sigh in surrender, knowing they're right. Dace is good. Cade is evil. And yet they're equally human. Which means I've got to find another way to stop Cade. But at the moment, I have no idea how to begin.

"It's still two against one," I venture, hoping to find comfort in the thought. Then seeing their confusion, I add, "What I mean is, I'm mostly good. Dace is all good. And since we're in love, and since love always wins—since the light always shatters the dark—we're destined for victory, right?" I glance between them, only to watch Paloma push away from the table and head for a locked cupboard I'd never paid any real notice to until now.

Retrieving an ancient, leather-bound tome, she plunks it down before us, and says, "Why don't we consult the codex?"

ten

Xotichl and I inch forward, sitting elbow to elbow as we lean over the tome. Its vellum pages crafted from thinly stretched cowhide that, while it's held up well over the years, bears edges that are showing signs of age and wear in the way they're beginning to wither and curl.

"It's illuminated!" Xotichl turns to Paloma for confirmation.

"It is indeed." Paloma nods. "Valentina was very skilled as both a soothsayer and an illustrator." Referring to one of the very first Seekers in the Santos family tree, who appeared to me during my vision quest, along with Django; Alejandro, the grandfather I never met; and a whole host of Santos ancestors along with their spirit animals.

I peer at the elaborately scrawled handwritten text that at first glance appears to be a convoluted mess of symbols and numbers and words so archaic, so cryptic, they're impossible to decipher.

"It's unreadable." My face droops as I turn to Paloma.

"It appears that way." She looks at me, a faint glimmer in her eye.

Xotichl's hands hover over the pages, palms down, her lips

screwed to the side. She contemplates for a moment, then says, "It has very pure energy. It speaks only the truth." She lowers her hands to her lap and sits back in her chair. "Though it came at great cost. A sacrifice was involved."

Paloma reaches toward Xotichl, eyes shining with pride. "You're making such progress!" She ruffles her hair, causing Xotichl to catch Paloma's hand with her own.

"Yes, but there's still so much more to learn." Xotichl grins.

I watch the two of them together—the teacher and the student. And yet they're so much more than that. They're family. My family. The realization filling me with a warmth I didn't expect. While Dace may be determined to avoid me in order to protect me, it's good to know I don't have to face this alone.

"Valentina was the sacrifice," Paloma says. "She suffered great trials to accumulate this knowledge, but she did so willingly. As one of the first to face the Richters, she knew the fight would continue—that her child would have little choice but to pick up where she left off. She was determined to leave some sort of guide. This book is the result."

"Did they speak in a special language known only to them?" I peer at the lettering, the strange symbols, still unable to make any sense of it.

"Valentina took great precautions to ensure the text would not fall into the wrong hands. All too aware that a breach of that kind would've proved disastrous for us, she invented an elaborate code that's not easily deciphered. Since the start of its existence, the book, along with the secret to reading it, has been passed down from Seeker to child. I presented this book to Django on his sixteenth birthday, as is the custom. Though, of course, as you already know, he wanted no part of the Seeker tradition. But now that you've accepted your calling, *nieta*, it's time I pass it to you."

Xotichl dips her head and sighs. "Looks like you've got some heavy reading ahead of you over Winter Break." She laughs, determined to make light of a heavy situation.

"Oh, no." I grasp the book by the edges and slide it toward me. "I've no intention of waiting. I'm starting now. That is, if Paloma's willing to show me how to read this thing."

I glance at Paloma, watching as she disappears into the kitchen, only to return a few moments later with a tray of homemade sugar-free cookies and freshly brewed tea. Placing a mug before each of us as we turn to the book—remaining like that late into the night.

The next morning I'm waiting outside Paloma's blue gate well before Dace is set to arrive. My grief from the night before lessened by what I now know.

It's like Paloma said, prophecies are tricky. They can be interpreted in a number of ways. And now that I've had a chance to read it in the book for myself, my mission is clear.

One must die. There's no getting around it.

But it won't be me.

And it won't be Dace either. I'll do whatever it takes to keep him alive. Even if that means thwarting a prediction made long ago.

Despite Paloma's telling me that killing is frowned upon, what she doesn't understand is that a new day has dawned. Now that I know what I know—seen what I've seen—it's clear that Cade Richter must be eliminated.

He may be human, but he's no ordinary human. And as soon as I've dealt with him, it's just a matter of time before I locate those undead Richters, since they're only as good as the guidance he gives them. Once they're gone, the Lowerworld will be free to heal and blossom again, the balance will be restored, and Dace and I will have nothing or no one standing in our way. We'll be free to love each other for as long as we want.

All I have to do is rid the world of his brother.

The thought providing a much-needed push for what I have to do next.

So when Dace parks his truck before me and hops free of his side to open my door, I remain rooted in place. My gaze fixed on his, I say, "Thanks for stopping by, but I'm getting a ride from Auden and Xotichl today."

He studies me with eyes that are even more fatigued and red-rimmed than they were when I left him. Speaking my name with a voice so hoarse, it takes all of my will not to barrel into his arms and beg him to forget what I said. Forget what he said. To forget everything and just be with me again.

He reaches for me, fingers straining toward mine, but I quickly withdraw from his grasp. I can't afford the contact. Can't afford to be swayed by the lure of his touch. If I'm going to kill his twin, I can't do anything that will enable Cade to become a more formidable opponent than he already is.

I have to be patient.

Have to believe in my heart that it won't be much longer until Dace and I are together.

I have to believe it, envision it, and think from the end.

I wave a hand before me, hoping he doesn't notice the way my fingers shake, the way my voice trembles when I say, "We're good, okay? Truly. I get why you have to do it. Really, I do." I choke back the sob crowding my throat, averting my gaze so I won't have to see his grief-stricken face.

He's about to speak again, when Auden and Xotichl arrive. Auden's eyes wide and uncertain, Xotichl's head tilted, when they find me standing with Dace.

I flash them the wait-a-minute signal, about to say good-bye to Dace when he grabs hold of me. Fingers circling my wrist, he peers at my finger and says, "You're healed."

"Looks like Paloma worked another miracle." I allow a quick

grin, then jerk free of his grip. The move costing much more than it appears on the surface. Bearing sole responsibility for the avalanche of ache that rages inside. "And you?"

I peer at the bit of gauze peeking free of his sleeve, marking the spot where Coyote made a feast of his flesh. Watching as he tugs hard on the fabric, dragging it down past the wound. "No miracle required. Not to worry, I'm good."

I squint, not quite believing it but choosing not to pursue it. I allow myself to hold his gaze for much longer than I should. Bargaining for just a few more seconds of being engulfed in the sacredness of his space—telling myself I'll do whatever it takes to make up for any damage that ensues.

It takes every last bit of my strength to drag myself from him, but I do. Heading for Auden and Xotichl without once looking back.

"Did you get any sleep?" Xotichl asks, when I slide onto the seat just behind them, trying to act nonchalant, though I'm pretty sure they're not fooled.

"Not really," I say. "But strangely, I'm not at all tired." *Determined but not tired.*

"Me neither," Xotichl says as Auden pulls onto the road and cautiously swerves around Dace.

"Well, I am," Auden quips. "There's not enough energy drinks in the world."

His words causing Xotichl to laugh in that delightful way that she has. Pressing her shoulder to his, she snuggles against him and says, "Epitaph had a gig in Albuquerque last night. The crowd loved them so much they played seven encores!"

"Two." Auden laughs. Yanking affectionately on Xotichl's ponytail when he adds, "But who's counting?"

"All I know is that he drove all the way back to Enchantment instead of staying over with the rest of the band, just so he could drive us to school. Isn't that sweet?" She cocks her head toward me, as I bite back the overwhelming surge of envy when I see the way they get to love each other so openly and easily. Forcing myself to agree that it is indeed sweet of him.

"Yeah, I'm sweet." Auden grins. "And the second I drop you off, I'm gonna go crash my sweet self until it's time to pick you both up again."

"I don't need a ride home." I stare out the window, taking in this dump of a town with its rusted cars, sagging clotheslines, and crumbling adobe homes.

For a brief time I'd fooled myself into thinking it was improving—fooled myself that I was the reason. But now, seeing it with untainted vision, there's no denying this place is a complete and total dead end. Bearing no hint of Paloma's claim that it was once a good match for its name. I can only hope that once I've properly dealt with Cade Richter, this place will be truly enchanting again.

"How you getting home?" Xotichl's voice is thick with suspicion.

"I'll find a ride." I unbuckle my seat belt and grab hold of my bag. "In fact, you can drop me right here."

"You skipping school?" Auden asks.

"Yep," I mumble, already distracted by what I now need to do.

"Again?" Xotichl swivels in her seat until she's halfway facing me.

Her voice colliding with Auden's, who blurts, "You seriously want me to stop right here?" He squints at me from the rearview mirror. Gaze narrowing further when he adds, "In the middle of the road?"

I nod, already opening the door and freeing a leg.

"What're you up to, Daire?" Xotichl's face darkens in a way I rarely see.

Since there's no use lying to her, I don't even try. I glance between the two of them and say, "Something that should have been done a long time ago."

Then I swing the door shut and head for Gifford's Gift Shop * Notary * & Mailstop. Planning to fill up on some of that freshly brewed coffee they advertise in the window, while I wait for the Rabbit Hole to open for business.

desecration

eleven

Dace

Daire walks away from my truck.

Away from me.

Determined. In a hurry. Her shiny brown hair sailing behind her in a way that seems almost mocking. As if to say: *You want me? You want to fold me in the palm of your hand, and weave your fingers around my soft, silken strands? Feel free—your demonic brother would love nothing more!*

I curse under my breath, kick stupidly at the dirt, and climb inside my truck. An ugly mess of scraped-together bits that, thanks to countless hours bent under the hood, and layers of grease on my hands, houses an engine that purrs.

I glance in my rearview mirror, watching as Daire settles onto Auden's backseat. Her deep green eyes shining like emeralds, her cheeks flushing pink—smiling so brightly I close my eyes and pretend she smiles for me.

When I open my eyes again, they're gone. Leaving me to stare into their dust, unable to do anything more than shake my head, spear a hand through my hair, and remember a time when I thought its length was the only thing that distinguished me from my twin.

Yesterday I was naïve.

Today, not so much.

Not after seeing the way he rose up before us—morphed into a freaking snake-tongued beast.

Then there was Daire—looking horrified, sure, but not one bit surprised to see him that way. Making me wonder if she had the dream too?

The one where Cade turned into a monster, stole her soul, and left her lying dead in my arms.

It's a dream I've dreamed too many times.

I drive my knuckles hard against my eyes in a failed attempt to stop them from burning—the direct result of a night spent in torment. Every time I tried to sleep, images of Daire swam in my head. Her eyes gazing at me—trusting me, loving me, giving herself in a way that frightened her more than me.

I was sure it was just the beginning.

Sure that our love could only grow from there.

I'd never felt happier, never felt more fulfilled than I did lying beside her. Vowing to dedicate the rest of my life to making her as contented as I was.

It was a promise I intended to keep.

Still do.

Our separation is temporary. A bitter necessity. It's what I have to do to keep her safe until I can find a way to deal with Cade.

And though every last bit of it's true—it leaves me no comfort.

Five minutes without her is unbearable.

A lifetime is completely unthinkable.

But while I can't risk going near her just yet, can't afford to even think about her without enabling Cade, I will find a way to end this. I've no choice. That recurring dream where she dies in my arms is hardly coincidence. It's a prophecy. There's no doubt in my mind.

A prophecy I plan to stop no matter the cost.

There's no way I'll stand by and watch as Daire dies. If anyone ends up dead, it'll be Cade. And if not Cade, then I'll gladly take his place. If I do nothing else with my ill-conceived existence, I'll make sure Daire goes unharmed.

I yank hard on the wheel—this ancient heap of rust and metal predates power steering by a decade. About to pull onto the street, when Daire's grandmother comes through the painted blue gate and looks right at me.

"Although I've long suspected, I couldn't be sure until now." Her voice is light and breathy, as though returning to a prior conversation I don't remember having. Confusing me further when she adds, "I'm so sorry."

I shrug. Rub my thumb over the wheel. There's a lot to be sorry for lately, but my guess is she's referring to my broken relationship with Daire.

"You are better than the circumstances of your birth," she says.

Oh. That.

"You must strive to rise above it. You hold the potential for greatness. You must never forget that."

She studies me, while I study my hands, unsure how to respond.

"Whatever you do, please don't beat yourself up. Your mother has indulged in enough self-recrimination for both of you, don't you think?"

I meet her gaze, wondering how she does it—how any of the elders do it. Paloma, Leftfoot, Chepi, and Chay—how do they remain so hopeful and optimistic in a world overflowing with pain?

"Because we have no choice." She smiles faintly, answering the thoughts in my head. "There will always be light and dark. How would we recognize one if not for the existence of the other?"

I hold her gaze, knowing I have her full understanding and support. But too overcome by the shame of her knowing what I am—how I came to be, the hideous truth no one bothered to tell me—to appreciate the look of compassion she gives me.

"You must fight the urge to fight fire with fire—no good will come of that. You must lean on your inner goodness and light." She pats my arm for emphasis, her touch brief, fleeting, but comforting all the same.

Then she steps away from the truck, pulls her cardigan tightly around her, and waves me away. The troubled look on her face blunted by the swirl of dust I stir in my wake.

When I pull into the school parking lot, the space next to Auden's is free. But I know better than to park there. Keeping my distance starts here. Now. So I start to drive on, making for the other side, when I notice only two people climb out of Auden's wagon, and Daire isn't one of them.

"Where is she?" I punch the brake hard. Search the area for some sign of her.

Eyeballing Auden, who turns to Xotichl, who turns in my direction and says, "She never made it this far—she had us drop her in town."

"In town—why?" I rub a hand over my chin, trying to make sense of why she'd do such a thing. Watching as Xotichl chews her lip, deciding just how much she should tell me.

Her shoulders rising and falling, she says, "Honestly, she's up to something—I just don't know what. All I can say for sure is that her energy was very determined. And, Dace, just so we're on the same page—I know what happened yesterday. Which just makes me even more worried."

The car behind me honks. It's Lita, lowering her window and greeting me with a sarcastic smile. "Hey—Dace. You taking that space or what? 'Cause if not, I'd really like to have it. Sometime today would be good!"

My eyes meet Auden's, seeing him shake his head and laugh as I wave Lita in. If Xotichl's worried, I'm worried. And that's all it takes for me to exit the lot as quickly as I entered.

Telling myself I just need to see her. Make sure she's okay. Once that's done, I'll head back to school, do what's expected, and I won't think about her again.

But no matter how many times I repeat it, I know it's not true.

twelve

Daire

The bell on the door clangs loudly behind me, causing a handful of customers to stop what they're doing long enough to give me a quick, appraising look.

Gifford peers up from his register, eyes widening in recognition. He calls to me in a cheerful voice, saying, "Hey there—miss your bus? Fresh batch of postcards just arrived—they're right over there." He points toward the rack bearing depressing pictures of this miserable three-block town. Completely unaware that he's just reminded me of one of the very worst times in my life. The day I nearly died just a few steps from here.

Still, bad as that was, yesterday was worse. Much worse. With Paloma's help, that broken leg I suffered outside the Rabbit Hole took only a few weeks to heal. If today doesn't go as planned, my broken heart may never recover.

I smile faintly. Reminding myself he means well—not everyone in this place is a Richter. Then I make for the space in back where the coffee is served. Hoping to grab one of those round tables with the bright pink tablecloths, use it as a temporary hideaway until it's time to make good on my plan.

Though the second I see Chay hunched over a coffee and

sweet roll while reading the paper, I start to head back the same way I came. Not getting very far before he's rising from the table and calling after me, leaving me with no choice but to own up and greet him.

"Hey," I say, hooking my bag on the seat opposite his.

He pushes his plate toward me, offering to share his danish. But tempting as it looks with the melted sweet cheese, the sugared fruit, and the overall promise of *yum*, I swore to Paloma I'd lay off the junk, and it's a vow I intend to keep.

"No thanks. I'm still on the wagon." I slide it back toward him. "Permanently on the wagon if Paloma has her way. But don't worry, I won't tell her how you spend your mornings."

He laughs when I say it, eyes crinkling and fanning in a riot of wrinkles. His good humor so infectious I can't help but laugh too, amazed by the way it instantly brightens my mood.

"How 'bout we make a deal," he says. "You don't tell Paloma I'm still indulging my sweet tooth despite all her warnings about the evils of sugar, and I won't tell her you're ditching school." When his gaze levels on mine, there's not one trace of mirth left in his eyes. "That is what's going on here, right?"

I lift my brow and shrug. No longer in a sharing mood. I push away from the table and help myself to the dregs of scorched coffee from a pot that's nearly empty. A good example of false advertising if I've ever seen one. So much for *freshly brewed.*

Taking a first, tentative sip, when Chay says, "And if that's the case, why'd you come here?"

"Not a whole lot of options this time of day. Or any other time, for that matter. After all, this is Enchantment we're talking about. Not exactly the excitement capital of the world." I add two creamers to my cup, hoping it'll take the edge off. It's dry creamer instead of liquid, the kind that would definitely not meet with Paloma's approval. But it's all I have to work with, and sometimes allowances must be made.

"I don't know," Chay says, "I can think of a hundred other things you could be doing."

"Name one." I dip one of those slim plastic sticks into my coffee and go to town with the stirring.

"Kachina loves an early morning ride." Chay studies me as I return to my seat.

"As do I." I take another sip that's better than the first, but only slightly so. "Guess I felt the need to be surrounded by people instead of nature. And what better place than right here?"

Chay pauses, a forkful of danish hovering between his plate and his mouth. "How about school? Lots of people there. People your own age, even." His eyes meet mine. He is not a man one can easily fool. "Daire, what's really going on here?" His voice turns sober and serious, having reached the end of the joke.

I stare into the clouds of clumpy coffee and sigh, saying, "Where to begin?"

"Wherever you'd like." He folds his paper in half and pushes it to the side, as I splay my hands on either side of my cup, weighing my options.

Chay is Paloma's trusted friend, and as I recently discovered, he's also her boyfriend. He's seen me at my absolute, sulkiest worst. Drove me all the way from Phoenix to Enchantment without a single complaint. Accompanied me to the place of my vision quest and gave me the confidence I needed to venture into that cave. He left Kachina in my care for however long I choose to look after her.

He's a good man.

Someone I can trust.

Maybe not with everything, but then I have no intention of telling him everything.

I lift my gaze to meet his, take a deep breath, and plunge in. Watching as he twists nervously at the eagle ring he always wears with the two golden stones standing in for the eyes, when I tell him all about the Lowerworld going to hell. Going on to explain about the Echo, how I finally discovered what it truly means, for Dace, for Cade, for all of us.

"And then, of course, there's the small matter of the prophecy," I say, voice filled with sarcasm, when the truth is, the prophecy looms larger than life—it's all I can think about. And it'll no doubt remain that way until I find a way to kick it to the curb—which is something I plan to do soon. Really soon. As soon as I can ditch Chay and cross the street to the Rabbit Hole. "You know about the prophecy, right?"

Chay leans over his coffee, purposely avoiding my eyes. "A prophecy can be interpreted in many ways."

I lean back in my seat, giving up on my coffee before I can take a third sip. "That's exactly what Paloma said." I regard him carefully, taking in the long, dark hair—not as long as Dace's but still long enough to pull back into a ponytail that falls just past his shoulders—the high cheekbones, the wide mouth, the brown weathered skin, and the kindest eyes I've ever seen—other than Dace's.

"Paloma is a wise woman." Chay grins. Taking a moment to finish the danish and clear the crumbs from his lips, before he goes on to say, "But that still doesn't explain why you're here."

"Doesn't it?" I cock my head, daring him to take a stab at guessing the truth, since I have no plans to reveal it.

He leans back in his seat, eyes narrowed in consideration. Clearly sensing my meaning, though probably not in its entirety, he tosses back the rest of his coffee and pushes away from the table. "Let's you and me take a walk."

I follow him outside, having no idea where he's taking me, though I'm pretty sure it won't be the Rabbit Hole. Or at least I hope not. I don't need an escort. Some things I'm destined to do on my own.

"Where we going?" I pause beside him on the curb, allowing a line of cars to pass before we cross.

"Bookstore." He trains his focus to the opposite side of the street where Dace watches me from his truck.

I know without looking it's him.

I can feel the stream of unconditional love that always surrounds me whenever he's near.

It takes every last bit of my strength to ignore it. To not look his way. To not jump up and down, waving my hands frantically over my head, as I shout out his name.

It's bad enough that I love him. Expressing that love is out of the question.

Or at least for now, anyway.

"I need to stop in here first," I say, grasping Chay by the elbow and steering him into the corner liquor store, where, once inside, I lean against the wall and fight to steady myself.

"You okay?" Chay peers hard at me.

I nod. Summoning the composure to say, "Would you mind grabbing a pack of cigarettes for me? I'm not old enough to buy them."

He quirks his brow, shoots me a dubious look.

"It's the demon snack of choice," I remind him. "And you never know when you'll need them."

thirteen

Dace

I slow when I see them. Sigh in relief as I watch them make their way down Main Street.

Chay's a good man. Solid. Dependable. Levelheaded. If Daire's skipping school to meet him, she must have her reasons.

I scrunch down in my seat when they stop at the curb. Feeling like a filthy stalker when Chay catches me watching. Though the look he shoots me is one of unspoken solidarity. Luckily, Daire's too busy talking to notice my presence.

I stare at her lips, straining to read them. Determined to punish myself when I imagine she's talking about us. How our love was doomed from the start. How I slept with her, then dumped her less than two hours later.

Maybe she thinks I'm choosing not to fight.

That I'm rolling over, letting Cade win.

God knows she insinuated as much last night in my kitchen.

And maybe that's why Chay fails to tell her I'm here. Staring helplessly out a dirt-covered window—already reneging on my word—unable to keep my own vows.

Maybe he thinks I'm not worthy of her.

When they disappear into the bookstore, I focus on the Rabbit Hole with newly informed eyes. Wondering how I'm supposed to continue to work there—step foot in there—now that I know what I know.

I hate the sight of the place.

I hate them.

But no sooner have I thought it than Chepi's voice slips into my head: *What have I taught you about hate, my son?*

Followed by the dutiful reply I spoke as a kid: *That it does more damage to the hater than the hated. To steer clear of it at all costs.*

I scrub my face with my hands. Wondering why she bothered to teach a child so presumably good, so supposedly incapable of such a dark emotion—what to do when faced with the specter of hate.

Did she suspect this day would come?

Was she preparing me for a time when my soul would be darkened by grief?

Whatever her reason, there's no doubt my soul could use a little darkening. If I've any hope of overcoming the circumstance of my birth—overcoming my demonic brother—then a little soul tarnish might come in handy.

Don't fight fire with fire, Paloma said. Claiming it comes to no good.

But how else am I supposed to fight?

Am I expected to glow so bright and good that Cade's destroyed by the sheer blinding sight of me?

Am I supposed to sit back and do nothing—allow my brother to kill Daire by stealing her soul like he did in my dreams? A dream I mistook for a nightmare. Couldn't imagine why I'd continually awaken, night after night, drenched in sweat and consumed with thoughts of a girl I'd never met.

Until she ran into me that night at the Rabbit Hole, and the sight of her flipped my world upside down.

Not long after that, when Leftfoot came to me, claiming that

Never imagined I would travel to the cave of her vision quest, convincing her to stay put, to see it through. Showing her the kind of greatness she could one day achieve if she could only hang in there just a little bit longer.

By the time it was over I was left with more questions than answers. *What did it mean? Why was I there? Why hasn't Daire ever once mentioned it? Not even the kiss that we shared?*

I glare at the Rabbit Hole with its stupid neon sign with the glowing arrow pointing down a steep flight of stairs.

The Richters are idiots.

When the portal failed to admit them to the Lowerworld, they tried to force their way in by digging deep into the earth. Not realizing they stood a better shot at reaching Australia than a mystical dimension inhabited by all things good.

When they finally realized their stupidity, they decided to put it to use by turning it into Enchantment's most happening place to hang out—Enchantment's only place to hang out. The drunks on the upper level, the teens on the lowest level, and it's a wall-to-wall crowd every night.

But now, thanks to Cade stealing Paloma's soul, and Daire's inability to sacrifice her grandmother's eternity for the greater good of all—they've found a way to breach the barrier. The story I was forced to cobble together from the scraps I managed to overhear—since everyone seems to think I need protecting, that I need to be shielded from the truth of my family.

Do they really think I'm so freaking pure I can't handle my own reality?

And worse, do they truly believe I'm incapable of defending myself?

I grip the wheel tighter, glaring at the side of the building as I punch hard on the gas, forcing the pedal all the way to the floor. Wanting nothing more than to crash through that fake adobe exterior, smash that stupid sign to bits, along with all the Richters inside.

But at the very last moment, I swing a hard U and head away from downtown.

Making my way to the reservation, in search of answers that are long overdue.

fourteen

Daire

By the time we exit the liquor store with the cigarettes secured in my bag, Dace is gone. Hopefully headed back to school, having realized the huge risk he takes by following me.

Thinking of me.

Loving me.

I follow Chay into the bookstore, where he proceeds to meander the aisles, peering at the kind of titles I'm pretty sure he has no interest in. Loitering in a way that makes me wonder why he decided to bring me here in the first place.

When the redheaded woman working the register calls to some unseen person in back—saying something about heading over to Gifford's to buy a roll of stamps—I can't help but notice the way Chay perks up as she exits. Darting for the counter the second the door closes behind her, he approaches it with a purpose I can't even fathom. Then smiles in greeting when a man with jet-black hair and eyes to match slips from behind the curtain, his gaze slanting toward me in question.

"Daire Santos." Chay bends his head toward me.

"Lucio Whitefeather." The man nods, gripping my hand in a nice, firm shake.

"Whitefeather?" I glance between him and Chay.

"Lucio is Leftfoot's son," Chay mumbles, as he guides me through the curtain, into a back room that, from the looks of it, seems to do triple duty as a storeroom, a break room, and a shipping center, judging by the number of large cardboard boxes strewn all about.

"Good timing," Lucio says. "Just got some new arrivals."

I watch as they hover over the box, cutting through thick bands of brown tape, only to reveal . . . *books*?

"I don't get it." I screw my mouth to the side. Try to make sense of it. "What's with all the secrecy?"

Lucio looks between Chay and me, taking the lead when he says, "The Richters don't just control the town—they control what's sold in town."

I gaze at the stacks of books with brightly colored covers— books about mastering one's destiny, creating a better world from the inside out—a far cry from the kinds of books I'd expect.

"So, you're saying that in addition to their long list of evil deeds—they're now book banners too?"

"They've banned anything they consider too inspirational or too informational." Lucio and Chay exchange a private look. "They don't want the people empowered. That wouldn't bode well for them."

"So they censor?"

"Ever listen to Enchantment radio?" Lucio asks.

I shake my head. It never even occurred to me to do so. I'm pretty much married to my iPod.

"It's filled with all the music and all the news *they* see fit to share. The town paper's no better."

"Okay, but still—why all the secrecy? Why not just order this stuff online and have all the self-help, inspirational books you desire delivered right to your door?"

"They run the local post office and the local Internet provider as well."

My eyes grow wide. *Sheesh.* I knew this town was bad. I knew the Richters were evil. But I guess I never knew just how far it went. They're complete and total fascists. One more reason to get myself to the Rabbit Hole and do what I came here to do.

"So, why do you stay?" I glance between them.

"Someone's got to fight the good fight." Chay grins, choosing a book from the stack and slipping it into my bag. Bidding a quick good-bye to Lucio and rushing me out the back door as soon as the redheaded salesclerk returns.

"So how about I take you home?" Chay broaches the question in a casual way, which stands in direct opposition to the probing look that he gives me.

"Home? Don't you mean school?" I quirk a brow, looking at him when I add, "Actually, I thought I'd just hang in town for a while. Find a quiet place to read my new book." I pat the side of my bag, though the look in his eye tells me he's not buying my act.

"I wouldn't recommend that. Best to keep that kind of thing to the privacy of your own home."

"So, you're saying our homes are private?"

A smile tugs at Chay's lips. "Paloma's is."

"What'd you give me, anyway?" I ask, having barely had a chance to look at it before he shoved it deep into my bag.

"Book about manifesting and intent nothing Paloma can't teach you."

I stare at him, feeling a little lost in his words.

He rubs his chin, casts a look around to ensure no one's listening. "Daire, I wanted to show you what you're up against. You're grossly underestimating El Coyote if you think you can just barge in there and do what . . . what I think you're planning to do. They're far more powerful than you realize. That pack of cigarettes in your bag may get you past the demons that guard the vortex, but what are you going to do once you're in? Do you even have a plan—or are you acting on an irrational blend of passion, anger, and adrenaline?" His gaze levels on me, waiting for me to respond, but when I don't, he goes on to say, "If you head over there now—you're only going to succeed in getting yourself killed."

"Not true," I say. "Cade won't kill me—he needs me. He knows I can't just will myself to stop loving Dace—it doesn't work that way. So the longer he keeps me around, the stronger he gets. He's the one who benefits."

"Don't think for a second he won't kill you in order to save himself because I guarantee you he will. Your drive to slay him is only as good as the strength you have to back it with. And, Daire, you're just not strong enough. I can't let you do it. Not yet anyway. Besides, you don't have to go this alone. You have plenty of resources in Paloma and me. Even in Leftfoot and Chepi and Lucio, who you just met. Let us help you. Let us show you how to do this the right way."

I stand before him, weighing his words.

"C'mon." He slides an arm around my shoulder and leads me down the street to his truck. "No shame in heeding an old man's wisdom."

fifteen

Dace

The last person I expect to see when I enter my mom's house is Leftfoot. Yet, there he is, sitting at her kitchen table, hunched over a steaming mug of freshly brewed piñon coffee. Caught in midconversation when he says, ". . . simply vanished. But we know that's not true."

He shoots Chepi a meaningful look, as her face goes grim in a way I don't often see. The two of them so lost in thought, it's a moment before they notice me.

"Dace!" My mother leaps to her feet, her expression arranging to one I can't read. Is it *guilt—surprise—reproach?* Before I can decide, she's rushing toward me, folding me into her arms and brushing a hand over my hair.

I return the hug. Clutch her tightly to me, then gently pry myself free. My gaze darting between them, I say, "I need answers."

"Why aren't you at school?" Chepi's large brown eyes narrow on mine. Attempting to deflect a conversation she'd prefer not to have. "Winter Break starts next week."

"Mother, please." My voice is as strained as the expression I wear on my face as I claim the empty chair between them, unwilling to play this particular game. "It's time you leveled with me and told me the truth."

Leftfoot mumbles something about needing to leave. But before he can get very far, I say, "As it happens, I need you here too."

He locks eyes with me and returns to his seat. Directing his words to my mother, he says, "Chepi, it's time. You can't avoid this day forever."

Chepi kneads the table with hands calloused from years of jewelry making—the turquoise and silver pieces once coveted by galleries and tourists alike. But over the last decade, the galleries have all closed, and Enchantment has fallen way off the tourist path. Forcing her to make frequent trips to Santa Fe, where she hawks her wares in the plaza, trying to keep us afloat.

"I know what happened to you on the Day of the Dead," I begin, hoping to spare her from reliving that hell. "I know what Leandro did. I know what I am, what Cade is, and how we were made. I know you were not at all responsible for what happened to you. I know how hard it must've been for you to look at me for the last sixteen years—"

"No!" Her hand finds mine, squeezing with surprising force when she says, "Don't you believe it—it's not at all true!"

I free myself from her grip, rock my chair back until it's balanced on two legs. An act that always resulted in a disapproving look followed by a verbal reprimand when I was a child but goes unnoticed today.

"You are my son. I have never once regretted bearing you. You were destined to come to me." Her fingers twist nervously.

Destined. Yes. I study my hands, deciding what to say next.

My thoughts interrupted by Leftfoot saying, "Dace, I'm sorry. There were many times I wanted to tell you, but—"

"But I wouldn't permit it," Chepi breaks in. "I thought that by ignoring it, I could avoid it. Stupid, I know." She shakes her head. "But when I saw you with the girl—"

"Daire. The girl's name is Daire." My gut twists in anguish when a vision of her blooms in my head.

"Yes." Chepi nods. "When I saw you with her, I knew it wouldn't be long before the truth was revealed. Still, even then, there never seemed a good time to tell you. Though please know that I never set out to lie to you or deceive you. I only wanted to protect you from the kind of regretful thoughts you're now having."

My gaze meets my mother's, and just like *that*, all the anger I'd cultivated during the course of a long torturous night dissolves as though it never existed. She's suffered more than any person rightfully should. There's no reason to rebuke her for hoarding her secrets. No reason to drag her any deeper into this than I already have.

Though when I try to tell her as much, insisting Leftfoot and I can take it from here, a long dormant strength rises to the surface. "You deserve an explanation," Chepi says. "You deserve to know the truth."

I steal a moment to steady myself. Despite barging in and insisting on this, I need time to prepare.

She stares at the opposite wall as though the memory is imprinted upon it. Her shoulders sinking, posture softening, as the corner of her lip lifts ever so slightly—in such contrast to the hardened jaw and clenched fists I would've expected.

"I was so very young then." Her voice lilts with fondness as a rueful smile lifts her cheeks, recalling an irretrievable version of herself. "Jolon—my father, your grandfather—fussed over me, coddled me, and protected me in ways I didn't even realize until he was gone."

"He spoiled you rotten," Leftfoot pipes in, inserting a welcome moment of levity into a story soon to grow dark.

Their eyes meet as though balancing the memory between them. The moment broken when Chepi tugs on her sleeves and returns to me. "I'd just turned sixteen. Though by today's standards, I was a very young and innocent sixteen. Believe me when I say I didn't possess even a trace of the worldliness of your generation. While I used to blame my naivete for what happened to me—Leftfoot was finally able to convince me it didn't matter either way. I was no match for Leandro. He was determined. I was his pawn. It's as simple as that."

My gaze drifts to Leftfoot, and I'm once again reminded of his selflessness—how quickly he stepped in to fill the fatherless void in our lives.

"There was a lot of excitement that day," she continues. "The entire reservation was abuzz with activity. But I was especially excited because Jolon had promised to take me to the Lowerworld so I could meet my spirit animal." Her eyes glitter with memory. "Although I'd always known I was guided by Hummingbird, I'd never made the journey to meet him face-to-face. I was so excited—I felt so grown-up, like I'd finally arrived as a full-fledged initiate. I'd always been fascinated by the mystical arts— I'd apprenticed with Jolon since I was a very young girl. But once I'd turned sixteen he agreed to step up my training. He was convinced I carried his gift. It was assumed I'd take over one day . . ."

She falls quiet, the tips of her fingers reading the table's wood grain, readying herself for whatever comes next. The sight of her prompting me to reach for her hand and cover it with my own, hoping it would provide the needed strength to continue.

"We'd planned to get an early start, but as was often the case with Jolon, we were soon delayed when a neighbor fell ill and needed his attention. Normally, I would've gone along to assist, but I was too excited, my energy too scattered to be of any use. So I hopped on my horse, an old mare named Lucky I was fiercely devoted to, and set out for the grove of twisted juniper trees, planning to wait for him there. On the way, I ran into Daniel—a shaggy-haired, brown-eyed boy I'd harbored a secret crush on. Or at least I'd thought it was secret; apparently I hadn't hidden it well." Her eyes flash, her face grows resigned, and she heaves a weary sigh. "At any rate, Daniel offered to join me, but first he had something exciting he wanted me to see. It wouldn't take long, he claimed, promising I'd be back at the vortex before Jolon ever guessed I'd been gone. He was so persuasive and I was so willing, that's all it took for me to agree. It was only later, when I found myself bound and gagged, that he revealed his true face. Turns out it wasn't Daniel I'd followed—it was Leandro Richter. He'd tricked me. Manipulated me by altering my perception and showing me what I most wanted to see. He held me captive for hours—aided by bleak and shadowy figures he conjured from the ether. Together they worked terrible black magick rituals that left me battered, beaten, and drifting in and out of consciousness. Until morning's first light when he tossed my unconscious body over Lucky's back and sent me home for Jolon to find me. A few hours later, Jolon was dead."

Her voice carries the quiet resignation of a survivor—one who's faced the worst life has to offer—the incomprehensible acts of cruelty humans choose to inflict upon each other.

"That day, I lost my innocence, I lost my faith, and I lost my beloved father."

I remove my hand from hers, clenching my fists tightly under the table, vowing revenge on Leandro, Cade, every last one of them. While she hasn't told me anything I didn't already know, there's no stopping the fresh wave of anger cresting inside me.

I'm derived from darkness. The spawn of an act so heinous it's hard to fathom.

How can she bear to look at me?

How can she stand to be near me?

As if sensing my thoughts, Chepi swivels in her seat until she's directly facing me. Pinching my chin between her index finger and thumb, she forces me to meet her gaze when she says, "Nine months later, when I had you, when I saw the light in your beautiful blue eyes, I knew that a small part of me had prevailed. While your brother has proved himself to be Leandro's creation—you, my beloved son, are mine and mine alone. It is *my* blood that courses through you. You are pure Whitefeather, and you must take great care to never forget that. Your grandfather Jolon was both powerful and gifted—he was linked to the divine—and I have no doubt you are as well."

"Yes, I'm the good half—the pure half," I say. The words bitter, rife with sarcasm as I wrench my chin from her grip, unwilling to meet her gaze, unworthy of her unconditional love.

"You've brought untold joy into my life." Her breath hitches, the words so full of emotion she needs a moment to continue. "You're the very reason I sit here today. Your arrival into this world gave me something to celebrate—something to live for. Dace, my darling boy, don't you know that now that you're here, I wouldn't have it any other way?"

It can't be true.

After all that she's been through, there's no way she means it.

But when my gaze finally, reluctantly, meets hers, there's no doubt she's speaking the truth.

I close my eyes, struggling to get a grip on myself. And when I open them again, I'm overcome with the need to apologize for making her relive such a horrible day. "I'm sorry for all of this— for everything. I'm sorry the past won't stay put."

Chepi shrugs. Her shoulders rising and falling, she says, "We've had sixteen peaceful years together—for that I am grateful." She reaches for my cheek with a palm that's soft and dry. And when she fusses at my hair, I don't try to stop it. Her touch brings great comfort. "Despite where we find ourselves now, I'm determined that more peace will follow. Leandro has claimed my past, but he will not claim my future—nor will he claim yours." Her voice is determined in a way I rarely hear, her irises deepening, reminding me of freshly turned earth. "I've already started the prep work."

I slant my gaze toward Leftfoot, seeing he's just as out of the loop on this one as I am.

"I haven't observed the Day of the Dead for many years. But after leaving you that morning with Daire, just after Paloma's soul was returned, I held a small ritual of my own."

I lean closer, trying to guess what that means.

"I called upon Jolon." She lifts her chin high. "I've sensed his presence through the years—his spirit is everywhere, just as I've taught you . . ." Her voice drifts as she absently rubs her thumb over the carved turquoise hummingbird she wears on her index finger. "I appealed for his protection, and ever since, I've felt the power of his lion looking after us. But, Dace, make no mistake— they exist merely in spirit. You and Daire are our last real defense against him and the rest of the Richters. There's no use denying it."

She falls quiet, leaving me to sort through her words. And though it wasn't at all what I expected to hear, I'm mostly caught on the part about Jolon's lion guiding us. Under the circumstances, that can't be good.

"The Lowerworld is corrupted," I say. "Daire and I were there yesterday. We've been going nearly every day—or, at least, Daire has." I pick at the crude bandage I wear on my arm, its edges already fraying, the middle stained red with my blood. All too aware of the way I used her name twice.

It's a sign of being in love. Acting as though the mere mention of a person can conjure their presence. When, in this case, the only thing it conjures is a breathtaking image of her lying beneath me—cheeks flushed, lips pink and inviting, eyes green and glittering, skin soft and welcoming under the press of my fingers . . .

I shake free of the thought. Vow to use her name as little as possible. There's no telling how much that little reverie cost me.

"The place is polluted," I continue. "And the spirit animals are infected as well. Horse is useless. He no longer guides me. They're all useless—skittish, freaked-out, inept."

That's all Chepi needs to remove the hummingbird ring she's worn for as long as I've known her. Plunking it down on the table, as Leftfoot makes a sign over the buckskin pouch he wears at his neck, the sight prompting me to think of Daire once again.

She's still wearing her pouch. Maybe I should tell her—warn her that it puts her at risk.

I shake my head. Scrub my hands over my face. I've got to stop this. Got to stop making excuses to think of her, see her. Paloma's looking after her. Chay too from what I saw earlier. She's in good hands.

I need to focus on protecting her in other ways.

Bigger ways.

Ways that truly matter.

I stare at Chepi's ring—a relic from my childhood I'd grown used to seeing, only now it looks different. As though it contains a whole cache of secrets I couldn't even begin to comprehend. My head so full, my thoughts so conflicted, I'm only half listening to myself when I say, "The animals are so corrupted they're no longer reliable."

My attention claimed by Leftfoot pushing away from the table. "Then we'll have to rely on ourselves," he says, heading toward the door and motioning for me to follow.

sixteen

Daire

When the drive goes on for too long, when Chay continues to meander down a series of unfamiliar dirt roads, taking increasingly confusing turns, I face him and say, "I thought you said Paloma was waiting?"

He shoots me a patient look. "She is."

"So—where exactly is it she's waiting? Clearly you're not taking me home."

"We're headed for the falls," he says, as though that makes perfect sense, when in truth it makes none.

"Can you give me a little more to go on?" I try to quell my growing alarm, along with the nervous chill running through me. This is reminding me an awful lot of how my vision quest went down. And despite getting through it and emerging renewed, that's not to say I enjoyed it.

Chay reaches toward me, his eagle ring glinting when he pats me on the knee. "I texted Paloma when I saw you in Gifford's. She told me to take you to the falls—said she'd meet us there."

"You guys text?" I swing toward him. I know it's not supposed to be the part I focus on—still, I never would've guessed.

Chay laughs. "Yeah, we text. We Facebook too. Though we draw the line at Twitter."

I shake my head. Force myself to focus, get back on track. "So, what will we do there, once we reach these *falls?*"

He looks at me. "Paloma will explain when we get there. I'm just the chauffeur."

I sigh. Slink toward the edge of my seat. All too aware there's no use pushing for more. Chay and Paloma are far too tight to fall for a game of Divide & Conquer.

A ribbon of scenery unfurls past my window—a smear of stark barren shapes in dark beiges and browns, set against a sky bleached white as bones. Despite the cold and dreary weather, Xotichl's claim that it'll snow by Christmas seems more improbable by the day.

We travel for miles. Travel over unfamiliar terrain that only seems to grow increasingly rugged the farther we go. And when we finally stop just a few feet from the water, I spot Paloma's Jeep parked near the shore.

I ease out of Chay's truck, watching as the two of them confer, with their heads bent together like fellow conspirators. Any chance of eavesdropping nixed by the rush of water raging so loudly it drowns everything out.

"Are you ready?" Paloma looks at me, her expression carefully guarded.

My eyes dart all around. Seeing a raging river and two people who may or may not have my best interests at heart.

"Ready for what?" I ask, though I'm afraid I already know. I begged Paloma to complete my Seeker initiation, to teach me as much as she could, as quickly as she could, and this is her way of making good on her word. "You seriously expect me to go in there? *Now?*" I point toward the river and shake my head. "You've got to be joking!" I fold my arms across my chest. "No way, Paloma. In case you haven't noticed, it's freezing. Not to mention, I'm not exactly dressed for it."

It seems like a good excuse to me, but the words are lost on her. Without so much as a pause, she says, "I brought you a change of clothes. As soon as you're ready, you will enter at this point here—" Her arm arcs before her, fingers pointing toward the place where the water meets the dirt. "And you will head downstream and find your way to the waterfall where you will endure its deluge until you manage to merge with its power and it reveals its song to you."

I blink. Shake my head. Blink again. Though it's not like it does any good. Every time I open my eyes I see them standing before me, waiting for me to quit wasting time and get started already.

"Remember what I told you: Everything is alive, *nieta*. The elements are our allies, a friend to all Seekers. They each have something to teach us, something to reveal to us. You've already met the power of Wind and Earth, and now you must learn the power of Water. There's an ancient saying that states: *The softest things in the world overcome the hardest things in the world*—and Water is a good example of that. It's silky, fluid, yet it's also responsible for carving those rocks at your feet. You must strive to listen to the Water, discover what it offers, and determine its song. If not, I'm afraid you'll succumb, and all will be lost."

I swallow hard. Try to determine what's worse—getting decapitated on an LA freeway like my dad or drowning in a murky New Mexico river, like I'm pretty sure I'm about to.

"One of the most important things you'll ever do as a Seeker, aside from keeping the balance between the worlds, is managing the weather by manipulating the elements. But before you can handle the elements, you must first learn to bond with them. And now it's time for you to bond with the water element. Many Seekers before you have undergone these trials, it's simply your turn."

She hands me the clothes she brought and tells me to change in her Jeep. When I emerge, she opens her arms as though to embrace me. And though I'm not feeling especially huggy toward her at the moment, I do so anyway.

It may be my last.

It may give me the strength I need to get through this.

When my eyes meet Chay's and he nods his encouragement, I square my shoulders, face the river, and wade in. Walking straight into the freezing cold water that soaks me in an instant, chilling my body to the verge of hypothermia in just a handful of seconds. Telling myself that if this is what it takes to kill Cade Richter, I'll do it.

At first, I fight the current, insisting on going at my own pace, my own way. Though it's not long before the effort exhausts me, forcing me to loosen my limbs and literally go with the flow. Clutching the buckskin pouch with one hand, I do what I can to keep my head above water as I'm carried downstream.

Fingers seeking the hard edge of the raven stone lurking inside, along with the spine of the feather, and the curve of Django's bear. Teeth chattering, lips quivering, I press the pouch between my palms, fold my fingers in supplication, and say, "If there's any good left in you, then please guide me through this. Please help me endure. Do not let me die. Not here. Not like this. Not before I get a chance to do what I was born to do."

seventeen

Dace

I grind my jaw hard. Cringing as Leftfoot pours more of that foul-smelling liquid onto my wound. Stuff burns like I can hardly believe.

"I think you've covered it." I push the words between gritted teeth. "Any more and I'll think you're just bent on torturing me."

"How'd you get this?" He squints, focusing on threading the needle he'll use to sew the gash closed.

"Had an unfortunate encounter with a crazy coyote."

He pauses, studying me for a long moment, then he jabs the needle into my flesh. "Relax. The more you resist, the worse it gets. That goes for everything in life, by the way, not just stitches."

I shake my head. Mutter a stream of curses under my breath. While it's hardly the first time Leftfoot's sewn me closed, this wound goes way deeper than most.

"I'm afraid it's even worse than you think." He weaves the needle and thread in and out of my skin.

I glare at the wound. *If that coyote was rabid, I'll kill it too!*

"No, not that." Leftfoot yanks on the thread before tying a knot. "The Middleworld is also suffering the effects of Cade's actions."

Oh. That.

"Yesterday a flock of ravens dropped from the sky. By the time they hit the ground, they were dead. That's the second time that's happened."

Ravens. Of course. How poetic.

Ravens equal Daire.

And dead Ravens equal Cade's plan to steal Daire's soul and leave her for dead—just like the prophetic dream that I had.

"And while it hasn't snowed in Enchantment for many years, now it's no longer snowing in the surrounding areas either. It's cold enough to snow. It feels like snow. But for whatever reason, it's not happening. Bad news for Angel Fire, Taos, and all the other ski resorts—but even worse news for us because we know what's behind it." He locks eyes with me. "And the one who's in charge of saving us isn't prepared for the job. Daire's training was cut short when Paloma lost her soul. They're just now picking up where they left off. But with Paloma's magick gone, Daire will have to face this thing on her own. And I hate to say it, but she's far from ready." He reaches for a roll of gauze, winds it snugly around my arm.

"I'll help her! I'll . . ." I clamp my lips shut and stare out the window.

How am I supposed to help her when I can't even get near her?

Can't even think about her without strengthening Cade.

The only way to help her is by replacing all loving thoughts of her with vengeful thoughts of Cade. Nurture my hate for him until my soul becomes dark enough to crush his.

"You're not ready either." Leftfoot's voice cuts into my thoughts. "You've been sheltered too long. Aside from a handful of parlor tricks we taught you as a kid, you have a long way to go."

I grit my teeth. That's hardly my fault.

He tugs on my sleeve, unrolling the fabric until it covers my wound. "Though, despite your lack of training, you must never forget you have one very distinct advantage over Cade."

Our eyes meet. I have no idea what that could possibly be.

"While the dark delivers suffering and chaos, the light is the only thing that can illuminate it well enough to stop it in its tracks. You don't have to become like your brother to fight your brother. Understood?"

I nod. Though the truth is, I'm willing to sacrifice anything—play dirty if necessary—if it means saving Daire. Now that she's a part of my life, there's nothing I won't do to protect her.

I study the hand-carved wooden santos filling the niches, the assortment of feathers, and crystals, and herbs lining the shelves. The tools of the Light Worker trade. The talismans Leftfoot swears by. Maybe it's good enough for healing the locals, but it's hardly a match for my beast of a brother.

I turn to Leftfoot. Catching him studying me with eyes that are hooded and deep. His gaze probing, as though reading my thoughts, he heaves a resigned breath and says, "Guess it's time you learn some new tricks."

"People are missing."

I sharpen my focus, unsure if he's being serious or purposely trying to distract me just so he can remind me, yet again, of the importance of intent. How it's magick's main ingredient. The force that makes it all happen.

I open my palm, fighting the urge to shout in triumph when the red-tailed hawk I'd been tracking lands on its center. Its sharp talons piercing my flesh as he settles for a few moments, taking a quick survey of the land, before spreading his wings and taking flight once again.

"Who's missing?" I ask, taking the bait now that I've nailed the part about connecting and blending with nature. Convincing that hawk to think, for a few short moments anyway, that I was a safe place to land. Hopefully the next lesson will provide a little more challenge. The last few were too easy.

"Mike Miller, Randy Shultz, Tessa Harpy, Anthony Lopez, Carla Sanchez—all of 'em gone. Seeming to vanish without a trace. And those are just the ones that I know of."

I frown. His words instantly reminding me of the conversation I interrupted between him and Chepi when I barged into her kitchen just a few hours earlier.

"Gone where?"

Leftfoot shrugs. "No saying. People don't often leave these parts, as you know."

"Some do." I stare into the distance, remembering how Marliz managed to flee a bleak future of waiting tables at the Rabbit Hole, and an even bleaker future of marrying my insane cousin Gabe by moving to LA—with a little help from Daire's mom, Jennika. And there was another girl I once knew . . . one who made it out and never returned.

"There haven't been many. And there's never been five in one day."

"Did their families report them missing?"

Leftfoot squints, his weathered face folding in a series of valleys and crags. "You think anyone in the police department is going to care, much less make a report? The whole town's run by Richters—they're probably behind it."

I work my jaw. Drag the bottom of my shoe across the dirt.

"You're nothing like them," he says.

I turn to face him, neither agreeing nor disagreeing. Unwilling to say anything that might result in his halting my training. There's so much left to learn, and he's the only one willing to teach me.

"What's next?" I study Leftfoot as he takes a moment to reassess. "Feel free to make it more challenging."

"You think you're ready for more, huh?" He considers me for a moment, his gaze so probing and deep I fight not to squirm.

The old medicine man may not be as legendary as his brother, Jolon, but he definitely holds his own, and I've never been able to fool him. "Fine. Though I warn you, this'll take most of the night; by tomorrow you'll be ready to return to your job at the Rabbit Hole."

eighteen

Daire

A hard blast of spray pummels my face well before I've actually
reached it.

That's the sort of power the waterfall wields.

From where I float, it looks scary, foreboding, and huge—an
ominous deluge thick as a highway. Leaving no doubt of its ability to crush me or transform me.

It could go either way.

I glimpse the place where Paloma and Chay track me from
the shore. Despite the fairly short distance between us, they seem
worlds away. Like two miniature figures looking on from the
sidelines, waiting to see if I'll live or die. Though it's not long before the current accelerates. The swiftly churning waters warning I'm soon to be delivered.

The constant drumming of water crashing onto itself vibrates
my insides, while outside, the river's icy embrace leaves my flesh
deadened and numb. Making for a predicament so miserable, so
unbearable, it requires every ounce of my resolve to ignore the instinctive urge to scramble for shore. To trust in the magick Paloma's taught me, the ancient Seeker traditions, and the elements to
see me safely through.

There's really no choice. No point in fighting my destiny.

Refusing to do this, refusing to complete my training, would end my life as surely as it did Django's. And somehow I feel like I'm doing this for both of us. Desperate to succeed where he failed. And while I may not survive this particular test, while it may plunk me into a horrible premature death, there's still a small chance I'll get through. And it's that thought I cling to.

I close my eyes tightly, focus hard on my goal, and tuck my chin to my chest.

Driven closer—

The spray blasts my cheeks like pounding fists.

Almost there—

Django—Paloma—please forgive me! I'm not cut out for this—I can't do this!

I'm under.

The water hammering so hard, it drives at my shoulders, pushing me down—and then down farther still. Plunging me into depths that surpass all reasonable limits, causing my lungs to swell so large, I'm sure they'll soon burst. And there's nothing I can do to stop it. The water's rendered me powerless, helpless—dissolving my strength until all that remains is my will.

My will to live.

My will to see this thing through.

My will to kill Cade—claim my birthright as a Seeker—and not die like my father.

Though, as it turns out, will alone isn't enough.

It's evanescent.

Fleeting.

No match against nature.

It just doesn't cut it.

Doesn't keep me from sinking. Arms flailing, legs kicking, unable to save myself from crashing hard against the bed of rocks far below, as slick, slippery, unknown things slither and skate all around me.

My limbs turned useless and weak, my lungs inflated far be-yond capacity—I struggle to gather whatever strength I have left, and strive once again to swim for the surface.

But, in the end, it's no more than a death dance: Frantic, pa-thetic, not nearly enough to save me.

Django was lucky—by the time he saw it coming, it was al-ready too late.

But this—this is horrible, made even more excruciating by the crystal clear awareness of the finality that awaits me.

The rocks turning first soft, and then spongy, until they com-pletely give way and I descend even farther. Delivered to a place that's no longer dark—where I'm no longer alone. Free of all the pain and suffering that plagued me mere seconds ago. Left to gaze upon a beautiful, luminescent figure that floats just before me. Emanating an energy so warm, so brilliant, so loving and healing, I no longer mourn what I lost.

I'm just grateful to orbit its presence.

Grateful this descent wasn't nearly as bad as I feared.

I linger. Floating slow circles around this wonderful, radiant being. An entity so glorious it's hard to comprehend.

My body strengthened, healed by the sheer purity of its innate power and goodness, I struggle to hold onto the feeling, never wanting it to end. But with no more than a slight shake of its head, and an upward tilt of its finger, I'm off and soaring again.

Rising. Churning. Thrusting through the waters so quickly, there's no time to protest before I burst free.

Free of the water.

Free of the current.

Left gasping and squinting through water-clogged eyes. Sur-prised to find myself in a calm, cool place on the waterfall's other side.

No longer menacing. No longer threatening. This inside view allows for a whole new perspective.

It's still shiny, slick, and gleaming, for sure—but from where I now float, it appears far more glorious than ominous. A brilliant cascade of crystalline waters glinting silver under the belly of a late-morning moon. The sound somehow muted—no longer the crashing crescendo I once found so deafening.

I reach for my pouch, relieved to find it survived the journey as well. Pressing the wet buckskin to my lips, I say, "Now what?"

Though I wasn't really expecting an answer, the silence that greets me encourages me to go silent too.

I silence my body. My mind. Forcing myself to grow quiet and still and see what the water reveals.

I have no idea how long I remain like that—with my body no longer cold, my skin no longer numb, time seems inconsequential at best. All I know is that at some point my pulse begins to quicken, my heart begins to thrum, until I can actually *feel* the raw power of the waterfall's energy becoming one with my own.

It surges inside me.

Merges with the very life force that drives me.

Its message coming faintly at first, though it's not long before it begins to ring clear. Rising into a beautiful harmony that wells up from the depths, until the sound of the watersong swells in my head.

I am comfort
I am death
I both take life and sustain it
I'm the lull and sway on a hot summer's day
I'm the hardened crust of a hard winter's spell
I'm adapting
Ever-changing
My attachments nonexisting
Follow my lead when you find yourself resisting.

The song repeats. Playing over and over until I'm singing right along with it. And once the lyrics are lodged in my head and etched on my heart, I find my way back. The once-raging water-fall slowing to a trickle—allowing me safe passage before it returns to full force.

Paloma and Chay meet me at the shore, warming me with a large heavy blanket she wraps snugly around me. Her hands moving over my shoulders and back, her voice thick with pride, she says, "*Nieta*, you made it!"

I gather my hair into my fist, squeezing large droplets of water onto the ground, along with a beautiful stone that glints up from below. Its color reminding me of Dace's eyes.

"A gift from the water." Paloma stoops to retrieve it, displaying it on the center of her palm as I gaze upon it in wonder. "An aquamarine—a water stone. This goes in your pouch, *nieta*."

She drops it beside the other talismans as I look between her and Chay, asking, "What's next?" Feeling more than ready to handle it, whatever it is. Sure it couldn't be any worse than the feat I just survived—okay, *barely* survived, but still.

Chay looks to Paloma. "I'll leave that to you," he says, giving her a brief kiss good-bye as he heads for his truck, and Paloma directs me to her Jeep, where I change back into the clothes I arrived in.

"Fire is next." She shields me with the blanket as she goes on to explain, "It's the last remaining element, and some would say, the most dangerous. We don't normally endure two trials in one day, but then again, these aren't normal circumstances, are they?"

"I'm ready." My voice is determined, as I allow her to weave my hair into a long braid that falls down my back much like hers. "Whatever it takes, I'll do it. Just tell me where to begin."

nineteen

Dace

After a tedious amount of nature hugging, blending, and merging, Leftfoot finally gets to the juice, saying, "Your twin is a skinwalker."

My first reaction is to freeze. It's instinctive, something I couldn't stop if I tried. My eyes darting frantically, on the lookout for anyone close enough to overhear, but of course it's just us. Though I still don't breathe any easier.

One of the first things I learned as a kid was that giving your attention to something by talking about it, or obsessively thinking about it, helps make it real by delivering it right to your door whether you wanted it or not. And it works for the bad things just as well as the good.

Because of it, I was steered away from unsavory topics—and the topic of skinwalkers counts among the most unsavory of all.

It's serious stuff, skinwalkers. Seriously scary stuff. If you're going to bring it up, you better have a good reason lest you draw the attention of one, which you'll live to regret.

If you're lucky enough to live, that is.

But, according to Leftfoot, I've already drawn the attention of one, who, as it just so happens, is also my twin.

I focus my attention on the old medicine man before me. In the fading afternoon sun, his hair glints like tinfoil. His hooded gaze deepening, he says, "Or rather I should say he's more like a hybrid of one. I doubt he completed the ritual. Not only because he lacks the patience for such a thing but also because it involves killing a relative—the usual price of admission for one's introduction to the black arts. And since Leandro is unwilling to spare even the dimmest Richter, it's my guess Cade isn't a full skinwalker yet. With a soul as dark as Cade's, the mere act of getting riled up, either by becoming very angry or very excited about something, is enough to result in a complete transformation of self."

I stare into the distance, needing a moment to examine his words. While I've no doubt what he's saying is true, the question remains—can I do it too?

"I've seen it." I switch my gaze to meet his. "Both in dreams and real life."

"As have I." Fielding my look of surprise, he says, "I've seen a lot of things in the sweat lodge, as will you. But first things first."

I look at him, feeling jacked up, ready for anything he's willing to teach.

"I'm going to share something with you that's long been forbidden. Something my brother, Jolon, taught me, that no one taught him. He just sort of *gleaned it,* as only Jolon could. He was very powerful that way." Leftfoot's eyes cloud with memory before returning to me. "I'm going to teach you to soul jump. How to immerse yourself in another person's essence by merging with their energy in order to share their experience. You will see what they see, hear what they think. And for the few who master the skill, they find they're able to wield great influence over those very same things."

Despite my eagerness to learn, I balk at his words. Standing before him in gaping-mouthed silence until I pull it together enough to say, "You're joking, right? How's that even possible?"

"Oh, it's possible." Leftfoot's expression and voice remain level and sure. "Much like you merged your energy a few moments ago with the birds and the snakes to share their experience—you will now learn to do the same thing with a human."

My eyes slide shut as I try to imagine it. Imagine myself making a soul jump into Cade.

What would it be like to to peer into that dark and hollow core and learn the secrets of his nature—go in search of his weak spots?

This is exactly the kind of thing I was hoping for.

It's a game changer, for sure.

If I can just get inside, get a peek at whatever darkness lurks there, I'll know exactly how to exploit it when it's time. Maybe I'll even claim a piece of it for my own. If my love for Daire strengthens him—then surely it can work the opposite way? Surely I can armor myself with his malevolence?

I focus on Leftfoot, eager to get started. Sure this'll prove to be far more useful than soaring over the landscape via that red-tailed hawk, despite how exhilarating that was.

"There is one caveat . . ." His eyes narrow on mine. "You must never teach another person what you've learned—not even Daire." He pauses long enough for me to agree, before he continues. "And you must never abuse the gift. *Ever.* I can't stress this enough. You use this gift if, and only if, you find that you must. You must first exhaust all other options. It is meant to be a last resort. The rest of the time you're to keep the knowledge locked safely inside. And you must vow to carry it to your grave. Even Chepi and Paloma have no idea that I know how to do this. As I've already said, it's been forbidden for years."

"I won't tell anyone." I'm quick to agree. "I swear." The vow sounding a bit too eager even too my ears, which is probably why Leftfoot shoots me a look that tells me he remains unconvinced.

"There's more." His brow droops low as his gaze travels a very long distance. "Something I hope will illustrate the seriousness of all this . . ."

I wait for him to spill it, but really I just want to get started.

"Leandro didn't kill Jolon."

I stare hard at Leftfoot, shocked by his words.

"That story is a disservice to Jolon. Though I've never tried to defend him because the truth is much worse."

He turns toward the Sangre de Cristo mountain range, grimacing when he takes in the lack of snow at the cap, or maybe he's grimacing at what he's about to say next. It's hard to tell with Leftfoot.

"The truth is, Jolon's defenses were much too strong for Leandro to penetrate, and Leandro was at least smart enough to know that. When Chepi arrived home that day, battered and bruised, Jolon decided to use the forbidden art we merely toyed with as kids to enter Leandro's experience. Remaining there long enough to view the contents of his wretched, debauched life—including the horrible acts he performed on Chepi. He thought he could handle it, and, at the time, Jolon was so strong I would've bet on it too. But the events Jolon witnessed were so horrific they weakened him in a way he never imagined. He died shortly after making the soul jump. So while the essence of the oft-repeated story is the same—that Jolon died from a broken heart over the things he witnessed—the truth is that Leandro didn't force Jolon to witness it. He didn't alter Jolon's perception like they claim. Jolon chose to make the jump. He *chose* to witness the dregs of Leandro's dark soul. And what he saw cost him his life."

I stand before him, suitably sobered by the tale.

"All magick comes with a price. You must never forget that."

I work my jaw, curl my fingers to fists, and nod like I mean it. I do mean it.

"Okay," Leftfoot says, finally convinced. "Here's how you do it . . ."

twenty

Daire

The second we spot Jennika parked outside Paloma's adobe, I'm not sure who groans louder, Paloma or me.

"Great. So much for fire starting." I stare incredulously as my mom leans against some generic rental car, furiously punching numbers into her cell. Probably calling me and getting my voice mail, since my phone has been off for the better part of the day.

Her chin lifts as she hears our approach—her expression changing from angry to relieved, before settling on completely annoyed. "Hello, Daire," she says, coming around to my side. Her arms spread wide for a hug, despite a demeanor that's hardly what I'd call welcoming. "Where the hell have you been?" She releases me from her grip. "I've been calling for hours. Even dropped by your school only to be told that you didn't bother to show. I was worried sick!" She grabs hold of my braid, then frowns when her fingers come away wet. Shifting her anger to Paloma, she says, "Well?"

"Please, come inside." Paloma ducks around her and leads us to the door. "I'll make us some tea, something to eat, and we can all sit and talk. It's nice to see you." She smiles at Jennika, but Jennika merely grunts in response.

I sneak a peek at Paloma, my gaze filled with questions. *How did this happen? How did my mom show up in Enchantment without my knowing—without any advance warning?* But Paloma seems as clueless as I am.

"What're you doing here?" I ask, claiming a seat at the kitchen table and motioning for Jennika to do the same, which she reluctantly does.

"I wanted to surprise you. And judging by the horrified look on your face when you saw me, I did."

I fumble for a grin. Try to act as though I'm not nearly as horrified as she thinks. A little surprised, but mostly just happy to see her.

Which I am.

Or at least I could've been with a little advance notice, some time to prepare. But then, Jennika's never been one to call ahead. She's all about the ambush.

"What's going on, Daire?" Her green eyes, nearly exact replicas of mine, study me in that all-knowing, all-seeing, motherly way that always leaves me squirming. "Why aren't you in school?"

"Why aren't you at work?" I retort, accepting the mug of tea Paloma places before me. If nothing else, it'll give me something to look at.

"We shut down for the holiday. So I thought I'd pay you a visit."

"You're staying *here*?" I ask, instantly regretting the way my face drops as my voice rings with panic.

Smooth, Daire. Way to keep her from guessing you're involved in the sort of activities she'd never approve of.

"I got a room in town." She taps her thumb against the cup, the silver ring I gave her for Mother's Day making a dull, clanging sound.

"There are rooms in town?" I squint, trying to imagine who would possibly stay in one. Who would choose to visit Enchantment and, once here, actually stay the night?

"Trust me, it's not much."

She picks at her hair, the bleached-blond strands appearing far more golden than the extreme platinum I remember. And her skin, normally as pale as mine, is now ever so slightly tanned. Must be the LA effect—the result of residing full time in the Golden State where the sun always shines.

Or at least that's what I think until I notice the faint row of lines crossing her forehead and realize she's not nearly as settled as I thought. She may have a permanent address and a permanent place of employment for the first time in a long time, but it's been a tough year, with too many changes to count. And not all of those changes were good.

Sometimes I forget just how hard it's been for Jennika to not only watch me deal with the kind of things she can't understand—and really doesn't want to—but to also leave me in the care of a woman she doesn't really know all that well.

She worries.

She means well.

And the longer she stays, the more I'll have to remind myself of that.

"I didn't want to impinge on you and Paloma," she continues. "But now I'm thinking maybe I should."

Great. I stare at my tea, as she stares at me. Once again, her timing couldn't be worse. She must have some crazy maternal instinct that tells her just the right moment to interfere. Nothing else explains it.

"So, now that I've answered your question, it's time for you to answer mine. What's going on with you and school? Why weren't you there today, when other than your inexplicable wet hair, you seem fine to me? Where were you and Paloma anyway? What's going on, Daire?"

I look to Paloma to save me, but she's returned to the stove. Her back turned toward us as she focuses on food prep.

Deciding to answer her barrage of questions as a whole, I say,

"I needed a mental health day, so Paloma took me on a field trip. Said a little time spent outdoors would do me good." I shrug. It's as good an answer as any and as close to the truth as I can afford.

"What do you mean, *mental health day*? Are the visions back?" Jennika's face pales, remembering the hallucinations that landed me here. But I'm quick to wave it away, reluctant to revisit that topic again.

"No. Nothing like that. I just . . . well, school's a whole new experience for me, as you know, and it's been a bit of an adjustment, that's all."

"Is this about that boy?" She frowns, her face darkening as the diamond stud in her nose twitches and winks.

"By *that boy*, I'm assuming you mean Dace?" I narrow my gaze on hers. Knowing full well she remembers his name.

"Dace Whitefeather, yes. So—is it? Did something happen between you?"

I lean back in my seat, not really wanting to discuss this but also knowing she won't let it go quite so easily. Jennika's a pit bull. She'll gladly sit here all night waiting for the answer she seeks. She can be unbelievably stubborn. I know because she's the one who taught me to be unbelievably stubborn too.

I sigh, already dreading her reaction. I admit, "We're not really together at the moment. We're taking a break."

"A break?" She cocks her head as a look of suspicion crosses her face.

"A short break." I nod. Inwardly rolling my eyes at myself, knowing that to her ears that hardly makes it any better or any more believable.

"And whose decision was this—to take this *short break*?" She folds her hands before her, waiting for me to spill the whole grisly tale.

I take a deep breath, wanting to say it was mine, but she'll never believe it. She knows me too well. She'll sense the lie the instant it passes my lips. So I go with the truth—or at least a partial truth. "His. It was his idea." Unable to resist adding, "Happy now?" Knowing full well that she is. She loves being right. Most people do.

She splays her hands on either side of her cup, unable to keep the self-satisfied glint from sneaking onto her face. "A short break—and so close to Christmas—how charming." She shakes her head, taps her cobalt-blue polished nails hard against the tabletop. "Does this mean you'll reconvene after the New Year? Or perhaps you can delay until well after Valentine's Day in order to steer clear of all the more romantic holidays?"

I gaze down at my tea. If only it was that easy.

She sighs long and loud, as though resigning herself to the burden of always being right. Adopting a cloying, singsongy tone, she says, "Well, I hate to say I told you so—"

"No you don't." I slide my elbows across the table and lean toward her, looking her straight in the eye. "You don't hate it at all. You practically live for those words."

She studies me. Probably trying to determine whether I'm angry, amused, or indifferent. The thought lasting a handful of seconds before she casts it aside. "True." Her shoulders rise and fall. "But in this particular case it would've been nice to be wrong. I know you don't believe me, Daire, but I truly am sorry, and I really do understand what you're going through. Dace was your first real boyfriend, but he won't be your last. So while it may feel bad now—"

"Could you please not do that?" I say. Responding to the confused look she gives me when I add, "Could you please not talk about other fish in the sea, stallions in the barn, roosters in the pen, or any other animal analogies and just allow me this moment to wallow? Like you said, it's my first breakup, so let me experience it in its entirety before you push me toward some phantom boy I have no interest in meeting just yet, okay?"

I slump low in my seat, surprised by the way my voice broke at the end. My intention was merely to play along, tell her what she wanted to hear, by pretending that it really is as simple as she thinks. Just your average high school romance gone suddenly south—all so Dace could be spared the burden of buying me a Christmas gift. But the longer I spoke, the more the words became real. And it's not long after that my paranoia sets in.

What if this isn't just a short break?

What if I can't find a way to overcome the curse of the Echo?

What if I can't overcome Cade?

How many people will suffer because of my failure?

Jennika moves toward me, starts fussing over my hair. Unraveling my braid, she gathers the strands into her hand before arranging them to spill in soft waves down my back. "I'd take you out for some ice cream, followed by some heavy-duty retail therapy, which, just so you know, are pretty much the two best cures for a broken heart. Except, we're stuck in this dump of a town with no good shopping to be had." Her eyes dart toward Paloma. "No offense," she says, but Paloma just waves it away and continues preparing our snack. "But while I failed to pack any ice cream, I did manage to bring a little retail therapy to you." Jennika kneels beside me, smiling so brightly it practically begs me to smile brightly too.

So I do.

This is Jennika trying.

Jennika doing her best to show me she understands.

Jennika determined to pull me out of my slump.

The least I can do is relent.

"I was going to save it for Christmas, but I see no reason why you can't have it now." She digs through a bag she's left by her chair, retrieving a hidden cache of designer jeans and a bunch of cute tops to wear with them, along with a tangle of silver jewelry, and a new pair of black boots. All of it chosen with Jennika's uncanny eye for all-things trendy and cool.

While the sight of it doesn't lift me in quite the same way it used to, I pretend like it does by crowding my fingers with rings and smiling when Jennika pulls out a new red wool cardigan she gives to Paloma.

Relieved to know that her suspicions are forgotten for now. Though it's just a matter of time before Jennika's back on course, determined to make me explain what Paloma and I have been doing.

twenty-one

Dace

By the time we arrive at the sweat lodge, the sun has dropped, the sky has turned the color of soot, and Leftfoot's apprentice, Cree, is already waiting for us. Focused hard on the blaze he continues to stoke, barely sparing a glance our way when Leftfoot says, "Cree will serve as the firekeeper."

I nod, aware of what an honor it is to keep the wood blazing and the river rocks properly heated for ritual.

"One is required to fast before a ceremony—when was your last meal?"

I go over the day, conducting a quick mental review. But unable to remember, I lift my shoulders in reply.

"Good enough." He turns to have a few words with Cree, instructing him on how he'd like to manage the ceremony, before returning to me. "Remove your clothing and shoes. The lodge is a sacred space."

Without question, I do as he asks. All too aware of what a privilege it is to receive Leftfoot's teachings. Despite his reputation for being kind, generous, and wise—when it comes to matters of mystical counsel and guiding one down the Red Road— the pathway to truth, peace, and harmony—he's incredibly discerning. Refusing to educate anyone he doesn't personally choose. It's an honor to be here. I won't let him down.

I kick off my shoes and shrug off my clothes. Leaving them piled neatly on the ground, I hop from foot to foot beneath the fattened belly of a December's full moon. Taking a moment to spread my arms wide and welcome the embrace of the frigid night air on my flesh.

With my skin prickly with chills, I distract myself from the cold by remembering what I was taught as a youth. The entrance to the lodge purposely faces east in order to greet the rising sun once the ceremony is concluded. The space is dug into the ground in order to symbolize the womb of the earth. And, most important, the experiences one has during the ritual are both powerful and transformative—allowing one to emerge fully purified and reborn.

While it's not exactly purification I seek, I decide not to share that with Leftfoot. If the experience is anything even remotely like the vision quest he guided me through, it'll be well worth my time.

Just when I think I can't take another second of being naked and shivering, Leftfoot ushers me toward the door but blocks me from entering. Declaring I must first seek permission from the spirits that guard it, he stands over me as I sink toward the earth and press my knees to the dirt. Appealing to my ancestors in my native tongue, and rising only when Leftfoot assures me I'm free to proceed.

He wields a bushy stick of sage across the width and length of the doorway. His voice rising in the melody of one of his traditional healing songs, as I descend the short ladder attached to the wall, and crouch toward the far end. Surprised to find the space so much smaller than I expected. Darker too. I guess I'd heard so many whispered stories over the years, I'd built up an elaborate vision in my head. Pictured it as bigger, roomier. When the truth is, its domed roof fastened by willow branches and covered with a tightly woven tarp swoops so low at the sides, I'm forced to inch toward the center in order to sit fully upright.

Leftfoot and Cree follow. Leftfoot claiming the space beside me, mumbling words of prayer. As Cree wields a massive pair of deer antlers piled with smoldering river rocks he lowers into the pit before dousing them with a liberal dose of water and herbs that infuses the space with a sweet, heady scent.

With the temperature swiftly rising, Cree closes the door, shrouding us in complete and utter darkness. Then he moves to the far side of the wall where he takes up his rattle, shaking it in a slow and steady rhythm as he chants a song I've never heard until now.

Thick rivulets of sweat begin to drip down my torso, forming small pools in the dirt just below. The incessant rhythm of Cree's chanting and rattling causing my head to thrum—my body to instinctively sway to its beat. The air all around me adopting a light, hazy feel—until the next thing I know, I'm no longer attached to my body.

I'm released of gravity's hold.

My physical form giving way to the astral version of me, I'm rendered weightless, freed of all restraints. Slipping easily through the domed tarp above me, I float through the ether. Surprised to find Leftfoot soaring alongside me, his ethereal form surrounded by a light film of gold, while my own is outlined with shimmering bands of blue.

Watch closely. His words swirl within me. *You will see what you are meant to see, so it's important to take careful note. You may not always like what you're shown, but you don't choose the journey—the journey chooses you.*

With a curt nod of his head, we drift downward. Ultimately landing in a long all-white hallway marked by a series of doors with no handles or knobs, no way to open them on our own.

I look to Leftfoot, unsure what to do, when his eyes meet mine and the word *patience* streams into my head.

A door to my right swings open, and I'm quick to look in. Surprised to see the moment I made a quick and quiet entrance into the world. Only to have the hush soon broken by Cade's noisy arrival just a few moments later.

To the casual observer, there's no discernible difference between us. Yet a closer look reveals the veil of darkness shrouding my twin.

Chepi knows it the instant she sees him. Her unease made visible by the way she flinches when he's placed in her arms.

Leandro sees it too. Evidenced by the spark in his eyes when he claims Cade for his own.

The image fades, dwindling and curling at the edges as though lit by a flame. Barely having a chance to digest what I've seen, when another door opens and Leftfoot guides me to an overstuffed chair set before a small screen. Where we watch a scratchy black-and-white reel of my most awkward childhood scenes.

I slink low in my seat, crossing and uncrossing my glowing blue legs. About to get up, try my luck in another room, when Leftfoot puts his hand on my arm and gestures toward the screen. And that's when I see it. That's when I see what I'd failed to grasp until now. Throughout my entire childhood—my entire life—every bleak moment, every humiliation, every episode of unhappiness was eased by Leftfoot's guidance.

He was there for me then, just as he's here for me now.

All along, he's known what I am and what it is that I'm headed for. And because of it, he's done his best to instill subtle lessons of magick and destiny, even when it opposed Chepi's wishes.

When the screen goes dark, I'm humbled by gratitude, overcome by the need to thank him. But he just waves it away and ushers me back to the hall, where we watch as a series of doors open and close.

Some allowing no more than a glimpse—while others offer much bigger reveals.

And despite having already lived it, seeing my life laid out before me so neatly, proves nothing was an accident.

Nothing was ever left to mere chance.

Each step flowed easily into the next—all of them pieces of a much greater plan.

The floor beneath our feet begins to move, propelling us toward the end of the hall, where we crash through the glass wall and swirl through a constellation of shiny crystalline pieces as we lift into the sky.

We sail over mountain peaks.

Glide across darkly glistening rivers.

Flying so much higher than I did as the red-tailed hawk I merged with just a few hours earlier. The sensation so glorious, so liberating, I can't bear to land.

Somewhere in the distance, Cree's rattle quickens—tiny beads bouncing furiously against rawhide. Calling us home. But I'm not ready yet.

We dip low.

And then lower still.

Veering toward a landscape that's drastically changed. A broken desert chaparral. A place of untold corruption and defeat. Its sagging homes and damaged people instantly identifying it as Enchantment.

A sad sack of a town, carelessly desecrated at the hands of the Richters—the bloodline I share.

We glide past the Rabbit Hole, seeing it cloaked in a cloud of murky brown haze I never noticed until now.

We sail past Paloma's adobe with the vibrant blue gate, the entire width of her property surrounded by a glorious wreath of light.

The town consisting of pockets both light and dark.

But mostly dark.

Primarily dark.

And then Cade.

We swoop into the alleyway that lies behind the Rabbit Hole. Going unnoticed as he pushes a girl hard against the wall and tugs at the neck of her shirt.

A girl with long dark hair that falls into her face, obscuring it in a way I can't see.

She turns her head—tries in vain to scream. Barely able to eke out more than a yelp, before Cade silences her with a hand slapped over her face.

His eyes blaze red. His mouth fills with snakes. Transformed into the beast that he is, he emits a spine-chilling growl and gouges her chest with his fangs.

Soul stealing.

Just like the dream.

I race toward him. Ram my energy hard into his. Hoping to throw him off balance long enough to allow the girl to escape.

But in the end, it's like tossing myself into foam—the landing is soft, malleable, bears no real effect.

Still, I keep at it. My quest to save her nothing short of relentless. Aware of a newfound power surging inside me, I crash hard into his side. Only to stare in horror when the girl falls away, revealing herself to be Daire, while my brother whirls on me with a shiny pearlescent orb balanced in the jaw of the two-headed serpent that springs from his tongue.

A scream rings out. The sound so rage-filled, so primal, I'm surprised to find I'm the source.

I continue to barrel into Cade, my energy repeatedly bashing into his. Though it's not long before I realize I'm swatting at air. Left to watch in astonishment when the entire scene pixilates before me. The shattered fragments dissipating into the ether as though they never existed.

I whirl all around, desperate to make sense of it. Until Leftfoot clamps a glowing hand on my shoulder and gestures toward the brick wall before us where a series of words scroll across it as though written by an invisible hand. Each line vanishing as soon as the next one begins. Though despite their brevity, the words remain emblazoned in my head.

It's the prophecy.

I know it the instant I see it.

It perfectly mimics the dream.

When it's done, when the words return to wherever they came from, Leftfoot speaks to me for the first time since this journey began. "Dace, I am truly sorry," he says, in a voice that reveals the full measure of his sorrow. "But the prophecy is written; it cannot be undone."

I start to respond. A long-winded protest ready to roll off my tongue, when the rattling quickens—my essence grows heavier—and the next thing I know I've sunk back into my skin. My limbs feeling foreign, fleshy, and stiff, I crick my neck from side to side, stretch my arms overhead. Trying to reacquaint myself with my physical form once again.

The sweat persists in fat droplets that race toward my eyes. Forcing me to swipe a hand across my brow as I focus on a curl of steam rising from the heap of rocks before me. Its snaking vapor beckoning like a finger, begging me to watch as it splits into two.

One side light, illuminated—the other so dark it's hard to perceive.

They waver before me in offering—demanding I choose.

I look to Leftfoot for guidance, only to find myself shocked by his invitation to soul jump.

"It's a one-time offer," he says. "Better make the most of it."

Without hesitation, I plunge. Eager to witness the code of his soul.

Everyone has a soul code.

Everyone has a soul and every soul a purpose.

Though the majority of people go about their lives completely unaware of this.

But not Leftfoot. Now that I'm given full access to the unedited movie of his life, I can't help but marvel at the sight. I thought

I knew him well, but the scenes that are revealed go far beyond anything I ever imagined.

It's a life where miracles are worked almost daily. Though that's not to say it's without its mistakes.

There were plenty of regrets. Plenty of situations he wished had gone differently. Though they were mostly in the younger years when he was ruled by his ego.

It's the cautionary part of the tale. The part I'm meant to absorb. And while I appreciate the wisdom and acknowledge it for the warning it is, I'm eager to probe deeper. Locate the place where the secrets are kept.

"Sure you're ready for that?" Leftfoot asks.

Ready or not, I'm greedy to absorb all that I can.

With a little more digging, I find it—the cache of arcane knowledge that could prove quite dangerous in the wrong hands.

In inexperienced, overeager hands.

Hands like mine?

Nonetheless, it's an irresistible storehouse of knowledge. Like panning for gold flakes and finding yourself swimming in nuggets.

One phrase in particular standing out above all the rest. So simple on the surface—yet seeming to speak directly to me.

Sometimes you must venture into the darkness to bring forth the light.

The moment it's uncovered, Leftfoot seals the vault and shuts me right out. His voice resigned, he says, "I've guided you to the best of my abilities. Shared with you all that I know. Now it's up to you to decide what you'll do with the knowledge you've gleaned. The path is yours to choose. But, Dace, you must always remember one of the most fundamental laws of the universe: Every action results in a reaction. It is a rule with no exceptions."

The water hisses—seething and whispering with impatience. Drawing my attention away from Leftfoot and back to the dueling curls of steam leaping before me.

Leftfoot's teachings circling my mind:

Every man must decide the kind of path he'll walk—now it's my turn to choose.

Every action has a reaction.

The prophecy is written. It cannot be undone.

It's that last part I refuse.

If the prophecy can't be undone—what does that say for free will?

Why even pretend I can choose my own path if it's already been determined for me?

The words contradict. Don't make any sense.

It's up to me to assemble the pieces of my life, call upon everything I've learned, put it all together, and prove the prophecy wrong.

Daire will not die.

Not on my watch.

I'll do whatever it takes to make good on that.

I narrow my focus, watching the curls of steam weave and gyrate before me. Then without another thought, I designate the one that I'll follow. Watching as it sparks and blazes, doubling in size as it consumes the other and leaps wildly before me.

I wish I could say that what I feel is relief. But the truth is, the sight leaves me unsettled.

Still, the choice has been made; there's no going back.

There will be consequences for sure, Leftfoot promised as much.

But it's nothing I can't handle. There's no price too big to save Daire.

By the time we leave the sweat lodge, the night is nudging well into dawn. Though, despite the lack of sleep, I'm not the least bit fatigued.

If anything, I feel renewed. Transformed. Like I grew from a kid to a man over the course of one night.

"I want you to go to school today," Leftfoot says, as we dress ourselves again. "Not only because your education is important, but also because it keeps Chepi from worrying, and it gives you the appearance of normalcy. Which is something you must work to maintain, now more than ever." He studies me closely, and I suck in my breath, ready for him to make mention of it. Give me grief over the choice that I made. But he just goes on to say, "Also, you must return to the Rabbit Hole and apologize for missing the last few days of work. Act contrite. It'll cost you nothing but a moment of pride, which is something you should try to rid yourself of. It's an overrated virtue that only serves to isolate, separating us from each other when we're better off working together. Then, once you're back in, I want you to locate that vortex I mentioned. Daire knows where it's located. But since it's best to avoid her at the moment, you might turn to Xotichl. She'll be able to guide you."

"And once I find it?" I ask, realizing that despite all he taught me over the course of the night, he never got around to telling me how he expects me to use what I've learned.

"I just want you to find it, that's all—or at least for the moment, anyway. They've already breached the Lowerworld, so that particular damage is done. For now, I just want you to keep an eye on it. Look for anything out of the ordinary, and report back to me with your findings."

I rub a hand over my chin. Surprised to discover a wide swath of whiskers that scratches my skin. Seems like days since I last showered and shaved.

"And Dace—"

I turn to face him.

"Get some rest. You're gonna need it."

Despite Leftfoot urging me to rest, despite the fact that I

haven't slept for days, when I get to my apartment, I'm way too wound up to do anything more than briefly consider it.

Sleep means closing my eyes.

And closing my eyes means dreaming of Daire.

Daire smiling.

Daire laughing.

Daire loving.

My head filled with the movie of her—culminating in the way she looked just after I told her we could no longer see each other. How she slumped over my kitchen table as though stabbed by my words . . .

I shake free of the thought, train my focus on getting cleaned up. Changing into clean clothes I pick from the laundry basket I never got around to unloading, and grabbing a quick bite to eat before I head out for school.

Fueled on nothing more than a bowl of stale cereal, weak coffee, and the adrenaline of pure determination, I glance at the clock as I make my way out. I'll be early—but early is better than sitting here trapped in my memories.

twenty-two

Daire

Jennika stops by early the next morning, under the guise of wanting to enjoy breakfast with us, but I know better. She wants to see me dressed and ready for school. Living the kind of life that won't cause her to worry any more than she already does.

She knocks on my bedroom door, barely allowing me enough time to respond before she barges in and plops down on my bed. Spouting some lecture she must have spent half the night composing. Her voice rising and falling as I dart from my bathroom to my closet in various stages of dress.

It's the same talk we parted with when she left Enchantment just a few months earlier. More warnings about the dangers of boys—especially the cute ones, like Dace. In "The World According to Jennika" boys like that live solely to sweet talk their way into your skinny jeans, only to dump you once they've had their way.

Kind of like what Django did to her.

Only Django didn't dump her.

He died.

And Jennika never got over it—never forgave him.

Which is why she's so desperate to stop me from repeating

her mistakes by giving my heart to someone who might die on me too.

But it's too late for that. I've already given my heart to a boy who died in my dreams, never mind the prophecy. Though if I have anything to do with it, he won't die in real life—not for many years to come.

"What about Vane?" I stand before her, one hand perched on my denim-clad hip, the other dangling the new boots she bought me. Fielding her blank look when I say, "You remember, Vane Wick? Global heartthrob—certified member of Hollywood's Youngest and Hottest—the guy I attacked in that Moroccan square?"

"What about him?" She picks at her sparkly blue fingernails. Peeling off the paint in the same way she always scolded me not to, claiming it weakens the nails.

"Well, I don't remember hearing this lecture back then." I shove my feet into the boots, smiling faintly when I see they fit perfectly.

"Because I knew you were too smart to fall for someone like Vane. You were never starstruck, Daire. You're far too savvy for that. I knew you could see right through his act, which is why I was never concerned about you two hanging out."

I turn toward the window, eyeing the dream catcher that hangs over the sill. Remembering the night Vane lured me into that alleyway, the expert way that he kissed me. How he nearly succeeded in talking me into doing the very things Jennika lectures about. How it was only the visions of glowing people that spared me from that.

But I don't share that either.

I shake free of the memory, listening patiently when she says, "I knew Dace was different the moment I saw you together." She frowns. Presumably remembering the night she caught us in his car. We were just about to kiss when she interfered and made sure that we didn't. "Daire, honey." Her green eyes slant toward mine. "You know I'm just trying to save you from making the same mistakes I made."

"Yes, I know." I turn away, angrily shoving a pile of books into my bag. "And, just so you know, I just love it when you refer to me as a *mistake*. Seriously. Makes me feel all warm and fuzzy inside."

She huffs under her breath. And though my back is turned, I know her well enough to know her eyes have slid closed as she silently counts to ten. "You know what I mean," she says, as soon as she gets there.

I frown. About to reply with a nasty retort, when I see her looking so small and defenseless, something inside me loosens up and gives way.

It's like I can actually *feel* how she felt when she found herself knocked up at sixteen by a boy who'd just died—only to lose her parents just a few years later.

Knocked sideways.

Kicked in the gut.

Left gasping and breathless—scrambling to build a new life.

I grab hold of the chair, fingers curling around the rail as I fight to steady myself. Overcome by the strength of this *impression*—of involuntarily diving into her experience.

It's the same phenomenon Paloma told me about, urged me to hone. Claiming it will help me to know the truth of a person.

The first time I experienced it was when I ran into Dace and Chepi at the gas station. Without even trying, I'd instantly tuned in to the cloud of sadness and grief surrounding his mom—along with the stream of pure, unconditional love that flowed from Dace to me.

And now, without even trying, it's happening again, only this time with Jennika.

After spending just a few moments beneath her steely veneer, I can no longer be angry with her. Can no longer take that same snarky tone. Like most people, she's just doing the best she knows how.

"C'mon." I lift my chin, making an exaggerated show of inhaling. "Smells like Paloma's making her famous blue-corn pancakes and, trust me, you don't want to miss them."

As committed as I was to being nicer to Jennika, when she insists on driving me to school, I can't help but shoot Paloma a pleading look, begging her to intervene in some way.

We need to talk. Need to continue my training. But now with Jennika's surprise visit, I've no idea when we'll be able to manage. By the time she left last night, it was too late and too cold for Paloma to teach me how to determine the firesong, so I was hoping we could do it today. But from the way things are going, that particular forecast seems doubtful.

Despite my pleading look, Paloma just tells me to have a good day—that she'll see me when I return. And though there's a hint of something deeper lying just beneath the words, before I can grasp it, Jennika's tugging on my sleeve, dragging me outside to her rental car.

"You really should learn how to drive." She climbs behind the wheel as I slide in beside her.

"I know," I say, hoping she won't offer to trade seats and teach me. We'll just end up arguing at a time when I'm really trying not to.

"Not that there's anywhere to actually drive to once you do get your license . . ."

She makes a frowny face. Letting me know, yet again, just how much she detests this place. Continuing to mutter under her breath, the same tired dialogue about how she can't understand why I would choose to live in this dump over the super-cool place she just got in LA. Stopping only when she sighs, fluffs her hair, and trains her focus on the car stereo.

When she asks me to look inside the glove compartment for her Hole CD, I know she wants to start over and find common ground. Nineties music, the songs of her youth, is always the go-to when she's looking for a reminder of less troubled times.

"You look cute in that top," she says, her mood instantly brightening after a few beats of Courtney Love singing "Celebrity Skin." "And those jeans are a perfect fit—I had a feeling they would be." She shoots me an appraising look, as I shrug, mumble *thanks*, and stare out the window. Watching a mangy stray dog plow through the contents of an overturned trash can, while an even mangier cat looks on, waiting to spring into action at the first opportunity.

"Dace Whitefeather is going to be damn sorry he dumped you," she says, in a misguided attempt to cheer me.

"I truly hope not." I peer at her. Satisfied when I see the flash of shock that crosses her face.

Her brow merging in an attempt to make sense of my words—make sense of me. Trying to find some trace of her teachings, the values she fought to instill.

"It's better if he doesn't think anything about me." I push the words past the sob clogging my throat—the one that's been permanently lodged there since that awful night in his kitchen. "It's better if he just moves on."

She considers me for a moment, her head bobbing back and forth as though weighing my words. Ultimately choosing to drop it, she says, "Where'd you get this?" She pinches the sleeve of the black down jacket I wear. "I'm not sure what's worse, Daire—that old army jacket you always wore or this thing." She shakes her head, having decided I'm an enigma who makes the kind of choices she'll never understand.

"It's Django's." I watch her jaw drop as her eyes grow bigger than I've ever seen them.

"Where'd you find that?" She stares at me, gripping the wheel so tightly her knuckles turn white.

"In a box full of his stuff. You should look through it while you're here. I think you'd find it interesting."

"No." She rips her gaze from mine, focuses on the bumpy dirt road ahead. "Maybe." She rubs her lips together, continues to squint out the window. "I don't know. We'll see." She sighs, her shoulders sinking in surrender and remaining that way, until she pulls into the parking lot and says, "Hey, aren't those your friends? And isn't that your ex standing with them?"

I follow her gaze to where Xotichl, Auden, Lita, Crickett, Jacy, and yes, even Dace, are talking and laughing. My eyes grazing over them, before settling on *him*—but only for a moment before I force myself to look away. I can't afford to allow my gaze to linger.

"Wow. I would've expected them to be on your side." Her eyes dart between them and me. "Do they even know about your breakup?"

"Probably not," I mumble. "Seeing as how I didn't go to school yesterday." My voice fading as I watch some new girl, someone I've never seen before, with a wild mane of dark spiral curls, cautiously approach them.

"Well, clearly he's not about to tell them what a jerk he is. So make sure you do it." Jennika huffs under her breath, looking like she's considering marching right over there and telling them for me.

But all I can do is stare at that slim, beautiful, exotic-looking girl with the halo of hair, the long almond-shaped eyes that tilt up at the sides, the dainty nose, and the generous full lips.

She looks like a dancer—sinewy, fluid—the very manifestation of grace.

She looks like several nationalities got together and decided to donate their most celebrated physical traits to one person, and she's the result.

"Who's that with them?" Jennika nudges my arm. "The one standing next to Jacy?"

I continue to stare, wondering why they all seem to know her—why she keeps looking at Dace. And why Dace can hardly bring himself to return the look.

About to probe deeper, try for one of those *impressions*, if only to get a read on the situation, when I catch myself. Stop myself. If anything, I should be building walls between us, not knocking them down.

Jennika's voice drones on, providing a long list of what's meant to be helpful hints on how to handle this breakup with my friends in order to gain the upper hand. Stopping only when I say, "Jennika—"

She looks at me, face expectant.

I gnaw hard on my lip, force myself to swallow the angry retort that comes far too easily. The one about boundaries—about allowing me the freedom to make my own mistakes my own way. The one where I remind her that she can't protect me from everything no matter how hard she tries. Instead, I just slip free of the car and wave to her from the curb. Watching as she exits the lot before I make for Chay's old blue truck parked at the side of the building, just under the cartoon picture of a wizard, our school mascot. This was what Paloma was hinting at.

"Get in." He leans across the seat to prop open my door. "Paloma's waiting. Looks like you've got more training to do."

I climb in beside him, and despite knowing better, I can't keep from taking one last look at Dace as Chay pulls onto the street.

Can't help but notice how quickly he senses me looking.

How swiftly he turns to meet my gaze.

I sink into the moment—allowing myself to bask in his presence.

Until I remember the high price of loving him and force myself to look away.

twenty-three

Dace

I sense her the second her mom pulls into the lot.

The rush of her energy, like a cocktail for the senses that leaves me thirsting for more.

So absorbed by Daire's presence, I almost miss it when Lita says, ". . . and then I'm like, *Phyre?*" She reenacts a scene from the day before, dramatizing the same expressions, the same hair swing, so we can see it just like it happened. Going on to add, "And sure enough, it was her. She's back in Enchantment. Can you even believe that? I could've sworn they were gone for good."

"Phyre?" I stare at Lita, though I don't really focus. The name alone is enough to reel me into a past I'd long since buried. Hardly ever think about.

Lita shakes her head, shoots me a dramatic roll of her eyes. "Um, hello? Yes, Phyre. What do you think I've been going on about?" She looks at everyone else, making a face she thinks I can't see even though I'm standing directly in front of her.

"So, she's back?" I say, knowing the question will only serve to annoy her, but I missed the details the first time around. I need the confirmation that it is what I think.

She adopts an overtly patient expression and the tone to

match. Acting as though she's been left to deal with a difficult child who needs everything carefully explained. "I saw her in town yesterday. She's definitely back. She's even coming to Milagro. Said she'll start up after Winter Break . . ."

She goes on from there, but I've already stopped listening. I've heard all I need to.

Phyre.

Here.

At Milagro.

I try to shake free of the thought, but it clings at the edges. Encouraging the blur of long-forgotten pictures that form in my head. The slideshow unfolding to the soundtrack of my own voice, warning: *You can never go back. And why would you want to?*

Then, just after I think it, I realize I wouldn't.

Go back.

Not ever.

"Wow," Xotichl says. Always amazing me with her ability to pack so much meaning into one single, seemingly innocuous word. Her head tilts toward me, no doubt reading my energy. Trying to assess how I'm taking the news. What it means to me—what it means for Daire.

I respond to her head tilt with a shrug. Hoping she'll sense it and rest assured that the news means nothing. I may find it interesting. Unexpected. But no more.

"Speaking of . . ." Jacy gestures toward the place where Phyre climbs out of a dusty white car. Her eyes lighting upon us, her face breaking into a smile.

She's changed. Looks really different from the way I remember. Her hair is still wild, but the red streaks are new. And she's definitely taller. Prettier too. Like the baby fat that once padded her cheeks migrated to other, more womanly places, allowing her face to rearrange itself into a series of sharp pleasing angles and curves.

I swipe a hand over my chin. Try to stop looking, but it's no use. It's like watching a ghost swoop down from the past, and all I can do is stand there and stare. Reminding myself it meant nothing, we were just kids, didn't really know what we were doing.

Okay, maybe not exactly kids.

Kids don't do what we did.

Still, a lot of time has passed. And during that time, a lot of things have changed. Actually, everything's changed. Or at least it has for me. And, from the looks of her, she's met with change too.

She says hello, allowing her gaze to move among us, before landing on me, where it stays long enough to take a full inventory. Holding the look just a few seconds too long—long enough for everyone to notice—before she clears her throat and says, "So . . . does this mean you guys are all friends now? How did that happen?"

"Daire made it happen." Xotichl tilts her chin and scrunches her nose as she accesses Phyre's energy. And from the way she fails to relent, I'm guessing she doesn't approve of what she *sees*. "Daire is Dace's girlfriend." The words so unmistakably pointed, Phyre rubs her lips together and shifts her gaze to her feet.

"Then I'm sure she's amazing," Phyre says, her eyes glittering just a little too brightly. "So, can anyone show me where the office is? I need to register."

She turns her focus on me, hoping I'll volunteer, but I pretend not to hear. I just watch as Lita nudges Jacy hard in the side, and a second later she and Crickett are leading her away.

Barely making it out of earshot when Xotichl frowns, and Lita says, "I don't like this." She stares after them, lips twitching from side to side. "I don't like what it could possibly mean for me." Her words purposely leading, practically begging Xotichl and me to ask her to explain. But we know we don't need to. Lita has every intention to continue. She's merely filtering the thoughts in her head. "I mean, look how she just waltzes right up and blends in. She was always flitting from clique to clique, blending with everyone so flippin' easily. It took me *years* to even consider acknowledging you guys." She stops, realizes what she just said. Then shrugging, she adds, "No offense. But still . . ."

She drones on, weighing the pros and cons of Phyre's sudden reappearance—how it might impact her own popularity. Either completely unaware that no one's really listening—or well beyond caring that Xotichl's lost in her own train of thoughts, as I fight like hell not to turn around and look at Daire.

Part of me aching to see her—part of me knowing it's the last thing we need.

Unfortunately, the first part wins. Driven by the weight of Daire's gaze upon me, begging me to turn. To look. And, without further hesitation, I do.

And I keep on looking long after Chay drives her away, blotting her out of my view.

twenty-four

Daire

"Once kindled, Fire is fast acting and quick to consume all in its path. It burns, scorches, singes, and transforms by altering the structure of all that it touches. In moderation, it provides comfort, warmth, and illumination. In excess, it blazes an unholy path of destruction."

Paloma bends toward the row of hand-dipped candles she's placed on the battered wooden table in her office. Their wicks sizzling and sparking when met with the flaming end of the long wooden match she wields in her hand.

"Fire can also be used for scrying." She looks at me, a small smile lighting her eyes. "Most any object can be used in this way, but fire adds a certain intensity, a certain animated quality you don't often get from a rock or a crystal. So, tell me, *nieta*, when you look into the flame, what do you see?"

I purse my lips and peer at the line of candles before me. Trying to take the exercise seriously, since there's so much at stake, but still not wanting to lie, I say, "Probably not what you want me to see." Lifting my shoulders when I add, "There's a base of blue that leads to a yellow-white tip that wavers about."

"Good." She grins. "That's all you're meant to see. Or at least for the moment, anyway. Much like you did with the pendulum, you will ask the Fire a question. But instead of the *yes* or *no* response of the pendulum, the Fire will show you images that will provide the information you seek."

I lift a brow, knowing better than to question her. Still, these lessons just seem to get weirder and weirder.

"And just like with the pendulum, it's important to remember that the Fire is only providing the wisdom that lives deep inside you. It's the same with the talismans you wear in your pouch. None of these things can impart attributes or answers you don't already possess—rather, they bring forth the powers that exist deep within you. There will come a time, *nieta,* when you are so in tune with yourself and your connection to all living things that you will no longer need to rely on these tools unless you seek clarification. But as you are not quite there yet, I want you to take a series of deep, cleansing breaths. I want you to clear your mind and center yourself. Then, when you are ready, I want you to choose one of the flames to gaze upon, allowing your focus to naturally settle. And instead of asking a question of the Fire, I want you to ask the Fire to reveal whatever it deems worthy of showing you. Just keep your mind open. Allow the information to flow. Can you do it?"

I nod. I'm already doing it. Already taking deep, calming breaths. Already aware of the way my muscles instantly soften and relax. The way my vision begins to widen before narrowing down to one single point.

Concentrating on a solitary flame snaking before me. Drawn to its heat, its essence, its spirited dance—striving to connect and merge with its very crux. Until everything fades except this lone flicker.

I've barely finished bidding a quick, silent plea for it to share its knowledge, when a face begins to form. A dark and haunted beautiful face with deep luminous eyes that gaze hard into mine.

Though just when I've grasped hold of the image, the face fades, allowing a fleeting trace of a raccoon to stand in its place.

"It's Valentina!" I gasp, gazing upon one of the first recorded Seekers in the Santos family tree. "And Raccoon—her spirit animal."

Paloma's whispered words of encouragement prompt me to lean closer, as I try to discern the message—convinced that there is one. And this time when Valentina's face appears before me again, her voice begins to sound in my head.

At first, the tone is faint, hard to discern. Though it's not long before the words begin to reverberate through the very core of me.

Listen—there is no time to waste! You must always remember that your intent fuels your will, and your will is your way. You must never look back. You must never regret. A new day has dawned—the old rules have changed. Unprecedented action is now required of you, and it will come at great cost. It is the creed of the Seeker and you must vow to heed it!

I nod vigorously, committing to every last word.

Watching as her face slowly fades, leaving me with the phrase: *It is your duty to protect them—look after them!*

As images of Xotichl, Auden, and Lita flash before me, followed by a bat, an otter, and an opossum, respectively.

Their spirit animals. It's got to be. Now that we're friends, now that I'm getting to know each of them, the animals that guide them make perfect sense.

Like Xotichl, Bat can see in the dark.

Like Auden, Otter is fun and cute, with focused intent.

Like Lita, Opossum is a good actor, quick to assess and adapt.

When the images fade, I'm left to watch the flame sway to the melody of the firesong:

> *At the whim of the wind*
> *I can smolder or singe*

Comforting as easily as I harm
A single lick of my flame begets irrevocable change
Be like me when you seek to transform

After the third repetition, the flame simply dies. Leaving me to stare at its ghost—a slim wispy finger of smoke undulating before me—as Paloma whispers into my ear, "Well done, *nieta*. Now extinguish the rest. You know what to do."

I reach toward one of the candles, raise my hand before it, and watch as it instantly burns itself out. Then I move on to the next, able to snuff it simply by blinking my eyes and willing it to be so. And when I reach the last one, I grab the double-sided knife Paloma placed by my side. Tightly grasping its smooth wooden hilt, I sanctify the athame by allowing it one slow pass through the candle's sacred flame. Aware of the chorus—the glorious symphony that swells in my head—as the fire blackens the blade as it passes, only to emerge shining like new.

When it's done, Paloma returns the knife to its case. Her fingers resting against the worn leather sheath, she employs a long pause before she says, "You were right."

I lean toward her, having no idea what she refers to.

"As much as I'd hoped otherwise, I'm afraid there's no denying Valentina's warning. A new day is among us. The old rules are now obsolete. Which means Cade must be killed. And I'm afraid you're the only one capable of doing it. The fate of this town—of your friends—relies upon your ability to slay him." Her fingers run the length of the sheath, as a flurry of conflicting emotions play across her face. And when her gaze finally meets mine, it's filled with an unfathomable sadness that's impossible to deny. "If I could take your place and do this for you, *nieta,* believe me I would. But my time as a Seeker is done. Whatever powers I had have been passed on to you."

I stare at her without blinking, without breathing. Startled by her sudden change of heart—the enormity of her words.

She slides the knife toward me. Looks me straight in the eye. "When you're ready to kill Cade, you will use this athame. You will also use it to rid the Lowerworld of undead Richters, by either removing their heads or cutting them clean at the waist."

I balk at her instructions. Unable to imagine committing such an act.

"I know the thought is unpleasant," she says. "I'm afraid the act will be too. But this time, unlike the last time, you will not have the aid of the Bone Keeper with you. Thus, it's the only way to release the souls that empower them. The only way to return them to the place where they belong."

"And Cade—is this the only way to kill him as well?" I remove the knife from its case. Studying it with newly informed eyes, testing the weight of it in my hand, sliding the wide smooth part across the width of my palm. Assuring myself I can do this—it's what I was born to do. I just have to find them, that's all. When the time comes, there will be no hesitation. I'll slay them all.

It's a promise I make to myself, to Paloma, to the people of Enchantment who don't deserve the kind of suffering they've endured.

I turn to Paloma with a determined gaze, wanting her to know I can handle the task. That I won't disappoint her. I will see this thing through. It's only when she returns my gaze with a deeply regretful look that I realize she's left my question unanswered.

"Will this kill Cade?" I repeat, voice pitching too high.

She presses her hands to her chest and steeples her fingers. "This is all new to me, *nieta*. And I'm sorry to ask this of you. All I know for sure is that the knife is now fortified with Valentina's essence. I've no doubt she will prove to be a formidable ally for you. From this moment on, you will keep the athame with you at all times. You will act when called upon. You will do whatever necessary to defeat Cade and his army of undead ancestors, no matter the stakes." Her gaze softening when she adds, "Now let's go see if we can't make it snow."

twenty-five

Dace

"Does anyone mind explaining just what the heck is going on around here?" Lita stares down the length of the lunch table, pausing on each of us. "First of all, where's Daire? Does she even go here anymore? And second, how strange is it that she disappears only to have Phyre show up? And not that I'm keeping track, so don't anybody get the wrong idea since I'm *totally* over him, but Cade Richter is still missing as well. And since nobody seems the least bit concerned by this series of strange events, I have to ask: Was there a memo I missed? Am I the only one who gives a flip about finals this week? And, for the record, I'm mostly looking at *you*, Whitefeather, since you're the one with the closest ties to all three of them."

The guys at the end of the table turn away, relieved to be off the hook. While I shrug, focus hard on my vending machine burrito, and say, "Daire's not feeling well. And Cade and I don't really talk, as you know."

Lita sits with the information. Head bobbing back and forth as though the scale of justice is embedded in there. "And the whole deal with Phyre? What's up with that?"

"Don't know," I mumble, knowing all too well where she's

heading with that but unwilling to take that particular trip. Phyre's a memory. A ghost. She has no place in the life I live now.

"Oh, no." Lita straightens, staring me down with her well-practiced, interrogation glare. The one that alerts Jacy and Crickett to sit up straighter too, unwilling to miss whatever comes next. "That does not work with me. Where does Phyre fit in—and how come you acted so weird around her?"

They stare. All of them. Even Xotichl's eyes dart suspiciously toward me. Leaving me with no choice but to flash my palms in surrender and say, "Phyre fits in wherever she chooses. She doesn't consult with me. She's been off my radar for years."

"Two years." Lita smirks, the words illustrated by the two fingers she shoves in my face. "It's been only two years since she left. And, my guess is, from the way she looked at you, she wants to pick up right where you guys left off. And from the way you acted all squirmy and weird around her, you don't know what you want. Or, even worse, you *do* know what you want, only now you have a little problem called Daire standing in the way. Which leaves you all . . . *conundrumed* and *kerfuffled*."

"Are those even words?" Xotichl asks, causing Jacy and Crickett to laugh into their hands, as Lita rolls her eyes and dismisses them all with a shake of her head.

"The problem with you, Whitefeather"—Lita pauses, demanding my full attention—"do you want to know what your problem is?"

I stare at my lunch. Wondering how I even got here. Why I ever agreed to befriend her, when it's clear she's barely changed since reclaiming her soul. But, instead, I just say, "Yeah, why not? Have at it."

She nods, crosses her legs and arms, taking on a defensive posture as though I'd even consider engaging in verbal combat with her. "The problem with you is you're not used to people thinking you're hot."

Xotichl frowns.

Jacy and Crickett gasp, barely able to contain themselves.

While my shoulders sink in relief. I expected much worse.

"Or, correction, you're used to only *one* person thinking you're hot. Phyre. And that was only because she was stuck on that reservation with you, where there weren't a whole lot of other options for a girl to choose from."

"Lita—" Xotichl swings toward her, trying to dissuade her from going any further, but Lita ignores it. She's on a roll. Won't be stopped 'til she's done.

"Anyway, back then, when Phyre was the only one who wanted you, the choice was easy. But now—now that Daire also thinks you're hot, along with a few other girls, who, although it makes zero sense to me, I've actually overheard them discussing the quality of your newly perceived hotness as well—you're suddenly faced with choices. As for me, I don't see it. You look way too much like Cade for my tastes."

"Um, yeah, because they're identical," Jacy says, causing Lita to frown and Crickett to shoot her a disapproving look.

"So, what I'm trying to say is, don't go getting all bigheaded just because you've had a little surge on the hotness scale. Don't be an ass. Don't be your twin. Do the right thing by Daire, or you will have to answer to me. *Comprehendu?*"

My jaw clenches. *Comprehendu? Guess that passes as Spanish in Lita Winslow's rarefied world.* I stare down the length of the table. Take a full inventory. Counting a group of guys I have nothing in common with, and who clearly want nothing to do with me—and a group of girls who have no problem dangling me over the burning hot coals they continue to stoke.

I was better off eating lunch by myself in the hall.

I focus on my food, refusing to answer. This is ridiculous. And despite my supposedly good and pure soul, I'm beginning to resent it.

But the thing with girls is, the silent treatment never works. They're too verbal to allow it. And they want me to be verbal too.

"Whatever," I say, knowing I have to say something, if only to put this to rest. "Phyre is history. No matter what's going on with Daire and me, we're solid. My heart beats for her, and her only."

"Solid, huh?" Lita squints, clearly not believing a word of it. "Then make sure you get her to the Rabbit Hole tonight for my Secret Santa party, okay? I don't care if you have to drag her by the hair like the caveman I'm convinced that you are. I want her there, Whitefeather. I want *everyone* there. I've worked my ass off to make this party my best one yet. And I don't think I should have to remind you that you're lucky to be invited. So don't make me regret my act of generosity, *K*?"

She shoots me a final look of warning, then turns her focus to Jacy and Crickett. Polling them on whether or not she should ditch her highlights for the winter: No. And if she should keep her Marilyn piercing or let the hole close up: They vote to keep.

When the bell rings, I swear it's never sounded so sweet. I push away from the table, eager to get the hell out of here and never return, when Xotichl grabs hold of my wrist and says, "We need to talk."

I close my eyes and stifle a groan. I don't know how much more grilling I can take. These girls are insane.

"Relax," she says, sensing my mood. "I'll leave that stuff to Lita; she does it better than I could anyway. What I meant was, we need to talk about the prophecy."

"You know about that?" I study her carefully.

"Have you read it?"

I hesitate, unsure how to answer. I settle on, "I've run across it once or twice. Still, I need to know whatever you can tell me. Specifically. Word for word. Leave nothing out."

"Then wait for me after school and give me a ride home. I'll fill you in then," she says, her gray/blue eyes veering away, but that doesn't mean she can't *see* me.

I sigh. Rake a hand through my hair, not wanting to wait, but not left with much of a choice, I agree.

The second I bail out of independent study I find Xotichl already waiting for me in the hall.

"I parked kinda far," I tell her, as she falls into step alongside me. Her red-tipped cane weaving before her.

"Good." She grins in a way that lights up her face. "Then you'll have plenty of time to tell me your side of the story. Everything. Start to finish. Leave nothing out."

I look at her, trying not to hate on the fact that yet another person has joined the ever-growing club of people who know about me. What I am. How I came to be. Not to mention, there's no way I'll tell her *everything*.

"I doubt it's any different from what Daire already told you." I reach toward her, about to help her navigate the curb, then pull away just as quickly. Xotichl does fine on her own. She doesn't need me to guide her.

"There's only one way to know for sure." Her face is determined, jaw set, mouth grim. For a tiny girl with a perceived dis ability, she's a force to be reckoned with.

She's also incredibly kind.

She was the first person to talk to me—scratch that—she was the *only* person to talk to me for what pretty much amounted to my first two years at this school—until Daire came along.

She's also the only one Cade's never been able to get to. And it's left me a little in awe of her.

I help her into my truck, see that she's settled, then I climb into my side. Starting the engine and backing out of the space when she says, "I'm still waiting . . ."

I yield to a few passing cars, then merge onto the street. "You really don't want me to go through the whole thing again, do you? There's really no point. Besides, the deal was I drive you home and you tell me what you know about the prophecy."

She considers for a moment, one tiny finger tapping the point of her chin. Enjoying my frustration, milking the moment for as long as she can. "Fine," she says, but only when she's sure I've suffered enough. "You win. I guess I learned everything I need to know from Daire. After all, she was pretty thorough."

Thorough? How thorough?

I grip the wheel tighter, work my jaw so hard it clicks in protest. Unable to relax until Xotichl says, "Listen, she's totally devastated, I'm not gonna lie. But it's not like she blames you. She knows you did the right thing. Besides, I'm pretty sure she won't stay devastated for long, she's a pretty tough cookie, you know."

While her words are meant to comfort, I'm not sure it's any better. *Is she insinuating that Daire's already getting over me—already moving on?*

I shake free of the thought. It's ridiculous. I'm ridiculous. I saw the way she looked at me today in the parking lot. Same way I looked at her. Besides, isn't that exactly what I told her to do? Stop thinking of me—stop loving me—for as long as it takes?

God, I hate my brother.

I swipe a hand through my hair, pushing strands away from my face. "Can we just move on to the prophecy?" I say, more than ready to hear it, even though I'm pretty sure I'm not going to like it.

She bobs her head back and forth, not entirely ready to give up on the game. Sighing in surrender, she says, "I read it in the codex."

I nod impatiently, not really sure what that is but eager to get on with it.

"It's an impressive book. Everything an ancient and mystical tome should be. With curling vellum pages and elaborate illustrations, it's like something you'd probably see in a fantasy movie. . . ." She pauses, probably just to torture me. She's a sweet girl, one of the sweetest I know, but she loves to play her little games. "Not that I could actually see the illustrations, though I could read their energy. Anyway, there's a lot to it. Loads and loads of pages, all of which are written in a special code that takes forever to decipher. I wish you could see it: its energy is so vibrant, so alive . . ."

My thumbs tap the wheel, as I bite back the urge to demand she just get to it and tell me already.

"Anyway," she says, a ghost of a smile lighting her face. "Here's the part that you need to know . . ."

When she's finished reciting, all I can think is how artless it seems.

How inconsequential.

With the sort of book she described, I guess I was expecting it to be bigger, more involved, than what I already knew.

Especially when you consider that actual lives are at stake.

Yet, according to Xotichl, the version in the codex is an exact match of the verses that were revealed during my sweat lodge experience.

A deceptively simple quatrain, stating:

> *The other side of midnight's hour strikes a herald thrice rung*
> *Seer, Shadow, Sun—together they come*
> *Sixteen winters hence—the light shall be eclipsed*
> *Leaving darkness to ascend beneath a sky bleeding fire*

"So it's true. The light will be eclipsed. One of us will die." I stare at the dirt road ahead, barely able to focus on anything other than the words that continue to play in my head.

Taunting.

Haunting.

Refusing to loosen their hold.

"But I guess we already knew that," I say, needing to remind myself that there's nothing new here. Xotichl's merely confirmed it, that's all.

"Daire's going to kill Cade," Xotichl says. "Not only so she can succeed as a Seeker, keep him from ascending, and set things right in the Lowerworld, but also to fix things with you. And while I totally get it, and while I completely support her wanting to do it—I also don't want her to get hurt. And I'm not sure what I can do to help keep her safe."

"She won't," I say, my voice determined as I veer onto Xotichl's street, parking outside the modest adobe home where she lives. "She won't get hurt. She won't have a chance to, because I'm going to get to him first."

Xotichl nods. It's the answer she was hoping to hear.

"There's a vortex in the Rabbit Hole." She props open the door and slides free of my truck. "If you enter from there, you stand a better chance of finding him."

"Leftfoot wants me to find it. Says you can show me where it is."

"It's tricky." She closes the door and leans through the open window. "It's also guarded by demons, so make sure you pack plenty of nicotine to appease them. But tonight, after the gifts are exchanged, I'll show you where it's located."

twenty-six

Daire

"Stop fidgeting. And stop eye rolling too. The longer you resist me, the longer this'll take." Jennika frowns, hooks her thumb under my chin, and tilts my head toward hers as she swipes an arc of deep purple shadow over my lids. "I thought you were in a hurry to get out of here and hang with your friends?"

"I am. And if you'll remember, that's exactly what I was trying to do when you barged in and insisted I needed a makeover." I shoot her a mock-scathing look that quickly turns to laughter when she returns it with one of her own.

"Well, excuse me for saying so, but no daughter of mine is going to a party looking like . . ." She cocks her head and squints, searching for the perfect way to both finish the sentence and properly offend me.

"Like *what*?" I take a surreptitious peek at my reflection. Seeing a left eye turned smoky and deep, while the right languishes in a state of semi-hazy with only the promise of sultry.

"No daughter of mine is going to a party looking like she's ready for *church*." Jennika smirks, pleased with herself for her ability to surprise me by saying something I didn't expect. Going on to add, "There are church looks, there are party looks, and then there are *holiday* party looks, which, I'll have you know, call for lots of drama, bling, and yes, deep smoky eyes. *Especially* deep smoky eyes. So if you can just bear with me for another ten minutes, I'll give you a look so killer, I guarantee *you know who* will keel over and die the second he sees you." She dips her brush into a pot of dusky charcoal shadow and comes at me again.

"Dace," I say. "His name is Dace. You're allowed to use it, you know?" Uttering the words through lips that barely move. A sort of ventriloquism I learned out of necessity when she used to practice her special-effects makeup techniques on me when I was a kid. "And if it'll help speed things along, feel free to make my eyes a little less *fatal*. I'd really prefer he doesn't *die* when he sees me. I like him better alive."

"Aha!" Jennika draws away. Her face lighting up as though I've just revealed something we didn't both already know. "You still *like* him—there it is." She wags her finger before me. "And therein lies the problem."

I open my mouth to speak, then close it just as quickly. Deciding against the way-too-defensive, not-at-all-believable reply that first springs to mind.

If defense is the first act of war, then anything I say will only escalate this into an argument I'd prefer not to have. If I have any hope of getting out of here in time to meet Dace, then I'm going to have to cooperate.

After today's session with Paloma, when I not only learned the firesong but actually whipped up a small little windstorm, followed by a brief burst of rain (though sadly the snow I tried to summon remained a wish unfulfilled)—I've got this surge of empowerment I'm reluctant to waste.

For the first time ever, I feel fully prepared to go head-to-head with Cade.

And I will.

Just as soon as I find him.

But before that can happen, I need to see Dace.

I have something planned. Something that, just yesterday, I wouldn't have had the courage to go through with—but now everything's changed.

I've changed.

And I can't wait to tell him.

Show him.

Now I just need to convince Jennika to hurry.

"*Et voilà!*" Jennika holds me at arm's length and inspects her work with a critical eye. Deeming the job a success, she smiles with pride. "You, my darling daughter, are perfection—a total knockout! You remind me of me when I was your age."

"And that's a good thing?" I joke, remembering the pictures I saw of her in her wannabe Courtney Love phase. All pale of face, red of lip, wearing a panty-skimming baby-doll dress and a tiara planted on the top of her bleached-blond head.

"It's a *very* good thing." She smiles. "And since you're new at this game, take it from an old master like me—*this* is how it's done. *This* is how all the best love wars are won."

"Love wars?" I can't help but scowl. There's just something really wrong about that. "So, all of this—" I arrow my finger toward my face. "This is really just war paint to you?"

She tugs her black long-sleeved sweater over her leather-clad hip and continues her scrutiny. Rummaging my features for traces of her traces of Django—too absorbed in the past to really see me.

"Honestly, Jennika, I think that's crazy. My feelings for Dace are no game. Love is not some old Pat Benatar song—it's not a battlefield or a war to be won or lost. And if you truly view it that way, then all I can say is *poor Harlan*."

The mere mention of her off-and-on-again but mostly off-again boyfriend shakes her out of her reverie, bringing an immediate frown to her face. "Really, Daire? *Poor Harlan*, you say?" She shakes her head, causing a spray of wispy blond strands to sweep across her delicate cheekbones before receding again. "Do you know he actually had the nerve to *propose?*"

I grip the bathroom counter to keep from toppling into the sink. Stealing a moment to absorb the surprising blow of her words. I didn't see that one coming. But now that she's said it, her impromptu visit makes perfect sense.

"When?" My voice rises with suspicion. "Exactly *when* did Harlan propose?"

She turns away, fumbles through her makeup case in a lame attempt to stall. Sighing in surrender, she admits, "Last week. On Malibu Beach. At sunset." She makes a face of distaste, as though he committed a detestable act in a hideous way.

"So that's why . . ." I shoot her a knowing look, purposely leaving the sentence to dangle unfinished.

"That's why—what? What're you getting at, Daire?" She dips a big fluffy brush in a pot of glittery bits and swirls it over my cheeks.

"That's why you're here. That's why you hopped the first plane to Enchantment. You're running away from Harlan—from commitment—from life!" My eyes blaze on hers. So caught up in the excitement of discovery, of being absolutely sure that I'm right, I almost miss the twitch of pain that crosses her face. Almost—but not quite.

"I'm here because it's Christmas and I wanted to spend time with my daughter." She insists on sticking to her story, despite the fact that the jig is up. "Why's that so hard for you to believe?"

"It's not that I don't believe it." I watch her closely. "It's just that it's not the full truth. There's more to it than that, and you know it. C'mon, Jennika, why can't you just admit that as much as you claim to hate it, Enchantment has become your new go-to spot when you can't take the heat?"

Her face grows dark in a way that tells me I've ventured way past her personal limits. But as someone who's recently freed myself from my own iron-clad cage, I know deep in my heart that she needs to hear it. So I go on to add, "Even you have to admit that now that you're settled full time in LA, it's getting harder and harder to escape all the things you once fled. You know, things like love. And commitment. And the very real, very tangible possibility of settling down with a guy as great, and talented, and nice, and patient—and, yes—even good-looking—or at least for an old guy—as Harlan." I smile when I say it, but she refuses to return the smile. "For the first time in a long time, you have a permanent address—a place for all of your personal demons to pile up on your doorstep, waiting to be dealt with. And now that you're all out of excuses—now that you can't just up and leave for the next makeup gig on the other side of the world—you're forced to face all of this and it scares the crap out of you. So, what do you do? You come visit me."

I fold my arms across my chest, challenging her to refute it. But she just rolls her eyes and says, "Well, who turned you into Dr. Phil?"

"Why don't you give him a chance?" I urge. "Why don't you plug your nose, close your eyes, and jump in? See how far you can fall without losing yourself? I'm pretty sure Harlan knows what he's getting into. I'm pretty sure he doesn't expect you to give up your career or even your name. I'm pretty sure he just wants you for you."

Jennika takes a moment. Whether to consider my words or wait for the subject to die an inevitable death, I can't be sure. All I know is that when she looks at me again, her voice is as resigned as the expression she wears on her face.

"You can either let me do your lips or you can continue to psychoanalyze me. Your choice, Daire. You decide just how soon you get out of here."

Our eyes meet and I decide to let her have this one. By planting the seed, I've already won.

Then I raise my chin, pucker my lips, and settle before her

again. Allowing her to swipe a thick layer of gloss across my mouth as I mumble, "I'm just sayin' . . ."

"Yeah, me too." Her voice rings tired and agitated but in a good way. In a way that tells me she's considering a future she's denied herself for too long. "I'm just sayin' too."

twenty-seven

Dace

From the time I leave my place to the time I get to the Rabbit Hole, I must've checked my coat pocket at least twenty times. But that doesn't stop me from checking again. Nor does it stop the sigh of relief when I find the small, wrapped package that contains Daire's Secret Santa gift is still there.

Despite the fact that the heart-shaped turquoise piece far exceeds the twenty-dollar limit, at first glance it probably seems underwhelming. The beauty of the stone—its obvious hardness, luster, and gleaming sky-blue color—all signs of quality of the highest grade—are all there, but the gem holds a deeper meaning as well.

It's meant to be an amulet—one she can add to her buckskin pouch along with all of her other talismans. It's meant to protect her when I can't be there for her. Turquoise is a healing stone. A protective stone. Said to ward off evil. And here in Enchantment, there's no shortage of that.

I just hope I can explain it in a way that makes sense without sounding stupid.

I park my truck in the usual space and shoot for the entrance.

Only making it halfway down the alleyway when Leandro steps out of the shadows, seeming to materialize out of nowhere.

"Dace," he says, in a voice as sharp as his gaze.

I glare at the monster before me. The horrible, evil, self-serving freak who sired me, accidentally created me, the day he violated my mother—messed with her perception and robbed her of her innocence, effectively derailing her future.

The beast I will never refer to as *father*.

"Haven't seen you in a while. You still work here?"

He keeps his tone casual, friendly, but I just shrug and check my pocket again.

He lifts his chin, peering down his nose in that probing way that he has. But instead of backing off like I usually do, this time I meet his gaze. Staring into those fathomless eyes—putting my new skills to use. Knowing I'll have to confront my brother's darkness before this is over, and choosing to meet it head-on.

"Sure you want to go there?" He grins in a way that pulls his lips wide, exposing a row of white teeth that gleam yellow under the glow of the streetlamps. "After all, you may not survive it. Your grandfather, Jolon, didn't."

I stare at him. Surprised to hear him admit it so freely.

"C'mon, son, surely you know the truth of your existence by now?"

"Don't call me that." I start to push past him, but he shadows me, gets right in my face.

"Don't call you what—*son*?" He lifts a brow. "But you are my son. Whether you like it or not, you owe your very existence to me. I gave you life. I brought you into this world, and, believe me, I could've ended you just as easily. I could've snuffed you out years ago, but I didn't. Ever wonder why?"

I stare into his eyes, not saying a word.

"I don't like waste. Don't believe in it. And I'm convinced that somewhere deep inside that pure and wretched soul of yours lurks a bitter black thorn that represents me, and I'm pretty sure you feel it too. You hate me. I can see the darkness growing inside you, and it pleases me immensely. Your hate gives me hope. If you nurture it, feed it, and allow it to grow, maybe you won't turn out to be such a lost cause after all. Maybe someday you'll be able to graduate from the lowly life of a Whitefeather to the exalted existence of a Richter. Of course, there's no guarantee, but for the first time ever, I'm beginning to think it could happen."

"You're crazy. Insane." I push past him, my shoulder butting hard against his.

"Have you seen your brother?" His gaze follows me, as I mutter under my breath and keep going. Aware of his voice calling from behind me, "If you do—tell him I'm looking for him. We need to talk before I head out of town."

When I reach the door, I slam my hand hard against it but stop short of entering. I need a moment to slow my breath to a more even pace, rid myself of my anger so I don't unload it on Daire. The last thing I want is to infect her with the bane of Leandro's dark presence.

Much as I hate it, Leandro and I share a bloodline. And just like he said—a piece of him lurks deep within me. As much as I hate him, loathe him, I'm determined to use our connection to stop him. If I sacrifice myself in the process, so be it. Saving Daire is all the legacy I need.

twenty-eight

Daire

After consenting to Jennika's curling iron, resulting in a series of soft loose waves that even I have to admit look pretty good, I allow her to style the rest of me too.

She runs a critical eye over the designer jeans, cute top, and the new boots she got me, before adding a few more bangles to each wrist and a few more rings to my fingers—some of them culled from her own hands. But when she offers to pierce my nose to match hers, I draw the line. Pushing her out of the house and into the bone-chilling night, where we slip into her rental car and spend the first few minutes shivering uncontrollably until the heater kicks in and warms us both up.

"The least it could do is snow." She glances over her shoulder as she backs down the drive. "Everything looks better under a fresh layer of snow, and God knows this town needs all the help it can get."

"I'm working on it," I say, fingers picking at the heavy brown paper shopping bag I hold on my lap. So busy with my mental inventory of its contents, I didn't realize I spoke the words out loud until Jennika calls me on it.

"You're *working on it?*" She shoots me a quizzical look. "Since when do you control the weather?"

Since today—since I learned to fully blend with the elements. As a Seeker, it's just one of my many duties.

But, instead, I just say, "What I meant was, I hope it snows too. Everyone wants a white Christmas, right?"

She shoots me a suspicious look, not quite buying my attempt at a cover-up. "Don't let Paloma fill your mind with weirdness," she warns. "Don't let her turn you into a younger version of her."

To that, I close my eyes and refuse to reply.

"Seriously," she continues, far from finished with this particular thread. "You have no idea how much I worry about leaving you with her. In fact, just earlier tonight, when you were in the shower, I actually saw her *spit* on a client."

I clamp my lips shut, determined not to speak until I've summoned my patience. "She didn't *spit* on the client, she merely . . ." *Ingested the client's bad energy then spit it out to be absorbed by the universe.* To Jennika's ears, that'll hardly sound better. "Whatever." I shrug. "All I know is she has a long list of clients who all seem to love her. It's not our place to judge her methods, is it?"

Jennika scowls. She hates when I act all righteous, especially when I truly am right.

"Anyway," I add, desperate to move on. "You remember how to get there?"

"How could I forget?" She slows to make a turn, then picks up speed. Bouncing in her seat as the rental car plows down a series of rough dirt roads. "Last time I was there, it was decorated with skeletons and skull masks. Hard to forget a thing like that."

"From what I hear, they've replaced the skeletons with twinkling fairy lights and a liberal dose of mistletoe—so be careful where you linger."

"Linger?" She balks. "Oh no, my job is to drive you. I've no intention of joining you."

I relax into my seat, trying not to look too relieved to know that our mother-daughter bonding won't extend beyond this car. The last thing I need is Jennika hovering over my shoulder, providing up-to-the-second tips on how to win my "love war."

"I thought I'd head back to Paloma's. Maybe check out that box you told me about. You know, that one with Django's stuff?"

"I think you should." I force back a smile, trying not to sound too excited by the prospect.

Jennika needs to look in that box. She'll never be able to forge a future with anyone if she can't reconcile the past.

"Or I might just go back to the hotel and crash." She drums her fingers against the steering wheel, accurately reading the true intention behind my words. "I haven't decided yet."

"Up to you." I pick at my cuticles, pretending not to care either way. Jennika's so stubborn, so obstinate that if she guesses this in any way relates to the conversation we had in the bathroom, when I tried to convince her to give Harlan a chance, she'll make sure to do the opposite.

We ride the rest of the way in silence, until she stops outside the Rabbit Hole and says, "I thought you said you hated this place?" She eyeballs me suspiciously.

"You sure that was me? 'Cause it sounds more like you." I flip down the visor, check my makeup in the small, lighted mirror. Barely recognizing myself, what with all the painted-on sultriness and big, frothy hair.

"Oh, I definitely said it." She frowns. "And I'm sure I'll say it a few more times before I head back to LA. I'll never understand your attraction to this place."

"And yet you still come to visit and offer to drive me around. So altruistic of you." I flip the visor up, grab the door handle, ready to say good-bye and get on with my night.

"Playing chauffeur seems to be the only way I can clinch any quality time with you. For such a dead-end town, you sure seem to keep busy."

"Yeah, it's called school. Homework. You know, the kind of

life normal people have. Crazy, I know." I shake my head, slide toward the edge of my seat.

"Is that what this is about—you wanting to be normal? Because we can do normal, Daire. You should see how normal my life has become." She swivels in her seat, looking at me with a face so full of hope I can't help but look away.

I stare hard at the Rabbit Hole, the very symbol of why I'll never be normal again. As long as there are Richters, I'll have no choice but to live the kind of life I'm only just beginning to understand.

Being a Seeker *is* my new normal. It's the life I'm going to have to learn to embrace. These lighthearted bickering sessions with Jennika are about as normal as my life will permit.

"So, Secret Santa, huh?" Jennika fusses at my hair, determined to reclaim my attention. "Whose name did you pick?"

"Lita's." Turning toward Jennika, I add, "But Lita got Dace so she traded with me." My voice sounds small when I say it. Prompting me to shake it off, remind myself how much has changed— how much I've changed—in just a few days.

"So, Lita got . . . *herself*?" When our eyes meet, we both burst into laughter, until she focuses on the bag I hold on my lap. "Are you going to tell me what you got him?"

"No." I gaze down at the bag, clutching it tighter, as though to keep her from snatching it. Which, she probably wouldn't do. Still, with Jennika, you can never be sure. "I'd really rather not."

She studies me for a long moment, heaving a sigh of resignation as she says, "You need me to pick you up too?"

"I'll find a ride. You just go do whatever you decide to do." I open the door, start to squeeze out of the car. But just when I step onto the street, I'm overcome by one of those *impressions*— astounded by the amount of sadness and loneliness Jennika holds in her heart. Enough to prompt me to turn back and say, "If you want to stop by tomorrow, I can saddle up Kachina, borrow a horse from Chay, and we can go for a ride?"

Jennika smiles. "Sure. Why not? It's been a while since I got my cowgirl on. But for now—" She fumbles through her purse, pulls me toward her, and dabs a dot of shiny, clear gloss smack in the center of my lower lip. Then she smudges a thumb over each cheek. "Okay, now you're completely irresistible. Go knock 'em dead."

I make for the entrance, but only because I can feel her watching me from the car. The second she drives away I dart for the back, where I busy myself with the prep work. Using every item I stored in my bag, before I run a self-conscious hand over the mane of curls I'm not used to wearing, and head into the club.

Barely having enough time to acclimate to the dim light and noise before Lita grabs hold of my sleeve. "Finally!" she says. "I thought for sure you were going to wreck my party!" She huffs, rolls her eyes, and shakes her head simultaneously. It's an impressive, dramatic display. "But—you're here now!" She engulfs me in one of her Lita hugs that, between the surprising amount of sincerity and the cloud of cloying perfume, always leave me reeling.

"So, where were you anyway? Why are you late? Did you come with Dace—because he's not here either. Or, correction, the old beater truck he drives is here, but I haven't seen him anywhere." She draws away and runs a scrutinizing eye over me. "And who did your hair and makeup? Is Jennika in town? Do you think she'll do me?" Not allowing me any time to respond, before she adds, "Whatever. We'll cover that later. Just come. C'mon!"

She tugs hard on my sleeve and steers me past a huge Christmas tree with branches so stuffed with ornaments they sag under the weight. Then she drags me down mistletoe row, scowling at any guy foolish enough to look at her with a gleam in his eye, stopping only when she reaches the group of tables nearest the bar, where pretty much the entire junior class sits. Including the people who, just a few weeks earlier, she'd deemed completely unworthy of noticing.

"Yeah, I know what you're thinking." She fields my look of surprise. "First I befriend you. Then Xotichl and Auden. Then Dace. And now, it looks like I'm willing to be friends with just about anyone." She lifts her shoulders, looks all around. "What can I say? I've turned into a complete and total friend whore. Then again, it is Christmas, and that always puts me in a giving mood. So I decided to expand my horizons and allow all of these losers to come to my party. " She smiles and waves at a small group of them, and the way they react to being noticed by her—overexcited and giddy—well, it's a good indication of just how much power she wields.

I may have the power of the elements and the power of my ancestors on my side, but Lita has the power of charisma— attracting people to her like bees to a flower.

"I have something for you," I say, once we've met up with Xotichl. "For both of you. Auden too." I dig through the contents of my purse, in search of the small, crudely wrapped packages I pass on to them. "Sorry about the wrap job—I didn't have much time."

"Who cares about the paper?" Lita says, not missing a beat before she's ripping into her gift. "It's the insides that count, right?"

I glance between them, noting Lita's disappointment and Xotichl's joy, when they discover a small carved opossum and bat respectively.

"It's a talisman." I bite down on my lip.

"I know what it is." Lita looks at me. "You can't grow up in Enchantment without being surrounded by loads of superstitions."

"It's not just superstitious," Xotichl says, curling hers into her palm. "These animal totems protect us, look after us, in more ways than you realize."

"Says the most superstitious person I know." Lita laughs, playfully bumping her shoulder against Xotichl's.

"Maybe so. But just so you know, these aren't like the ones they used to sell in the tourist shops—back when we had tourist shops. These are—"

"Fortified," I cut in. "They hold the power to protect. But only if you wear it, keep it nearby, and try not to share it with anyone else. Present company excluded, of course."

Xotichl tucks Auden's gift into her pocket, and her bat into the soft buckskin pouch she recently started wearing, while Lita looks on with a skeptical expression. "I don't have to start wearing one of those, do I?" She jabs a thumb toward Xotichl's pouch. "I mean, don't get me wrong, I'm appreciative of the gift, and those pouches look okay on you guys, but I wear a lot of deep V-necks. It's gonna stand out—and not in a good way."

"You can put it in a pocket," Xotichl says. "Or . . ."

Lita gazes down at her outfit, in search of a good place to stow it. But her red velvet dress with the faux white fur trim around the sleeves and hem is so tight, short, and pocket-free, it doesn't allow room for anything more.

"Oh, I know—I'll put it in my boot!" She grabs onto my shoulder for balance, leaning forward as she wedges it deep into the shaft of her shiny, black, knee-high stilettos. Enveloping me into another one of her infamous perfumey hugs, she says, "I love it. Truly. I was just giving you grief. Guess I'm a little shocked at how easily you're fitting into the way things are done around here." She pulls away, runs her palms down the front of her dress. "And now, I leave you with Xotichl. She's the only one I truly trust to look after you and make sure you stay put. And if either of you happen to find Dace, make sure you grab hold of him and make him stay too. Secret Santa is an exact science, you know? Everyone must be present and accounted for or it doesn't work." She leaves us with that, storming toward the stage where Auden's band Epitaph plays. Waiting impatiently for them to finish their set so she can take their place.

"Dace isn't here?" I face Xotichl, trying to keep the worry from my voice, but it's no use—she sees right through it.

"He's around. I felt his presence earlier. But you better not go looking for him. Lita's kind of scary when she's in party dictator mode. And now that she's made you my responsibility, you need to stay put." Xotichl laughs. "Bet you didn't realize you held the fate of the entire gift exchange in your hands?" She cocks her head to the side. "Or—did you?"

I laugh when she says it, though the truth is, it's not entirely sincere, and Xotichl, true to form, is quick to catch on to even a hint of falseness.

"There's something different about you." She reaches toward me, places her hand over mine.

"I'm wearing makeup—lots and lots of makeup—courtesy of Jennika," I tell her. "Oh, and I also let her curl my hair. And while I kind of like it, it's also kind of weird to see myself this way." I toss my hair over my shoulder, hoping I'll soon forget about it, stop messing with it. I've got way more important things to focus on than the sparkly, new, holiday party look my mom foisted on me.

"I'm sure you look amazing," Xotichl says. "But that's not what I meant."

Oh. I look at her, wondering just what her blindsight is telling her.

"Part of you is stronger." She lifts her hand from my mine, allowing it to hover as she assesses my energy. "And yet, part of you is *not.*"

"You wouldn't say that if you saw me earlier today. Paloma taught me to manipulate the elements. If it's up to me, you'll have your white Christmas and then some . . ." My voice drifts along with my gaze, claimed by the girl just a few tables away.

The new girl.

The one with the wild hair and exotic good looks.

She's talking with Jacy and Crickett and a handful of boys whose names I keep forgetting.

"Daire—" Xotichl squeezes my fingers. Trying to stop me from staring, stop me from asking the question we both know is coming.

But I can't stop either of those things.

"Who is she?" I ask, knowing there's no need to explain who I'm talking about.

Noting the way Xotichl's voice grows soft and resigned when she says, "Her name's Phyre. Phyre Youngblood. Pronounced like fire—but spelled with a *P H Y*."

Phyre.

Pronounced like fire.

The very element I bonded with—learned to control. And yet, Phyre the person leaves me feeling completely outclassed.

"How do you know her? How come all of you seem to know her?"

I'm still staring, unable to look anywhere else. Watching as she laughs in a way that sends a cascade of curls bouncing over her shoulders, exposing a long, graceful curve of neck. Her movements so fluid, so elegant, so endlessly watchable—the boys can't help but stare with unbridled longing, while Jacy and Crickett look on with unabashed envy.

She presses a hand to her mouth, hushing herself, as the boy standing before her—Brendan? Bryce? whatever—all I know for sure is that the sheer sight of her causes him to inch just a little bit closer, as though warming himself in her glow.

But the second she turns toward me, catching me staring, I tear my gaze away. Feeling awkward, stupid, and clumsy— wondering if I should maybe add the word *jealous* to the quickly growing list of my faults.

"She used to live here," Xotichl says, pulling me back to my original question. "Then her mom disappeared and her siblings, Ashe and Ember, went to live with their aunt, while Phyre moved away with her dad. But now, apparently, they're back. Or at least that's the nutshell version."

"Yeah? And what's the other version—the one you're keeping from me?"

I study her closely, knowing she's only trying to be a good friend and protect me from things like "wrong ideas" or "hurt feelings," but it's too late for that. My mind is already spinning with ideas—both wrong and hurtful—and only the truth can set me straight.

The fact is, I saw the way Phyre looked at Dace.

I also saw the way he could barely bring himself to return the gaze.

There's a story there.

One that probably has nothing to do with me—one that's no doubt none of my business. And yet I still need to hear it, so I can try to make sense of the strange way I'm feeling.

So I can determine if there truly is something odd about Phyre—or if I'm just acting petty and feel threatened by the arrival of a girl who just so happens to be unbelievably pretty. One who may or may not share a past with my boyfriend.

Am I just pulling a Lita?

Or is there something substantial to worry about?

Having never been in this kind of situation before, it's hard for me to read. Still, I'm really hoping the blame falls on Phyre—not me.

"You have nothing to worry about. Dace loves you and only you, you already know that."

I look at Xotichl, seeing the veil of regret that crosses her face at revealing even that much. Knowing whatever she tells me only serves to add fuel to my fire—Phyre?—it's now one and the same.

"Just tell me," I plead. "What's their connection? I mean, obviously they were together, but just *how* together?" I stare hard at Xotichl, remembering what Dace told me the other day at the not-so Enchanted Spring. How he'd only been with one other girl. And knowing deep down in my heart it was Phyre.

Xotichl sighs, toys with her bottle of water. "They both grew up on the reservation."

"*And*—" I watch as she squirms, shifting uncomfortably on her seat. And while the sight of it makes me feel bad, that doesn't stop me from pushing her further. "Look, I get it, okay? Everyone has a past. Heck, practically the whole school knows about my Vane Wick flameout."

"No, not *practically*. *Everyone* knows. Even the teachers were talking about it."

She grins. I laugh. But then I'm right back at it again.

"There's something different here. I get the feeling she's not quite done with him—not quite . . . *over* him. Or am I being paranoid? Am I acting like some pathetically jealous girlfriend who freaks at every pretty girl who so much as looks at her boyfriend? Because if that's the case, you need to tell me right now, so we can stage an intervention and find a quick way to eradicate it."

"Look," Xotichl says. "I'm not up on all the dirt, but yeah, I heard the rumors, and Lita pretty much confirmed they had a thing. And when she confronted Dace about it today at lunch, he didn't exactly deny it. She really gave him hell about it too. Told him he better not mess with you, or he'd have to answer to her."

We turn toward the stage where Lita stands to the side, ready to grab the mic the second Auden's guitar solo ends.

"She's a very strange but surprisingly loyal friend. I can never quite get a handle on her. Anyway, it was impressive stuff. It's too bad you missed it."

"So, then you're saying it's true. I am being a jealous freak." I turn toward Xotichl and slouch on my stool. Wondering if there's a quick fix for envy—maybe a spell or an herb I can take?

"No," Xotichl says, voice lowered to a whisper. "I'm not saying that at all. There is something weird about her just showing up out of the blue. And so far, I can't quite get a grip on her energy. But I will, just give me time. Though as far as Dace is concerned, you have nothing to worry about. Or, should I say, nothing but Cade, anyway."

Oh yeah. Him. As awful as it felt to be mired in my pathetic pool of jealousy, it did provide a nice respite from obsessing over a much bigger threat that looms large before me.

"Think he'll show up for the gift exchange?"

The question wasn't meant to be serious. It's just something I said to lighten the mood. Though before Xotichl can reply, we're interrupted by Lita wrangling control of the mic.

She stands before us, her Santa hat tipped low over one eye, giving an extra edge to her sexy Mrs. Claus look. Roaming the length of the stage, allowing everyone an equal view. "I just want to thank all of you for taking the time to come to my Annual Rabbit Hole Christmas Party!" She pauses in a way that prompts the audience to whistle and cheer, shushing them when she deems it's gone on long enough. "There's a lot of new faces out there, and I know how excited you must be to finally be included. Just think of it as my little gift to you!" She pauses again, and when the cheers are a little more subdued than the last time, she places a hand on her hip and frowns until they kick it up enough to prompt her to proceed. "And speaking of gifts, for all of you Secret Santas out there, it's time for the gift exchange—so, no need to delay, you know the drill—let the wrapping paper fly!"

She passes the mic back to Auden and exits the stage, as Epitaph breaks into a chorus of "We Wish You a Merry Christmas" that sounds a lot like the Weezer version Jennika has on her iPod.

"So—how'd I do?" Lita stands before us all breathless and pretty as she readjusts her hat.

"Great!" I say.

"Excellent!" Xotichl confirms.

But Lita just chews on her lip, unconvinced.

"You know, I really thought he'd show." She crosses her arms over her chest, as she does a quick scan of the club. Responding to the questioning look on my face, she says, "Cade. I'm talking about Cade. He's gone completely MIA."

"Lita, you're not . . . you're not still into him, are you?" I peer into her eyes, searching for signs of soul loss, which only seems to annoy her.

"Stop with the probing stare. You're freaking me out. But to answer your question, *no*—I'm not into Cade. Not at all. Not even a teensy, weensy bit. But at the same time I can't help thinking how he's all too aware of just how hard I work on this party. He knows how much it means to me. Heck, I've been organizing this thing going all the way back to sixth grade. And broken heart or not, it's completely rude of him to just blow me and my party off like we don't exist."

"But maybe it's too painful for him to be around you," Xotichl says, giving me a swift kick under the table that warns me to play along.

"Yeah, maybe he doesn't want you to see what happens when he gets really upset?" I say, which only succeeds in garnering a weird look from both Xotichl and Lita alike.

"What's that even supposed to mean?" Lita frowns. "I swear you are such an enigma to me. Anyway, the thing is, if Cade's going to continue to pine over me, then the least he could do is have the decency to show up and pine in person. He could at least give me the satisfaction of seeing it firsthand!"

Xotichl and I nod, as though we totally understand.

"Well, at least his twin's here. That should make *you* happy, right?"

I follow the length of her gaze all the way to where Dace stands, looking tall, lean, strong, gorgeous. His gaze instantly finding mine as an uncertain smile lights up his face.

"Listen—" I force myself to look away as I retrieve a small envelope from my pocket and shove it into Lita's hand. "I'm not really sure how this Secret Santa thing works, but can you give this to Dace?"

Xotichl leans toward it, attempting to read its energy, while Lita pinches it between her index finger and thumb, her voice as disdainful as her expression. "What'd you do, Santos—write him a twenty-dollar check?"

"Just—" I turn toward Dace. He's heading toward me, only a few feet away. Then I turn back to Lita, my voice hurried as I say, "Can you please do it?"

"Whatever. Your wish is my command." She tucks the envelope under her arm as I shoot for the back door. Calling after me to say, "Oh, and just in case you were wondering, I put my money toward these boots, cool, huh?"

But I just keep running, plowing through the exit before Dace can reach me.

twenty-nine

Dace

When I'm ready to face her, I push through the door. Calling on all of my senses, just like Leftfoot taught me, to locate Daire in the throng. And the second I see her, everything stops.

The noise dims.

The light fades.

The room goes quiet and hazy except for the nimbus of soft golden light that surrounds her.

She's beautiful.

I already knew that, of course. Yet seeing her now, with her hair tumbling over her shoulders, and her gaze burning on mine, I'm instantly transported to the day at the Enchanted Spring. Reminded of the way she looked lying beneath me, just after we . . .

I shake my head, check my pocket again to ensure that her gift is still there and make my way toward her. Covering more than half the room in just a handful of steps, only to watch her turn on her heel and bolt for the back door, as Lita steps before me and says, "This is for you." She shoves a small, rectangular envelope into my hand. "Please keep in mind that it's not from me. So, if it's as lame as I think, don't shoot the messenger. And don't say I didn't warn you."

She waves to someone across the room and leaves me flipping the envelope back and forth in my palm. It's from Daire, that much I know. But since I can't sense its contents, I'm reluctant to open it.

Is it some kind of official breakup letter?

Some change-of-heart memo that states: *I know you think you broke up with me, but really I'm breaking up with you*—?

Is that why she ran out the back door the second she saw me?

Or am I just being paranoid?

"Maybe you should open it and see," Xotichl says, reading into my energy as she comes over to join me.

Of course, she's right. No use standing here guessing. I slip a finger under the flap, and retrieve a heavy piece of cream-colored paper featuring a hand-scrawled map, which, though it doesn't make any immediate sense, at least is not as bad as I imagined.

"Can I guess?" Xotichl asks, grinning when Auden comes up from behind her and plants a kiss on her cheek.

I hand her the map and stare down at my feet. I can't watch them together. Their happiness makes me long for Daire so much it aches.

Xotichl screws her mouth to the side and runs her fingertips back and forth across the page. "Oh, it's a map! Like a treasure hunt—how fun!" She returns it to me.

"How do you do that?" It's not the first time I've asked such a thing.

But, like always, Xotichl just laughs as Auden jabs a thumb over his shoulder and says, "I think she went that way."

I make for the door. Pushing past everyone who gets in my way, eager to be with Daire once again, see what she's planned. When Phyre purposely inserts herself into my path and in a whispered voice says, "Hey, Dace."

Her lips begin a slow curl as her gaze travels over me. But I don't have time for this, and I'm quick to tell her as much. "Yeah, hey. Listen, I'm kind of in a hurry, so—" I start to move past her, but just like Leandro did in the alleyway, Phyre shadows me, insisting on having her say.

"Can't you spare a few seconds for an old friend?" She cocks her head to the side, her eyes gleaming flirtatiously, but it's wasted on me. Daire is my present. My future. Phyre is history. "It's been such a long time." She adopts the kind of timid demeanor that just doesn't suit her. She's not shy. Never has been. This is how she operates.

I mumble something incoherent and check my pocket again.

"So why do I get the feeling you're trying to avoid me?" She places a hand on either hip, determined to keep me from where I most need to be.

I rub my lips together and glance all around. Seeing Lita glaring at me from halfway across the dance floor, Xotichl turning toward me with a curious tilt of her head, as Phyre stands before me, demanding an answer.

"Look—" I start, the words dissolving on my tongue the instant she steps closer. Gazing at me through a thick fringe of lashes, her catlike eyes tilting up at the sides. "A lot's changed," I finally manage. "Actually, no, scratch that—*everything's* changed, and I think you should know that." I meet her gaze straight on, hoping that'll suffice. Let her down easy and work as my Get Out of Jail Free card, so I can get on with my night.

"You're right." She smiles, unfazed by my words, ignoring the determined expression I wear on my face. "A lot has changed. Including me." She sort of swivels before me, encouraging her dress to sway around her legs in a way that's meant to be enticing. Begging me to see her, appreciate her, in the way that I used to.

I turn away. Steadfastly refuse her. Wishing I could stomp out this tired old memory she insists on resurrecting.

"And I haven't just changed on the outside," she says, her determination proving to be a good match for my own. "The inside's different as well. And I get the feeling you're different too."

I huff under my breath. Swipe a hand across my chin. This is ridiculous. Daire is out there somewhere, waiting for me in the freezing cold night, while I'm stuck inside this stupid club, trapped in a nightmare visit from the Ghost of Christmas Past.

I lift my gaze to meet hers. Determined to end this quickly and easily, I say, "Phyre, it's good to see you. Really. But, I'm not sure what you're after. We were kids when we—when you left. We're not kids anymore."

She inches closer, runs a purple painted nail from my shoulder to my elbow. The chill of her touch penetrating all the way through my heavy down jacket and the wool sweater beneath, leaving my skin pricked with cold. Her voice soft and lilting, she says, "Funny, I didn't feel like a kid when I was with you."

I flinch at her touch, aware of her sharp intake of breath as her hand falls back to her side. But I don't feel badly. It's all coming back to me now. The way she manipulates. Calculates. The wave of regret that washed over me the instant it was over.

"Are you well?" I figure I owe her the courtesy of asking.

She nods.

"And your dad—is he well too?"

"He gets by." She shrugs, tilts her head from side to side.

"Okay then. I'm glad to hear it, but I really have to—"

"You really have to go. I know." She stares at me for a long time. Too long. Her features darkening, she steps aside and says, "Don't let me stop you."

I push past her. Push into the night. Glad for the bite of frigid air blasting my hands, my face. Overcome with relief to finally be rid of her.

After a quick consult with the map, I navigate the path Daire outlined. Stopping before two long rows of glowing luminarias lighting either side of a trail that ultimately leads to the place where she stands huddled against the bitter night air.

When she sees me—when her eyes meet mine—it's all I can do to keep from sprinting down the trail and taking her into my arms. But I force myself to walk it instead. Force myself to take the time to appreciate the stage that she's set.

"Merry Christmas," she says, once I'm standing before her. Her cheeks flushed and luminous, her eyes flickering with amusement. "I'm your not-so-Secret Santa."

I smile. Content to just stand there and fill my eyes with the glorious sight of her.

Screw Cade.

Screw all the Richters.

This is all that matters.

This beautiful girl standing before me.

I'm hollow without her. Just barely existing. I know that now.

And while I know that what we're doing is right—that this is the way it has to be until Cade is stopped—I also know that when this is over, there will be no more shutting her out of my life. The last few days without her were hell, with thoughts of her haunting me at every turn.

If it's the last thing I do, I'll find a way to make this work.

Or die trying, anyway.

I find her eyes once again. Realizing she's waiting for me to react to her news, I say, "Oh, and I'm yours."

"Really?" She cocks her head in a way that encourages a spray of curls to fall across her cheek. And it takes all of my strength not to pull her tightly to me and sink into the softness of her. "Well, actually, Lita drew your name, not me. But then she asked me to trade, so I did."

"Lita pulled the same thing on me." My eyes fix on her mouth—those soft inviting lips I ache to taste again and again. "I hear she puts her name in twice so she can spend the money on herself."

"So the whole thing was rigged?" Daire grins in a way that's infectious. "And here I thought it was fated." Her eyes move over me, leaving a trail of warmth that starts at my head and wanders all the way to my feet.

"This is really beautiful." My voice sounds hoarse, unused. "I can't think of a better gift than to find you waiting at the end of a candlelit path."

"I'm not your gift." She smiles. "I'm not that poetic."

"No?" I take another look around. "Could've fooled me."

"*This* is your gift." She hooks a thumb toward the chain-link fence at her back.

I squint, try to think of a reply, but its meaning is lost. So I go the jokey route and say, "I'm pretty sure you've gone way past the twenty-dollar limit. The permits alone—" My words halted by the finger she presses to my lips.

"Not the fence, silly—*this*." She flicks the small golden lock that's fixed to one of the links.

Still, I look at her. Not really getting it—but not caring either. My lips burn from her touch. It's all I can think about.

"You probably don't realize it, but today marks six weeks since we first got together. And, well, I wanted to observe it in some way. This is pretty much a first for me."

"It's a first for me too." I want so badly to kiss her, right here, right now. But something tells me to wait. There's still more to say.

"Is that because you're usually long gone by this point?" She chases the words with a grin, but it doesn't take much to spot the vein of worry that pulses just underneath.

"That's Cade's game, not mine," I say, hoping to convince her I will do whatever it takes to be with her—now and forever. I was a fool that night in my kitchen. I won't be anymore.

She nods, takes a deep breath, and says, "Anyway, I wanted to do something special, and then I remembered *this*."

She points to the lock again, but I still don't get the significance.

"There's a place in Paris with an old chain-link fence, much like this one." She hooks her finger around one of the links and rattles it for emphasis—the move, along with her words, leaving me even more perplexed than before. "Only that fence, the one in

Paris, is completely covered with locks. The entire thing is crammed chock full of locks of all kinds. And, well, it's one of the most beautiful things I've ever seen. Or at least it is once you realize what it is the locks symbolize."

I look at her, clueless as to where this is going.

"It's a fence for lovers." Her voice softens. "It's a place where couples go to declare their love for each other. As a show of devotion, they attach the lock to the fence, and then each person gets a key. If at any point one of them decides their feelings have changed, they're free to use their key to remove the lock. But from the looks of that fence, it rarely happens." She stares down at her feet, taking a moment to collect her thoughts. "So, I guess what I'm trying to say is—I'm declaring my love for you. And this lock, on this fence, is a symbol of that love. I love you, Dace Whitefeather, and whether we're together or apart, it doesn't change the essential truth. If there's one thing I've discovered over the last few days, it's that suppressing my love for you doesn't make it go away or weaken it in the slightest." Her lips lift, but her eyes suggest the tinge of sadness that dwells just under the surface. "I know what we're up against, and I know you know too. But—" She takes a deep breath, and it's all I can do to stand patiently before her, not crush my lips to hers. "But the thing is, I'm willing to do whatever it takes to be together. And, well, I was hoping you feel the same. But in case you're not on board . . ."

She dips inside her top, retrieving one of two long black cords with a small gold key attached to its end, which she's quick to drape around my neck. Leaving it to lie against my chest, just like the one that she wears.

I pinch the key between my fingers. "I won't use it." My gaze burns on hers. "I will wear this for eternity. They'll bury me in it."

She bites her bottom lip, as her eyes go so bright and glittery, her cheeks so flushed and pink, I'm just about to kiss her. Just about to pull her into my arms and taste her in the way I could only dream about yesterday. When I remember I have something for her.

I place the small package into her hands, watching as she works the stone free of the red-and-green wrapping paper. "It's a—"

"I know what it is." She rubs her finger over the top, then flips it over and examines the back. "It's your version of the lock and key." She smiles at me.

"It's also meant to protect you, keep you from harm. It's an amulet. May I?"

I hook my finger around the soft buckskin pouch that hangs from her neck. Waiting for her to nod her consent before I loosen the string and open the top just wide enough to add the stone to her collection of talismans. My fingers lingering in the place where it lies. Finding it impossible to pull away now that I've touched her.

Mesmerized by the warmth of her skin meeting mine. The rhythm of her heart beating hard against my palm. Her breath coming soft and fast as she stands just before me. Looking so beautiful, so radiant—I draw her into my arms and cover her mouth with my own.

Aware of nothing more than the way her body melts and conforms against mine—the way she returns my kiss with an equal amount of desire and need. Allowing everything else to skew out of focus—Cade, Leandro, the Rabbit Hole—screw it all. *This* is all that I care about.

Daire.

In my arms.

Loving me and needing me as much as I love and need her.

She breaks the kiss, catching her breath as she says, "I've loved you since the first time you appeared in my dreams—long before I even heard of Enchantment."

My eyes narrow, surprised by her words. Never once guessing that she had the dreams too.

"So you know how it ends?"

She shakes her head, allowing her hair to spring into her face, making her even more irresistible. "No. I know how the dream ends. But that's not how we end. Dace, I was thinking, can't we give ourselves this night? I know we can't be together full time, or at least not until after Cade is defeated. Still, I was thinking maybe we could give ourselves this one gift—this one night—just you and me. Tomorrow we'll separate and do what we have to. But tonight . . . well, I guess I need something to go on. Something to carry me through. Something to ease the ache of loneliness and pain that comes from missing you."

I kiss her again. Fully. Deeply. It's the only thing that makes sense.

Love is meant to be shared—not hoarded. That's the whole point of it.

No wonder there are so many love songs on the radio. It's a never-ending attempt by artists to describe the indescribable.

Somewhere inside the Rabbit Hole a party rages.

Somewhere inside that club Epitaph rocks the stage, while Xotichl waits for me to return so she can lead me to the vortex.

Somewhere among the crowd Leandro roots for my dark side, as Phyre pokes through the embers of a passion that died long ago.

But none of that matters right now.

Because Daire and I are together.

As we should be.

As we're meant to be.

And when I bundle her into the crook of my arm and usher her into my truck, I watch as she snuffs out the candles lining the path with merely a nod of her head.

Leaving no doubt she's right.

We'll get through this. The prophecy doesn't define us.

Tonight we'll give ourselves the gift of each other.

Tomorrow will come soon enough.

———

I wake to the sight of Daire sleeping beside me. Her breath soft and even, her skin fair and gleaming under the slant of light that seeps in from the window. And as much as I long to touch her, fill my fingers with the promise of her—I climb out of bed and leave her to slumber.

I pull on the jeans I'd left on the floor and swipe a clean T-shirt from the laundry basket and yank it over my head. Chasing it with a gray sweater culled from the back of a chair, I look around my place for the first time in days, horrified by the colossal mess that it is.

The last week has been chaotic at best. And because of it, my apartment is trashed. While Daire and I were a little too preoccupied last night for her to really take notice, there's no doubt she'll notice now. There's no place to hide under the harsh glare of daylight.

I hit the kitchen first, determined to deal with the pile of dirty dishes crowding the sink. Not getting very far before there's a knock at the door and I open it to find Xotichl and Auden loaded down with pink boxes and white bags embossed with the logo of Nana's bakery, one of the few places in Enchantment that's not owned and operated by the Richters, which means the bread is pure heaven.

"We bring sustenance." Xotichl finds her way past me as Auden follows and plunks the bags on the small kitchen table. "But we're counting on you for the coffee, so please don't disappoint us. You're not the only one who had a late night. I'm desperately in need of my morning fix."

"That's the one thing I do have." I return to the sink, working the scrubber side of the sponge over the stubborn film of crud on the bottom of the coffeepot. "Just, uh—give me a second and we're good to go."

Xotichl stands in the middle of my living room, head swiveling from side to side, as though she doesn't know where to sit, even though this is hardly her and Auden's first visit.

"Something wrong?" I watch as Auden tears off a piece of bread, plops it into his mouth, and shoots me a guilty look, while Xotichl stays rooted in place, nose pitched high, face scrunched in disapproval.

"Dace—this place feels like a mess. Like a serious, chaotic mess."

"That's because it is," Auden says. Looking at me when he adds, "Sorry, bro, but I can't let you continue like this. Clutter makes for bad energy. You should know that."

"Funny—I didn't even notice the clutter 'til you just now mentioned it. How'd you manage to slip that past me?" Daire stands in the doorway, looking adorable in one of my old, red flannel shirts that falls halfway to her knees.

"Lots of things go unnoticed in the night, but surely you notice now?" Xotichl says, unable to find a place to sit until Auden clears a space off the couch and guides her to it.

"Nope. I'm focused solely on breakfast." Daire veers past me, teasing a finger along my spine as she makes her way to the table where Auden's arranged a pile of freshly baked rolls, danishes, and fat loaves of oven-warmed bread. "I'm famished." She bites into a roll, closing her eyes to savor the flavor. Lids fluttering open when she says, "So, how'd you guys know I'd be here?" She wanders into the living room and perches on the arm of the sofa, next to Xotichl.

"Dace stood me up." Xotichl nods her head in my direction as Auden laughs. "I was going to show him the vortex, but then when he didn't show and you never returned . . . well, let's just say that as far as mysteries go, this one was easy to solve."

"Sorry," I mutter, checking on the coffeemaker. "I should've called."

"No worries." Xotichl shrugs. "It's not like it's going anywhere."

"Though you did miss the excitement." Auden makes for the table, filching a danish this time. "Cade showed."

Daire and I exchange a look.

A look Auden catches when he says, "Yeah, I know all about it. Demons—vortexes—multiple worlds—the Richters are evil beasts out to dominate Enchantment . . ." His cheeks fill as he takes another bite of pastry. Covering his mouth as he adds, "I'm all up to speed."

"So, what happened?" I reach into the cupboard, searching for mugs that aren't chipped. But not finding any, I'm forced to settle on four that bear the least amount of damage and wear.

"Yeah, and is Lita okay?" Daire crosses her legs, distracting me with a quick glimpse of thigh I try hard not to stare at.

"Lita's fine," Xotichl says. "In fact, she's more than fine. I think she spent over an hour working the mistletoe line, giving away free, one-time-only Christmas kisses just to annoy him."

"And did it?" Daire's face lights up at the thought.

"Not in the way that she hoped," Xotichl says. "Cade's beyond jealousy. Though I do think it bugged him that he couldn't control her in the way that he used to. He's pretty much a control freak."

"So—that's it? Cade showed up, Lita kissed a bunch of guys she's known all her life, and the party ended normally?" I distribute mugs filled with coffee while apologizing for the clumpy sugar and lack of milk.

"Pretty much," Auden says, sitting beside Xotichl and clasping her hand in his. "Though he asked about you—about both of you."

"And?" Daire peers at him from over the rim of her mug.

"And—nothing," Xotichl says. "I blew him off. Said I hadn't seen you."

"But it was weird," Auden says. "He actually looked pretty happy about that."

"Yeah, he would." I exchange another look with Daire.

"And then what?" Daire leans against my chest when I move to stand behind her. "Did he stay—leave—what happened?"

"Actually, it was weird. He pretty much spent the rest of the time talking with Phyre." Xotichl takes a long grateful sip of her coffee.

"What'd they talk about?" I rub Daire's shoulders, noticing the way they stiffen at the mention of Phyre's name. Leaving me to wonder how much she knows—versus what she might've guessed on her own.

"I don't know," Xotichl says. "I wasn't close enough to hear. But the energy they had going between them was certainly weird."

"Weird how?" Daire leans forward, her voice sounding worried.

"Frenetic. Off. Kind of murky and gray-brown in color."

"You could *see* it?" Daire asks. "I thought that only worked with music?"

Xotichl shakes her head, takes another sip of coffee. "Paloma is teaching me to see the color in all forms of energy. Music was just the gateway."

"Speaking of—" Daire grabs hold of my wrist and consults my watch. "I should get dressed and head back. I'm supposed to meet up with Jennika, so we can spend some quality mother-daughter time together."

"I'll drive you, if you want," Auden says. "I'm heading that way."

"And I figured I'd stick around and finally show Dace where the Rabbit Hole vortex is located."

"I don't want you going there." Daire pauses on her way to the bedroom, her words directed at Xotichl.

"I figured as much," Xotichl says. "But I'm not sure that'll stop me."

"Seriously," Daire says, refusing to give in so easily. "It's totally corrupt. It's too dangerous. Dace—promise me you won't let her go with you. In fact, promise me neither of you will go."

I swipe a hand over my chin, purposely ignoring that last bit. "Have you ever tried to keep Xotichl from doing what she's determined to do?"

"I have." Auden raises a hand. "It's not pretty. My flower is a stubborn one."

Daire shoots me a warning look, but all I can do is shrug in response.

I'm going in.

Without Xotichl.

Without Daire.

Without anyone.

Last night clinched it. Now that I've been with her again, I don't ever want to be without her.

I'm going to confront the prophecy and see that it's done.

And by the time I'm finished, Cade will be dead.

thirty

Daire

When I get to Paloma's, I'm not sure what to expect after staying out all night without telling anyone.

At the very least, I expect they'll be worried.

At the very worst, they'll be really, really angry.

Though maybe not Paloma. As a fellow Seeker, her expectations of me and my comings and goings differ from that of the average grandmother's.

But Jennika? She'll be in a frenzy for sure. My absence will hit all of her triggers. She'll put two and two together and come up with three: Me + Dace = an unplanned pregnancy. Never stopping to think that I've got my own story to live—one that reads nothing like hers. Besides, Dace and I were careful, it's not a baby we were making.

Though the scene I'm confronted with when I push through the door is not the one I expected.

Jennika is curled up on the couch, staring into the fire with a blanket wrapped snugly around her, while Paloma sits in an adjacent chair, sipping from a mug of fragrant herbal tea. The two of them sitting quietly, as though they weren't even thinking, much less worried, about me.

I mumble a quiet greeting. Shooting a tentative, questioning look at Paloma, who merely smiles and nods in return.

"Did you have a good night?" Jennika asks, her eyes dark and sooty from the makeup she must've slept in. Breaking her own cardinal rule of: Thou shalt go to bed fresh of face. Leading me to believe she spent the night here.

I fill the space beside her and fold my knees underneath me. "The party was good."

"And the after-party?"

We exchange a look. That's not a question I intend to answer.

"At least tell me you were careful?" she prods.

I take a deep breath, unable to believe I'm having this conversation in front of my grandmother. "Of course." I bite down on my lip, fingering the shiny gold key at my chest as I stare hard at her. She looks different. Vulnerable and soft in an almost malleable way. Like a long occupied space has suddenly vacated inside her. My voice softening, I add, "For the record, I really was listening during all of those awkward sex talks you forced on me."

A ghost of a smile crosses her face as she wraps an arm around me and pulls me tightly to her. Burying her nose in my hair and inhaling deeply, she says, "Guess this means you're back together?"

She pulls away and looks at me, and I nod in reply.

"You're all grown up now." She trails the pad of her thumb down my cheek. "I've got nothing left to teach you."

"That's not true," I say, surprised to realize I mean it.

But she just shakes her head. "As it turns out, it appears I'm now learning from you."

I squint, unsure of her meaning.

"I went through the box."

I look to Paloma, seeing her smiling faintly as she nods toward my mom.

"And then Paloma and I had a long talk."

I clamp my lips shut, not sure what that means.

How much of a talk?

About Django?

About me?

About me choosing to accept the biological inheritance he fought to deny?

Does this mean she knows I'm a Seeker?

She pushes a lock of hair from her face and levels her gaze on mine. "I think I'm beginning to realize just how much I don't know about the world. Not to mention how much I've denied what I couldn't bear to face. And while I won't claim to like it—while I don't like it one single bit—while I can barely wrap my head around the kind of future you face—I'm also left with no choice but to accept it. If I could do something, anything, to change it, I would. If I could volunteer on your behalf and take your place, I'd do that too. But Paloma tells me I can't. Says I've done all that I could the last sixteen years, and now I need to leave you in the care of a force far greater than me." She swallows hard, plants a kiss on the side of my head. Her voice a mere whisper, she says, "You know, I think Django would be proud of you—to know that you're trying to complete the very thing he tried hard to flee . . . I think he'd be amazed by your courage and strength. I know I am."

"I met him," I say, seeing the way her gaze widens at the words. "During my vision quest. He came to me. Helped me. I couldn't have survived it without him. He was so handsome too. I can see why you fell for him as hard as you did."

Jennika's gaze travels to a distant place—smiling faintly at his memory.

"He's everywhere, you know. Paloma taught me that. You can talk to him wherever and whenever you want. But, honestly, I think he'd prefer you move on."

She nods, pulls me back to her. "Don't let that boy hurt you again." The words are a fierce whisper.

"Still calling him *that boy?*"

Her shoulders lift, as she flips open the blanket, inviting me in.

"He didn't mean to hurt me the first time. It was a misguided attempt to protect me, that's all." I inch closer, allowing her to envelop me in a cozy layer of wool.

"And don't forget that you're not just a Santos—a Seeker—you're a Lyons as well. I'm part of that equation too, you know."

"How could I forget?" I snuggle against her. "Besides, I wouldn't have it any other way, would you?"

She shakes her head slightly, tightening her blanket around us, as we gaze into the flames. Watching as they crackle and spit, devouring the vertically stacked logs in Paloma's kiva fireplace.

Our reverie broken when Paloma says, "Look—it's raining!"

I look toward the window and, sure enough, the panes are streaming and wet.

"Not quite the snow I tried to manifest, but it's a start, right?" I glance between my mother and grandmother.

Smiling with contentment when they say, "It is indeed."

We remain like that for the better part of the morning. Three generations of females, staring into the rain—contemplating a future that yawns wide before us.

"I can't believe you're leaving." I glance around the tiny hotel room while Jennika packs up the few things she brought. "I mean, I can see why you wouldn't want to stay—this place is pretty dismal. Still, I'm going to miss you. It's nice having you around. Especially now."

"Why *especially now*?" She starts to fold a T-shirt into thirds, then gives up and squashes it instead.

"Because I hated lying to you. It feels so much better to have it all out in the open. It's good to know you're on board."

"Did I have a choice?"

We exchange a look.

"At least you know for sure I'm not crazy. The visions—the crows—the glowing people—it's all real."

She sighs in a way that tells me that just because she accepts it, doesn't mean that she likes it—doesn't mean she wants to delve into the details. Then she motions for me to sit on top of her suitcase so she can zip it shut.

"So, where do you go from here?" She grits her teeth and tugs hard on the zipper.

"The Rabbit Hole. You?" I push down with both hands in an effort to help her.

"First home and then Harlan's." She secures the shiny black lock with a satisfying *click*.

"Yeah?" I look at her, my smile growing bigger when she swats at me, pushes me to my feet.

Doing her best to nix my hopes, she says, "I'm committing to meeting him for a drink. And if that goes well, I'll let him buy me dinner. We'll see where it leads. Baby steps, right?" She heaves her bag off the bed and yanks hard on the handle, pulling the bag upright. "Need a ride?"

I shake my head and follow her to the door. "It's not far. Besides, I could use the walk."

"It's still raining," she warns.

"Yeah, and I'm still trying for snow."

She hugs me to her. Crushing me so tightly, I'm left gasping and laughing, as I croak, "I can't breathe!"

"You be careful out there." She slowly draws away. Fussing with my hair, rearranging the tumble of curls that survived the night surprisingly well.

"You be careful too." I follow her to the car. Waiting until she drives away before I cross the street, ready to make good on my destiny.

thirty-one

Dace

"You know I can't let you go any farther," I say, seeing Xotichl standing beside me so tiny and frail she looks like she's about to be swallowed by the heavy blue parka she wears.

We were lucky to have made it this far without being seen. Managing to slip past a horde of undead Richters too absorbed in the task of setting up some so-called job fair to take notice of us. Though that doesn't mean our luck won't run out. And I'd never forgive myself if Xotichl got hurt on my watch.

"Honestly, I can't say that I want to," she says. "Something strange is going on around here." She tips her chin, sniffs at the air. "Stranger than normal, that is. Those people we passed earlier, the ones setting up the tables and hanging the signs?"

"Yeah?" I slant my brow and lean toward her.

"They're undead."

I exhale, amused to find I'm relieved by her words. Shows how much my life has changed in just a handful of weeks. "I know." I tell her. "It's Cade's pet project. He reanimated a bunch of long-deceased Richters on the Day of the Dead, fueling them on bits of souls—both animal and human. Just one more reason he has to be stopped. The last thing we need is more Richters lumbering around."

Xotichl squeezes her cane, shoulders cringing inward, as she says, "I think the job fair is bogus. I think it's a front for something far more sinister." She pauses, allowing me time to respond, but I have nothing to add. I don't disagree. "Maybe I should go with you," she offers. "You know, like a bodyguard." She grins at her joke, but the effect is short-lived when the weight of the situation settles upon us.

"I hate leaving you here. Are you sure you can find your way back?" I glance between her and the wall that's not really a wall. Musing at how long I remained oblivious to its presence, despite having passed it hundreds of times. How I needed a blind girl to point me toward the truth that was always right there before me.

We see what we want to see. And when we can no longer afford that luxury, we see what we must.

Now that I'm faced with the truth, I'm torn between my desire to charge it head-on, and worried about leaving her behind. Afraid she'll get lost in this dark and cavernous space that practically reeks of evil and malevolence.

"Never make the mistake of underestimating me. I'll be fine." She quirks a brow in a way that leaves no room for doubt. "If anyone catches me, I'll say I was so excited about the job opening, I got here early so I could be among the first to fill out an application. And if they deny me that right, I'll threaten to sue them on grounds of discrimination." She taps her cane hard against the carpeted floor for emphasis. "You have the cigarettes?"

I pat my pocket, confirm that I do. "I always thought that was a myth. You know, the whole tobacco offering for the demons thing."

"And where do you think myths originated?" she asks. "They began as truths. They only turned to myths when we decided it was easier to live in denial of the things we don't understand."

"Okay, Little Wise One." I clasp a hand to each shoulder and turn her 'til she's facing the opposite way. "It's time for us to part ways. You find the exit while I go explore."

But no sooner have I started to leave than she turns back and says, "Dace—" Her face creases with worry. "What do I tell Daire? You know, if I run into her?"

I study Xotichl's face. She looks so tiny and vulnerable in this hollow space, I have to remind myself that she's right—underestimating her would be a mistake. Then I palm the cigarettes, squeezing my fingers around them, as I make for the greasy, pulsing veil, saying, "Not to worry. Thanks to you, I've got a solid head start. While Daire probably just walked in the door only to be faced with a full interrogation about how and where she spent her night. By the time she escapes, Cade will be dead. If nothing else, I'll make sure of that."

thirty-two

Daire

By the time I get to the Rabbit Hole, the stairwell is crowded with a large group of people forming a somewhat orderly line under a banner that advertises a job fair.

A job fair?

Here—in Enchantment—where there are no jobs to be had?

This is not what I expected.

I was hoping to get here early. Blend with the cleaning crew so I could do a little investigating while hopefully going unnoticed.

I'd planned to enter the Lowerworld directly through the Rabbit Hole vortex. Thinking their point of access would lead me directly to Cade.

And then, once I'd found him, I'd kill him.

A plan that made loads of sense—up until now, anyway.

Despite my late start, I never once considered a scenario where I'd be greeted by a bouncer doling out single-sided job applications.

Still, I decide to go with it and see where it leads. Carrying my form to one of the tall round tables surrounding the dance floor, I take in the mob of job seekers, most of them middle-aged, all of them wearing the same tired, glazed look. Other than dragging themselves here, no one appears all that motivated to do anything more than wander around in a daze.

"Numbers one through twenty—come this way!" I turn toward the voice shouting from behind me. My gaze landing on a man I've never seen, but who definitely bears the dark swarthy look of a Richter, scrutinizing the group he just summoned as they slowly file past.

I stare down at my slip, the hand-scrawled 27 in the upper right corner placing me in the next group to be called.

Should I go?

Should I fill this thing out and see where it leads?

Will I live to regret it?

Will I live?

I bury my face in my hands, unsure what to do. Comforting myself with the thought that at least I don't have to worry about Dace and Xotichl. Even though they probably ignored my protest and came here the second I left, I'm sure they turned back the instant they saw this.

My thoughts interrupted by a woman asking to borrow a pen. Her eyes so tired and with wrinkles so deep they seem to recede into her skull.

I dig through the contents of my bag. Locating a pencil, I hand it over and say, "Not exactly a pen, but I doubt they'll care."

Without a word, she takes it from me. Her hand shaky, jaw clenched, as she concentrates on the simple task of writing her name.

"So, what kind of jobs are they offering?" I ask, desperate to get a handle on what I'm about to get myself into.

"Dunno." Her voice is as flat as her gaze. Returning the pencil, even though, other than adding her name, the remaining boxes are blank. "Heard it offers free room and board. 'At's all I care about."

She slumps toward the stage where she waits for the next

group to be called. And while I'm still no closer to knowing what this is about, it's safe to assume that this so-called job fair is not what it seems. The Richters aren't exactly known for their altruism—there's always something in it for them. Still, there's only one way to be sure.

I fill out my form with a false name and address. Having a little fun with the ruse until I reach the part where the questions start to get weird, asking things like: *Any diseases? List them here.*

And just under that: *Maximum weight you can easily lift?*

Though the one that really disturbs me is: *This job requires you to be gone for an indefinite period of time. List the names of all those who might miss you. If necessary, feel free to continue on the back of the page.*

What the heck kind of job is this?

A moment later, when my group is called, I unzip my hood from its hiding place in the collar and sling it over my head. Then I slump my shoulders, crumple my application into my hand, and join them. Giving my best impersonation of a lonely, defeated, downtrodden person with a talent for weight lifting and no serious diseases. Which is not nearly as easy as it seems.

I merge with my group. Shrinking deeper into my hood when I pass the stage where the Richter with the microphone studies us with a sharp eye before waving us down the hall that ultimately leads to the demon-guarded vortex beyond.

Shuffling along with the rest of them, I manage a few covert peeks at my fellow job seekers. All of them bearing the same glazed look, reminding me of the patrons who sat at the bar the first time I came here. How they looked like they'd been teetering on their bar stools for the better part of the day—if not the better part of their lives. Numbed from the endless stream of alcohol pickling their brains.

A new group of applicants join us, and it's not long before several more are told to follow. Too many years spent under the

Richters' control have left these people hopeless, desperate, and all too eager to trade the hell they know for one they can't even imagine.

A muffled sound comes from the front, and while I can't quite make it out, its tone is familiar in a way that sets me on edge.

I rise onto my tiptoes, straining to see over the tops of too many heads. Getting a glimpse of yet another undead Richter, before the bodies surge forward and I'm forced to slouch along with the rest of them. Bearing the sort of poor posture Jennika sought to break me of as a kid, I slip the pack of cigarettes into my palm and shove the athame up my right sleeve. Ready for any number of possibilities, since I have no idea where this might eventually lead.

We trudge down the hall, heading straight for the wall that disguises the vortex, where we're stopped by that same undead Richter I glimpsed a moment ago. From what I can tell by peering over several rows of shoulders, he's in charge of inspecting the applications and deciding who gains admittance.

But after watching a bit, I realize it's really just a ploy intended to heighten the tension. Make people yearn for admission, then breathe a sigh of relief once they're in. From what I can tell, no one's rejected. No matter how they fill out the form, the Richters will find a way to squeeze 'em dry before they discard them.

When it's my turn, I hand over my application and stare blankly ahead, trying not to cringe under his scrutiny. All too aware of the sound of warning bells ringing in my head, urging me to run—to ditch this place and never look back. Imagining all the horrible ways this could blow up in my face.

My heart begins to race. My weight instinctively shifts onto my toes. Driven by my most primal instinct to save my own skin no matter the cost, I'm just about to flee when that creepy undead Richter grabs hold of my chin and tilts it toward his. His gaze probing mine while his dry, papery, undead fingers squeeze so tightly it hurts.

I can't breathe. Can't speak. Can't run. Can't do much of any-thing but meet his stare with my own. Overcome with regret for the situation I find myself in.

I shouldn't have come here.

I've completely underestimated them.

And now, because of it, I'm just seconds away from being con-quered and crushed.

His gruesome lips tug at the side, but otherwise, his expres-sion remains so unreadable there's no way to guess what he's thinking. All I know for sure is that I have to get the heck out while I still have a sliver of a chance of surviving.

I turn my head sharply, desperate to wrench free of his grip, when he slams his other hand hard against my back and shoves me smack through the vortex.

thirty-three

Dace

I creep through the cave, relieved to find it free of undead Richters and demons—guess they were needed to set up the job fair—yet disappointed to find that I'm still in the Middleworld.

Another dimension of the Middleworld—but still a far cry from the Lowerworld I was hoping for. Though I'm sure it'll lead there eventually.

The place is luxurious. Plush. With its rare antique furniture and priceless art covering the walls, it's clear they've spent a great deal of time here. Plotting. Planning. Waiting for the entry to yawn open again.

Throughout history, whenever they managed to invade the Lowerworld, this is the place that served as their main point of entry. Once in, they immediately set out to corrupt the spirit animals by contaminating their land and stripping them of their power and light, rendering them incapable of guiding their human attachments. The loss resulting in horrific episodes of madness, chaos, and war across the Middleworld—and untold riches for the Richters.

Or at least that's the story according to Leftfoot.

And its just one more reason why I need to kill Cade.

Then as soon as that's done, Leandro is next.

With his sights mostly confined to ruling Enchantment, and not exactly interested in Cade's broader goal of world domination, he may not be as dangerous, though he still has to go. If for no other reason than I can't bear to look at him after knowing what he did to my mom. Despite what the elders say, keeping him balanced and contained just isn't enough.

Not for me.

Never will be.

It's time to redefine a few things.

Time to shake up the prophecy.

Time to make sure the whole lot of them dies.

This is so much bigger than my being with Daire.

And yet, while I know this is true, as I make my way through this long, hollow space, ultimately pushing through the far wall, where I find myself surrounded by sand, Daire is all I can think about.

I stop. Gaze all around. Remembering what Leftfoot taught me—to seek the truth that lies beneath the things that I see. To question my sight just as I should question all of the thoughts I've been conditioned to believe.

There is much more to this world than meets the eye. A whole other truth people strive to deny. Don't be blinded like them. Look deeper. Think deeper. Allow yourself to go quiet and still, and allow the truth to reveal itself to you.

I close my eyes and do as he said, and when I open them again, it's as though a path has been laid out before me. Seeming to end at the crest of a very large sand dune that, once reached, drops straight into the Lowerworld.

I slip through the earth, ultimately landing hard on my side. I'm quick to pull myself up and survey the place. Not having been here since my last hunt with Daire—I'm stunned to see how much it's deteriorated in only a handful of days. The spirit animals, once happy and active, are now sluggish and listless—barely able to attend to their most basic needs. And the more I explore, the worse it appears. Every step revealing further corruption, spoilage, and ruin—all of it unfolding under an eerie hush that's soon broken by the unsettling sound of branches snapping, trees toppling, and the amplified hum of animalistic grunting and huffing reverberating all around.

I dart behind a large boulder just as a flash of beige fur and red glowing eyes bursts into the space where I stood.

Coyote.

Cade's coyote no doubt.

He skids to a stop with his snout pitched high, catching my scent. And it's only a moment later when another coyote appears—its fangs and fur coated with blood and the slimy remnants of some unfortunate kill.

The second I see them I know Leftfoot was right.

While Cade may not be a skinwalker in the traditional sense, he is able to assume other forms.

My fingers snake into my pocket, in search of the blowgun Leftfoot once gave me that was given to him by Alejandro, a Brazilian jaguar shaman, who also happens to be the grandfather Daire never met. According to Leftfoot, the weapon was carefully carved from a rare wood found only in the Amazon rain forest. But before he agreed to hand it over, he forced me to promise that I would only use it for self-defense.

The coyotes crouch side by side—noses twitching, eyes darting—just seconds away from discovering the place where I hide.

So why let it get to that point?

Why wait for them to attack me—just so I can claim self-defense—when I can easily snuff them out now?

I reach for a dart, pinching it by its raven-feathered fletch as I load it inside.

Then I slide one eye closed, narrow the other in focus, lift the small tube to my mouth, and take aim.

Watching as Coyote snarls. Lunging in a flash of gleaming eyes, gnashing teeth, and hot rancid breath pelting hard against my cheek. His jaw widening, ready to take another chunk out of me—

When he falters.

Stumbles.

Collapsing to the ground and howling in pain.

I smile triumphantly, though the smile soon fades when I lift my gaze to find Cade looming naked and bloodied before me, bits of animal carcass clinging to his skin.

I've hit the wrong mark.

"What the hell are you doing?" He drops beside Coyote, cursing bitterly as he drags on the fletch, yanking the dart from his neck. And damn if he isn't smart enough to know it doesn't end there. He lowers his head to the hit, molds his lips around it, and siphons the poison I'd placed on the tip, before spitting it onto the ground. "You're a real idiot, you know that?" He shakes his head and glares, watching as I reload the blowgun and take aim once again. "Trust me," he says. "You do *not* want to do that."

"You have no idea what I want." I wrap my lips around the tube, inhale a deep, purposeful breath, and blow once again.

Blow with everything that I've got.

Letting loose my own stream of curses when Cade dances free of the dart's path, and turns into a coyote again.

The other one now fully recovered, they stand in solidarity before me—shoulder to menacing shoulder.

Eyes blazing with vengeance, leaving no doubt it's my blood they're after. And before I can run, before I can reload and take aim—they descend on me in a frenzy of ragged claws and sharp fangs.

thirty-four

Daire

The first thing I notice when I burst through the wall is the demon.

Or should I say, *demons*. After all, there's an entire army of them.

The second thing I notice is how no one seems to be the least bit alarmed by the giant-sized, malevolent beings that surround them. Barely sparing a glance at the variety of tails, and hooves, and horns, and misshapen heads. Not to mention the faces that appear to be a grotesque mix of animal, human, and some other unidentifiable beast that originated in a very dark place.

The crowd just continues to shuffle along in their numbed and glazed state. And when it's my turn to pass, despite my best efforts to blend with the rest, it's not long before one of those long, ragged claws reaches toward me, as he shoves his face close to mine. Its dark slitted eyes peering so close, I break into a sweat.

This can't happen.

I can't afford to be outed.

Not now.

Not after getting this far.

I steady my breath and stare straight ahead, covertly wagging the pack of cigarettes before him as I send a silent prayer to my ancestors, the elements, my talismans, anyone who might be willing to listen. Praying the tobacco offering will work as well as it did the last time I was here, and heaving a sigh of relief when he accepts the bribe and tosses it into his mouth, plastic wrapper and all.

We pass through the tunnel that leads to the cave, then we slip through the entry and on past the den. Making our way down the long hall where we crowd into a semicircle, listening to, from what I can make out, some sort of initiation speech.

The words a bit muffled from where I stand, though I'm still able to discern things like: *Great opportunity . . . rare blue tourmaline . . . a fortune to be made . . . free room and board . . .* None of which leaves me with any more insight than I started with.

Though one thing's for sure—the only fortune to be made will be for the Richters. These people won't see a dime of it.

A moment later, we're moving again. Pushing through the second wall that leads to the valley of sand, where we begin our trek across the desert terrain. My fellow travelers so glazed, so obedient, I wonder if they even realize what they're doing, where it is they're going. It's as though they're caught in a trance, programmed to do what they're told and not to react to anything unusual.

When we reach the point where the hill crests and the ground gives way, I'm careful to shield myself from the mass of flailing limbs as we tumble toward the Lowerworld, where I leap to my feet and scramble behind a guy twice my size. Adjusting my hood so it shields the better part of my face, hoping to go unrecognized until I'm ready to be seen.

"Welcome!" Cade calls, his voice deep and sure. "I'm glad you all could make it—that you've decided to reach a little higher—do something more meaningful with your lives than spending your days slumping over the bar, getting sloshed out of your minds. Our cause is a great one, and you should be proud of your part in it . . ." He drones on, reciting a speech that's completely unnecessary. These people are captive. His to command. There's no reason to go on like he does, other than the fact that he loves to hear himself speak. Finally reaching the end when he says, "So, it's time we get started. I see no reason to delay. But first—your uniforms."

He reaches into a large cardboard box an undead Richter has placed by his side and goes about tossing heaps of black, short-sleeved T-shirts bearing a picture of him into the crowd, like he once tossed souls to the army of undead Richters.

"Take one and pass the rest," he barks. "This is so you never forget who you've sworn fealty to." His gaze grows darker as he takes in his subjects assembled before him.

When the guy in front of me hands me a T-shirt, I take a moment to examine it. Noting how the grin in Cade's picture is a perfect match for the one he wears now.

Fake.

Empty.

A meaningless void.

It's the smile of a psychopath.

An egomaniacal freak with no access to human emotion, so the best he can do is imitate.

I crunch it into a ball and discard it at my feet. I have no intention of wearing it. No intention of working for him. My immediate goal is to determine what he's up to. And then—

And then I'm no longer sure.

This wasn't part of the plan.

"You'll be mining for tourmaline. Pure blue tourmaline. Which, just so you know, is one of the most precious, rarest, and therefore most costly, stones on earth. Though make no mistake— you will enjoy all of the labor and none of the profits. And any of you even considering pocketing a rock you think no one will miss—think again. We are watching you at all times. The price for that kind of treason is immediate death with no questions asked. And any of you wanting to turn back—it's too late. There is no escape."

A few grunts of protest erupt from the crowd, but it's not like Cade cares. He expects nothing less than their absolute submission, and there's no doubt he'll get it.

He turns on his heel, confident that we'll follow (we do), as he leads us across a blackened scorched land to an elaborate mining operation guarded by an army of more undead Richters. The sight of which leaves me gaping in astonishment.

I'm out of my element.

Out of my league.

The double-sided knife I've stashed up my sleeve is a joke, no matter what Paloma claims.

There are way too many Richters—way too many heads to remove—versus only one of me.

While the athame may hold the power to slay Cade, I won't even get that far before I'm overcome by the rest of them.

I've completely miscalculated.

Ignored common sense in favor of anger and thoughts of revenge.

Despite Valentina's claim: *Your intent fuels your will, and your will is your way*—I don't see how either one of those things will bring me to victory when I'm so outnumbered like this.

I crouch behind the guy before me, tipping my hood just enough to see what a mess this place is.

The mine is the cause of this environmental disgrace. The very reason why the ocean is polluted and the fish are all dying. But Cade won't care. Violating the Lowerworld will not only result in profit for him but will also ensure that the Middleworld will soon fall to ruin—just as he planned.

When my fellow travelers crowd into the shaft, I slip free of their ranks and hide among a grove of burned-out tree carcasses. Stealing a moment to observe the goings on while I decide my next move.

There's no reason to take any chances. If I've any hope of help-ing these people—of getting them out of here—I have to make it back to the Middleworld, where I can consult the elders and come up with a much better way to handle this.

When the entire group disappears inside the mine, Cade looks around with a creepy self-satisfied grin.

A creepy self-satisfied grin that fades the instant he tips his nose in the air and captures my scent. Whirling in my direction, his eyes deep, opaque, and fathomless, he says, "Do you know what I find most fascinating about ravens?"

I swallow hard. Slip the athame into my hand. Watching as he snaps his fingers and raises his arm, smiling in triumph when a moment later Raven, my Raven, obediently lands on his finger.

"Not only can they be trained to come on command, but they're also exceedingly gifted at mimicry. They can repeat all manner of sounds and phrases with absolute perfect pitch. For example—" He peers at Raven, cooing softly when he says, "Go ahead, tell Santos what you know."

Right on command, Raven's purple eyes glimmer as he croaks, "The Seeker loves the Echo." His voice a perfect match for Cade's.

I remove the sheath from the blade, keep it close to my side.

"Cute, huh?" Cade gives Raven an affectionate tap on the head. "Of course, we've only just started, got a ways to go still." He releases Raven, watching him lift into flight only to land on a branch just a few feet away. The sight of it causing Cade to make a face of distaste. "He's so nosy." He shakes his head and returns his attention to me. "How did you stand it?"

He strides toward me, as I grip the hilt tighter. Fingers press-ing into the smooth black wood, ready to use it at the first oppor-tunity. Allowing myself to exhale only when he stops a few feet away.

"But then you're not here to watch stupid pet tricks, are you? And surely you're not seeking a job, or at least I should hope not.

It's mind-numbing, soul-crushing work that wouldn't even begin to utilize your many talents and skills." He tilts his head, runs his tongue across his front teeth. A move so lurid, so obscene, I have to force myself not to react. "It's not exactly what I had in mind when I approached you about working together. So, why don't you just admit it, Santos, you're here to see me."

He shoots me one of his smug grins, and before I can stop myself, I say, "You're completely delusional!" I step free of the tree, seeing no point in hiding when my cover's been blown.

"Am I?" He regards me carefully. "And yet you can't stop thinking about me—what's up with that?"

I roll my eyes in reply. "You can't do this. Despite what you think, the Lowerworld is not yours to control."

He smirks. Looks all around. Gesturing to a surrounding landscape that would seem to beg otherwise. "Perhaps you should take another look," he says, observing all the damage and destruction he's caused. Clearly pleased by the bleak state of wretchedness he's single-handedly wrought.

I ready the blade in my hand. One eye fixed on the army of Richters keeping a close watch on me, the other on Cade.

"I'm guessing you've come here to kill me." He smiles patiently, like you do with a very slow child.

I clamp my lips shut. Refuse to confirm or deny.

"That's the second assassination attempt in one day." He runs a hand through his hair, his lip curling as though amused by the idea, while my own reaction is anything but.

If I'm the second attempt, then Dace was the first.

It also means he failed.

Failed in the way of the prophecy?

My body stiffens. My heart fails to beat. Aware that the game has just changed, and yet there's a part of me that refuses to believe it.

If something did happen to Dace, surely I would have felt it. Surely I would've sensed it in some way.

Wouldn't I?

"I always forget what a newbie you are." Cade slips behind a mask of chagrin. "So, allow me to give you a little piece of advice that might spare us this brand of awkwardness in the future. You're not going to kill me, Santos. Dace isn't going to kill me either. Believe me when I say that any attempt on my life will not bode well for either of you. Not to mention that your pathetic little Wiccan pruning knife is hardly up to the task."

I shift the knife behind my leg, secure it from view.

But he just laughs. "What—you think I can't see it?" He studies me closely, sighing as he adds, "Maybe I've overestimated you. You're a much slower learner than I thought you'd be." His eyes slew over me, lingering in all the wrong places. "Do us both a favor and run along so we can both try to forget this ever happened. I'm a patient guy, Daire. And I'm truly trying to work with you here. But you need to work with me too. You need to accept the fact that there's no point in going after me. You're in way over your head. It's my world, Seeker—you're lucky I allow you to live in it."

Despite what he says, I remain right where I am. Imagining the thrill of rushing toward him—the satisfaction of slamming this blade straight into his heart. Assuming he has one.

"In case you don't get it, this is me being altruistic. We've got a lot of work ahead of us. And, other than these little transgressions you seem to insist on, I'm thrilled to see you turning out to be a much better business partner than I ever expected. In other words, I'm not ready to kill you just yet. Believe me, you'll know when I am."

"But perhaps I'm ready to kill you." My voice rings surprisingly steady as I make a move toward him, noticing how he fails to so much as flinch.

"Well then, I'd say you're about to find yourself faced with a major dilemma." He grins, purposely swiping a hand over his chin in the way Dace often does. The sight so disarming, I have to force myself to take the next step. "What would you rather do, Daire? Kill me—or save the life of my twin?"

With only a handful of steps left between us, it's a distance I can easily close in one single leap.

"Yours to decide." His voice grows bored as he focuses on a space just past my shoulder, challenging me to follow.

At first I refuse, convinced it's a trick.

But when I hear a low rasping moan—the sound of someone in pain—chased by a trickle of Dace's usual swarm of warm loving energy, I raise the knife high over my head, determined to do it—slay Cade while I can.

Then I abandon the idea just as quickly.

Instinctively knowing that the reason Dace's energy is so faint is because his life force is fading so swiftly that in the time it takes to kill Cade, I'll run a serious risk of losing Dace too.

I race toward him. Dismayed to find him discarded, left for dead, just a few feet away. His torso shredded and blood-soaked, his hands covered in bite marks, his arm awkwardly jangled and skewed at his side.

I sink to my knees and pull him to me. My need to save him the only thing driving me. It's all I can focus on. All I can see.

My love for him completely consumes me.

Unfortunately, it consumes Cade as well.

Allowing him to morph. Grow. His clothes shredding at the seams, as his body bulges and stretches—undergoing a transformation that's as spectacular as it is gruesome. Transmuting into a scaly-skinned, snake-tongued beast three times his normal size.

And when he turns—when he raises his hands to his sides and focuses his attention toward the mine—a horrible rumble roars through the land. Prompting Raven to squawk and lift into flight as the earth begins to loosen and shift until it becomes a harsh roiling tremor that causes me to lose hold of Dace.

The ground splits between us—stranding us each on our own hellish islands. My panic scored by the boom of Cade's malevolent laughter as he throws his head back, yawns his mouth wide, and allows those soul-stealing snakes to shoot free, turning toward me in full demon glory.

His mouth a jagged, obscene gash of snakes and gums, he says, "Thought I'd shake it up a bit. Loosen the tourmaline and make the stones easier to retrieve. We may lose a few miners in the process, but hey—that's the price of business, right, *partner?*"

I look toward the mine, longing to help in some way. I can't let him do this. Can't let those poor people suffer any more than they already have. But the ground continues to split, further separating me from Dace.

"You're no good to them dead. You're no good to me either. Save yourself, Santos. While you still can. And while you're at it, save my brother too. And the next time you come here to kill me, remember that it's because of you that I'm stronger than you." A crude smirk further distorts his demonic face. "Speaking of which, I should probably thank you for the latest infusion of power. Thanks to you, I'm stronger than ever. I can only imagine the kind of dirty deeds you two have been up to."

The tremors intensify. The earth shaking so violently, the trees I once hid behind crash and fall all around me. And when one of them narrowly misses crushing Dace, I'm left with no choice but to risk the leap toward him.

My focus narrowed as I flail through the air. My legs kicking wildly as the toe of my boot finds purchase, but only briefly, before the soil crumbles and loosens beneath me. Sending me into a free fall—tumbling into a yawning dark chasm that offers nothing to grab hold of.

The pull of gravity dragging me down until the earth shifts again, moving toward me this time. Offering a hardened piece of packed earth I'm quick to grab hold of, followed by a succession of rocks. And the next thing I know, I'm seeking handholds and footholds, as I cautiously work my way up.

When I'm over the ledge, I rush to the place where Dace lies.

Sparing a second to ensure he's still breathing, I toss his good arm over my shoulder, heave him up alongside me, and drag him along as I seek a way out.

Chased by an ever-increasing crevice splintering behind us and the sound of Cade's mocking laughter singing, "Run, Seeker, run!"

thirty-five

Dace

When I wake, I have no idea how long I've been out.

All I know is it must've been bad, if the heady shroud of incense and candles are anything to go by.

Chepi reaches me first. But then I'm pretty sure she's been there all along. Never really left. Her exhausted, tear-streaked face hovers over mine as one hand fusses at my hair, smoothing it off my forehead, while the other clutches an overused tissue she presses hard to her chest. Murmuring soft words of gratitude and relief—wanting me to know how much she loves me, how much she prayed for me, that Jolon's spirit stood by me—until Leftfoot pushes her aside and stands in her place.

His own ministrations not nearly as loving, he says, "I thought for sure you were dead on arrival."

I start to speak, but my mouth is so dry I have to force my tongue to separate from my teeth. "So, these are funeral candles?" I croak, my voice hoarse, underused.

"You can't afford to make jokes." He frowns. "You have no idea just how bad off you are. But soon, the medicinal herbs I gave you to numb your pain will wear off, and you'll be newly enlightened."

I slide my eyes shut, straining to remember exactly how I got here. My mind requiring a handful of seconds to warm up, wake up, and piece together the hazy remnants of a distant memory. And a moment later, when the scene comes barreling toward me in its hideously detailed entirety, I'm left wishing I'd been smart enough to leave it alone.

The hellish encounter gleefully unfolds in my head, lingering over the scene where Daire had to physically drag me out of the Lowerworld. Insistently rewinding it again and again, if only to punish me.

Humiliated doesn't even begin to describe it.

Mortified doesn't work either.

There's not a single word I can think of that accurately states how I feel.

Though the question remains: *Is she here?*

I try to sit up, desperate to see her. Stopped by the stabbing pain in my side, along with Leftfoot's hand pushing me back toward the mattress.

"Where is she?" I force the question between gritted teeth. Leftfoot was right—the herbs are starting to fade.

In an instant, Daire is beside me. Her hair disheveled and wind-tossed. Her clothes filthy and bloodstained. And yet, beneath the layers of dirt, her cheeks are flushed pink, her eyes bright and hopeful, and to me, she's never been more beautiful. I've never been more happy to see her.

"I'm here—I'm always here," she whispers, words intended only for my ears.

But when she bites down on her lip and sweeps a cautious hand over my cheek, I'm quick to close my eyes and turn away. Imagining how repugnant I must look to her.

Battered.

Broken.

Defeated and weak.

Someone she was forced to rescue.

A far cry from the hero I was striving to be.

And it's not like Leftfoot has any interest in sparing my ego. He's made it all too clear what he thinks of my pride.

"How many times will I have to patch you up before there's nothing left to patch?" He continues to mutter under his breath as he motions for Chay to help prop me up.

I steel myself against the pain, but mostly I'm embarrassed for Daire to see me this way.

"We need to remove your shirt," Leftfoot commands. "Or what's left of it, anyway. You were in such bad shape when they brought you in, all I could do was a quick patch job. I was afraid anything more would send you over the edge. But now that you're on the mend, it's time to put you back together again." Responding to my hesitation, the furtive look I shoot Daire, he says, "She's been here all along. It's nothing she hasn't seen before."

Daire flushes pink and looks the other way, as Leftfoot wads up a red bandanna he pulls from a drawer, shoves it toward me, and says, "Here—bite down on this. You're gonna need it."

I turn my cheek in refusal. My gaze drifting from Chay, to Chepi, to the back of Daire's head, before traveling back to Leftfoot again. Nothing more emasculating than a roomful of elders judging me in front of my girlfriend. The very least I can do is tough it out and reject the pacifier.

"Your call," Leftfoot says, never one to force me, despite how foolish he deems my behavior. "You're lucky it's only a dislocation and not a break. Breaks take longer to heal." He places one hand on my shoulder, as the other grabs at my arm. Muttering one of his healing songs under his breath, he pushes with a great deal of strength, wrenching the joint back into place.

The sudden jerk of bone meeting bone resulting in a pain so staggering, I force myself to focus on the niche full of santos on the other side of the room. Biting back the scream that crowds my throat, I fight like hell not to pass out.

Not like this.

Not in front of Daire.

Though there's nothing I can do about the constellation of stars that swirl bright and shining before me.

"Funny, I don't feel so lucky." I grind the words between clenched teeth, as I fight to steady my breath and get a grip on myself.

"And now . . . the wounds." Leftfoot lifts the blood-caked key from my chest. Pausing to give it a thorough inspection, he shoots Daire a look of reproach, then goes about the business of removing the gauze and poultices that held me together like a mummy so he can better inspect my torn and ravaged flesh.

The sight of my wounds causing Chepi to sob into her already soggy tissue, as Daire looks on with a face crowded with guilt-laced sympathy.

It's a look I can't bear.

A look that proves just how much I've failed her.

"You're lucky Chay found you when he did," Leftfoot says.

"How did you find us? How'd you know where to go?" I ask, unable to recall that particular detail.

"Intuition." Chay's words are directed at me, though his eyes remain fixed on Leftfoot. "I was out riding when we had a small earthquake and I instinctively headed for the vortex, sensing it wasn't the usual shifting of the earth. I'd only been there a few minutes when you two appeared."

"What were you doing down there?" Chepi asks.

Daire and I exchange a look. I have no idea what she told them, so I bypass the question, and tell them about the mine instead. Explaining its connection to all those disappearances Leftfoot told me about.

Glad for the chance to concentrate on something other than the sharp sting of potions Leftfoot uses to sterilize my wounds, before he gets to stitching them closed and mummifying me again in several layers of gauze and herbs.

When he's finished, he tosses me a clean shirt, tells me to get dressed, and damn if I don't need his help. As if I wasn't emasculated enough for one day.

His words directed at Chepi, he says, "Take him home. In order to mend, he's going to require serious bed rest." Then turning his focus to Daire, he adds, "Chay can drop you off at Paloma's. It's time you two stay away from each other. For good this time. I guarantee you, next time you won't be so lucky."

bleeding

sky

thirty-six

Daire

When I lose count of the number of times I've called Dace only to have Chepi pick up and refuse to put him on, I know it's time for another approach.

While she may have succeeded in confiscating his phone, while the elders may be working together, doing whatever it takes to keep us apart, there's no way they'll prevail.

I need to see him.

Need to check in and make sure he's okay.

Last I saw, his body was as battered as his ego. And I need to tell him that I don't think any less of him for being beaten by Coyote.

Twice now Dace has purposely jumped in the path of that psychotic, demonic, bloodthirsty beast—willing to sacrifice himself in an effort to save me.

It's touching beyond words.

It's the very definition of heroic.

But the look in his eyes when I left Leftfoot's adobe, made it clear he felt far more ashamed than valiant.

It's a look that continues to haunt me—one I'm desperate to change.

The question is how?

How can I possibly get to him when he's under Chepi's round-the-clock surveillance?

I heave myself off my bed and move toward the window. Tapping a finger lightly against the feather trim that hangs from the dream catcher over the sill, I gaze at the courtyard beyond. The thick layer of freshly poured protective salt, the coyote fence made of tall pieces of juniper branch, and the thick adobe wall that surrounds the entire property. Remembering a time just after I got here, when I used the strange setup as a reason to run—having no idea just how much it would come to serve and protect me.

I consider sneaking out, tossing a saddle on Kachina, and finding my way to Dace's window, but Dace isn't the only one under surveillance. Having decided to heed Leftfoot's warning to keep Dace and me away from each other, Paloma's spent the past few days keeping serious tabs on me. There's no way to escape without being found.

I watch as the sun begins to sink, painting the sky a brilliant orangey hue.

I watch as my cat creeps across the fence, pausing a moment to look my way, before crouching low and leaping onto the street.

I watch as a raven swoops onto a branch, taking a moment to settle as a gentle wind stirs and ruffles its feathers.

Raven.

Wind.

It's so obvious, I can't believe I didn't think of it before!

Raven is my spirit animal. Wind my guiding element. It's no accident this seemingly innocuous scene is unfolding before me.

There are no accidents. No such thing as coincidence. This is an offering, pure and simple.

If I've learned nothing else, it's that life is full of synchronicities—brimming with all manner of omens and signs we choose to ignore. Until we've become so accustomed to denying the barrage of miracles occurring all around us, we can no longer recognize them when they unfold right before us.

But not this time. This is exactly the opportunity I've sought all along.

I check to make sure the door is completely shut, since the last thing I need is for Paloma to come in and find my body lying inert on the floor while my soul journeys alongside a raven's. Then I turn toward the wind-ruffled bird and focus on him with all of my might. Much like I merged with a cockroach the first time I followed Cade to the vortex—I meld my energy with his until our souls sync as one and our hearts beat in tandem.

As soon as I'm settled, we're off. Lifting from the branch and soaring high into the sky. Carried by wings as light and fluid as gossamer, we glide across a landscape that unravels like a ribbon beneath us. The experience so glorious, I can hardly believe I allowed so much time to lapse since the last time I did this.

When we reach Chepi's property, the raven circles in a wide careful arc before landing just outside Dace's window. The gentle swish of his wing brushing the pane, enough to cause Chepi to look up from her reading with a suspicious gaze. The intensity of her stare so startling, so unexpected, my energy spikes and I nearly lose the connection.

She doesn't know it's me, I tell myself in an attempt to rein in my panic. *I'm just another raven. It's not like there's a shortage of them.*

Though clearly it's a mantra heard only by me. Chepi's scrutiny continues to deepen. Convinced I'm no random bird. That the scene isn't nearly as benign as it seems.

The raven grows anxious, starts to scramble about. Tired of playing host, he goes to great effort to evict me by hopping from foot to foot, emitting a low, guttural croak, and thumping his tail feathers hard against the glass. The commotion causing Chepi to frown and Dace to awaken with a gaze that veers straight for me. Intuitively sensing my presence, he directs a subtle nod my way, then says something to Chepi I can't quite make out. But it's enough for her to abandon her book and exit the room, as Dace bolts from his bed.

Crossing the room in just a few steps, he shoves the window open and offers his hand. While the raven's most primal instincts prompt him to flee, I'm able to convince him to creep closer, until he's nudging his head against Dace's welcoming fingers. And it's all I can do to contain myself when Dace responds by lowering his lips to the dome of raven's head. His kiss so intoxicating it reverberates throughout me.

"I knew you'd come," he whispers. "I knew you'd find a way. Still, I have to say, this is genius. Wish I'd thought of it. I would've visited you."

Despite the fact that ravens are known for their amazing vocal abilities, this particular raven refuses to cooperate, refuses to speak the words I urge it to share. After too many frustrated attempts, I resolve to convey it with a look. Hoping my gratitude, admiration, and love will somehow beam through the raven's small beady eyes.

Dace runs a finger down the length of raven's back, whispering, "There's no reason to worry. I'm getting better and stronger every day." He continues to stroke the shiny black feathers, causing me to melt under his touch. "It won't be long now before you and I are together again." His voice rings with determination. And though he means to reassure, somehow the words bear the opposite effect.

He's planning something. That much is clear. But whatever it is, I can't let him go through with it. Can't let him go after Cade. Can't let him get to him first.

To do so would be to play right into the prophecy. And that could only end in tragedy.

"Soon, Daire. Soon . . ." His voice drifts along with his gaze, traveling to some unknown future event that plays out in his head.

In a desperate bid to get through to him, I urge the raven to head for Dace's shoulder. About to take another crack at whispering into his ear, when Chepi pokes her head into the room and says, "Dace? Why are you up and who are you talking to?"

And that's all it takes for the raven to flit back to the ledge.

"It's nothing." Dace turns away from the window. "I just needed some air. And a little reminder of the world outside this room."

Chepi approaches with a gait full of purpose and an all-knowing gaze. "And now that you've been reminded, it's time to get back to bed." She reaches for the window sash and shoves it down with such force, the bond between the raven and me is instantly severed.

Allowing raven to shoot free of the ledge, as my soul reunites with my body.

thirty-seven

Dace

Daire's visit was exactly what I needed.

Her showing up on my windowsill via the raven wasn't just pure inspired genius, it gave me the push I need to get out of this house and make good on my plan.

But first I have to get past Chepi. She's a formidable obstacle—an eagle-eyed sentinel. And since I've already sent her on all the food and water errands I can without arousing her suspicions, the only ruse I have left is another round of feigned sleep. Needing her to think I'm down for the night, that I won't stir again until morning, I pull the blanket over my head and force my breath to fall slow and even. Remaining like that until she finally relaxes enough to leave.

The second she's gone, I toss the covers, peer down the hall to ensure it's all clear, and race for the door. Nearly free of it, when she rushes up from behind, grabs hold of my arm, and demands, "Where are you going?"

I close my eyes briefly. Overcome with regret for what I'm about to do next. Wishing it didn't have to be this way. But wishing is futile. It's action that's needed. And no matter how hard she

fights me, there's no way she'll keep me from doing what I most
need to do.

Still, I make a point to soften my tone when I say, "I need to
step out. You've kept me housebound too long and I'm feeling
hemmed in. I need to swing by my place and take care of some
things."

Her face darkens with disapproval. Causing the lines that
cross her forehead and fan either side of her mouth to deepen, as
though she's aged ten years in a matter of seconds.

"C'mon, Ma—you know you can't keep me cooped up here
forever." I shift my weight from foot to foot, never wanting to
leave a place as badly as this.

"You're going to see *her*." Her voice is accusatory, eyes sharp
and knowing.

"I don't even know where she is." I swipe a hand over my chin,
hiding the lie to come. "We haven't talked for days. But then you
already knew that. You've made sure of it." I swallow hard, force
myself to meet her gaze.

A fleeting expression crosses her face—a mixture of sadness
and apology that's gone in a blink. "You're still healing." She
reaches for my arm, attempts to inspect a wound that's already
faded. "I can't let you go until you're well. I promised Leftfoot I'd
make sure you got plenty of bed rest."

"You can tell Leftfoot I'm fine, fully healed." I yank on the
hem of my shirt, pull it up over my torso so she can see that not
only are the bandages gone, but also, thanks to a thick layer of
Leftfoot's poultice, along with a little magick I've worked on
my own—magick that's better left unmentioned—I'm left with
only the faintest trail of scars, that promise to fade, if not disappear.

I drop the hem, allow the shirt to fall to my hips. Wondering
what argument she'll try to wage next. Sure there will be one.

Her concern for my health replaced by the plea: "But it's
Christmas!" She stands before me, refusing to let go of my sleeve.

She's playing the mom card—playing on my sympathies. But tonight, it won't work. Can't work. I need to get out of here. Need to handle my own business, my own way.

"*Tomorrow* is Christmas," I say. "And I'll be back to spend it with you. I promise." I bend toward her, depositing a soft kiss on the top of her head as I gently curl my fingers around hers. Giving them a meaningful squeeze, hoping to convey what I've failed to say with words. Then I loosen her grip from my sleeve and make for the porch as she calls after me.

I turn. Try to contain my annoyance by reminding myself her intentions are good.

"Be careful." She steps toward me. Studying me with a critical eye, as her hand finds its way to my cheek. "Don't let your regard for others compromise your safety. I need you here."

I close my eyes briefly and send her a silent apology for the hurt I may cause her. But when my gaze meets hers, I just say, "Good night, Mother."

There's no need to cause any further alarm.

No need to inform her that during the past several days spent holed up in my room, it wasn't just healing I'd been focusing on.

She stands on the stoop, one hand hanging loose by her side, the other clutched close to her heart. The bright overhead light falling languidly upon her, engulfing her in an incandescent veil of white light that makes her appear luminous—radiant—angelic and saintly.

Her tortured image the last thing I see before I head for my truck and ease onto the road. Ready to put my newly honed skills to the test.

thirty-eight

Daire

Paloma pokes her head into my room, frowning when she finds
me sitting cross-legged in the middle of the floor amidst a scatter-
ing of feathers, crystals, candles, the pendulum, my rattle, the
drum, and the athame, its blade polished and gleaming. The trap-
pings of the Seeker trade—along with the codex propped open
beside me. "Any luck?" She leans against the doorjamb, surveying the mess.

I lift my shoulders. Allow my eyes to meet hers. "Sure. I'm
loaded with luck—at least where my magick's concerned. Thanks
to you and all that you've taught me, I'm amazed at how far I've
come, and how quickly. And yet, I'm not sure how it's going to
help me defeat Cade."

"Every bit helps, *nieta*. Every piece fits neatly into the other."

I sigh. Having no doubt it's true, though the pieces I seek seem
to lie just outside my reach, and I don't hesitate to tell her as
much.

"What does the book say?" She crosses her arms before her,
tilting her head in a way that encourages her braid to slip over her
shoulder and fall to her waist.

"The book says plenty, most of which I don't understand. You've read it, so you tell me, what is it I'm missing?"

She glances down the hall, as though she's worried about someone overhearing, then in a lowered voice says, "I'm not sure that you're missing anything. I'm not sure Valentina was able to foresee all that you're up against. Some things are for you to discover on your own. That is always the way."

I sigh. Wishing this wasn't always so difficult—wishing that just this once, the answers would come easily. Then I discard the thought just as quickly. Easy has never been part of the equation, and from what I've experienced so far, it's foolish to expect such a thing. It's up to me to figure this out and prove that I'm worthy. No one else can do that for me.

"Thing is—Cade's freakishly strong." I shudder when I say it, remembering the way he held Dace off with one hand that horrible day at the not-so Enchanted Spring. "And when he's not guarded by his creepy coyote, he's surrounded by his army of undead yet very loyal ancestors. And despite feeling so much stronger, so much more empowered, than I did a week ago, I'm worried it won't be enough. Chances are I'll have to get through them in order to get to Cade, and I'm not sure I can do it. Also, I know I haven't mentioned it, partly because I didn't really know what to make of it, and partly because I didn't want to give it any more power than it already has, but—" I pause for breath, my eyes meeting hers. "The dream is back." I study her expression, but Paloma fights to keep her face as unreadable as ever. "It's haunted me ever since we left Dace at Leftfoot's adobe, and it's always the same. Dace and me enjoying ourselves in the Enchanted Spring, until Cade arrives, turns into the beast that he is, and steals Dace's soul, leaving him dead in my arms." I cringe, the memory so clear it's as though it's occurring before me. "While Cade's made it clear that he knows about the dream, what I can't figure out is if he's found a way to manipulate my dream state, or if it's a prophecy all of us share? And speaking of the prophecy, I was hoping to find a different way to interpret it, but it's pretty clear-cut, isn't it?"

The grave look on Paloma's face provides all the confirmation I need.

"So anyway, what about you guys?" I ask, eager to steer the subject away from me and onto her, hoping they've met with more success than I have. Aware of the constant ritual and vigil the elders have engaged in ever since the day they learned about the level of havoc and destruction Cade's wrought. "Have you and Chay made any progress? And what about Chepi and Left-foot?"

She looks at me, both of us all too aware of the name I failed to mention.

Dace.

I can't risk speaking his name. Can't risk her guessing what I've done. That I went behind her back, used the skill she taught me, and visited him via the raven.

Still, it's impossible to lie to Paloma, and one look at her face tells me she knows more than she lets on.

My fingers fumble for the small golden key at my chest—remembering the feel of Dace's skin, his lips pressing against the feathers, the weight of his touch . . .

I shake free of the thought, shove the key back under my sweater, and return my attention to my grandmother.

"Chay just returned," she says. "He and Leftfoot ventured into the Lowerworld to conduct a little reconnaissance. From what he tells me, it's settled for now. And by that I mean that the mine is still operating, the spirit animals are still listless and dull, and the Lowerworld is sorely polluted. Though our combined efforts seem to have worked in stabilizing it and keeping it from getting any worse. Or at least for the moment. There's no telling how long our magick will hold. Fixing this will require something more drastic." She chases the words with a pointed look.

"In other words, the next move is mine?" I pose it like a

question, though we both know the answer. It's entirely up to me to fix this. It's what I was born to do.

"Soon, you'll be ready, *nieta*."

I lower my gaze to the mess of tools. *Soon* isn't quite good enough. I needed to be ready right now. Time is a luxury I just can't afford.

I knock the book closed with my knee, vowing to face Cade tonight. There's no more delaying. The longer this goes on, the more people will suffer. Besides, I heard what Dace said, saw the determination in his gaze. I have to get to his brother well before he can. As long as he's under Chepi's watch, he's safe. The prophecy can't possibly play out if she's keeping him under lock and key.

Which is why I have to move now.

To delay any longer is to risk everything.

I lift my face to Paloma. "It's time," I say, my voice determined and sure. "My training's complete and my magick . . . well, it could probably be better, but it's still pretty dang good. At any rate, I have to act now, before it's too late."

She regards me sagely. Relaying so much emotion in one single look: Her regret that my life requires so much sacrifice—her pride that I'm embracing the challenge despite all the dangers— her fears for my safety, the very real possibility that I won't live to see twenty.

"It's not enough just to have a goal, *nieta*. You need to have a plan to see it through."

I consider her words for a moment, knowing there is no strategy, no plan, and no time to come up with one. Then I look at her and say, "I don't have a strategy. So, I guess I'll just do as you taught me and think from the end."

Her fingers fidget with the buttons running the length of her cardigan. Taking a moment to consider, she nods her assent and says, "Well, first you'll have to do something about this room.

Your friends are waiting in the den. I doubt you want them to see
you like this." She gestures at the mess, her grin growing wider
when I set my room into a frenzy of motion. Straightening my
bedspread, restacking the pillows, and returning all of the random, loose objects into the trunk where they originated. Everything tucked neatly away, despite the fact that I haven't so much
as lifted a finger.

"Do not underestimate your abilities or your readiness, *nieta*.
Especially not after such an impressive display. Your telekinesis
has come a long way." Her voice grows hoarse with emotion. "It's
really quite remarkable." She pulls her sweater tightly around
her, observing me for a long quiet moment, before she swipes a
hand across her cheek and goes to summon my friends.

By the time my friends reach my room, I'm lounging on my bed
with my back against the headboard and my legs stretched before
me. Running a quick hand through my hair, as Lita saunters in
first, saying, "So this is your room?" She tosses her hair over her
shoulder and takes a good look around. Surveying the space
through squinted eyes and lashes caked with a liberal use of mas-
cara. "I have to be honest, Daire—it's not at all what I expected."

"What were you expecting?" Xotichl navigates her way to my
bed, where she sits at the end.

Lita shakes off her jacket, drapes it over the back of my chair,
and drums her fingers hard against her hip. Inspecting my desk,
the dream catcher hanging over the window, the tall dresser
with the picture of Django displayed on its top. "I mean, it's not
like I haven't been here before, though I never made it past the
den. I guess I didn't expect it to be so much like the rest of
the house. I thought it'd be more stylish. More fashionable.
Maybe even—dare I say—glamorous. I thought there'd be at
least some small smidgen of something, anything, that might

hint at your former Hollywood past. But, nope. The only word to describe this four-walled box is *efficient*. Your room is *clean, tidy,* and *efficient*. It does what a room is supposed to do and no more."

"Sorry to disappoint. Guess my Vane Wick poster got lost in the move." I push deeper into the row of pillows at my back, reminding myself that this is just Lita being Lita, there's no use taking offense. And when she turns to me with flashing eyes and curving lips, I brace for whatever comes next.

"Speaking of . . ." She pauses dramatically. "You never want to talk about it. But since it's Christmas and all, I was hoping you might relent and toss a little Tinseltown morsel my way."

She steeples her hands under her chin, striving for a hopeful, angelic expression, which only makes me laugh. "I knew it!" I shake my head, pretending to be far more upset than I am.

"Knew what?" Her eyes grow alarmed, though she keeps her hands firmly in place.

"I knew that's why you befriended me. I'm just surprised you held back for so long."

Her hands drop to her hips, as the look of feigned innocence fades. "Not only is that not fair, but it's also not true, and you know it. I mean, how about showing a little mercy for the less privileged among us? This is the only place I've ever lived. I grew up in Enchantment and I'll probably die here as well. The most I can hope for is the occasional shopping trip to Albuquerque. I'll never have the opportunities you've had, so the least you can do is throw me a bone."

"You have to admit, it's a pretty good argument," Xotichl says. "Besides, we're your friends, and that's what friends do. They dish about the past—whine about the present—and fantasize about the future."

"You guys really know how to wage one heck of a guilt trip," I grumble. Though the truth is, I've already decided to spill. What harm could it do? "What do you want to know?" I ask, directing the words mostly at Lita, watching as she gnaws her bottom lip in feigned consideration, although the answer comes so quickly, it's clear she's rehearsed it.

"Two things."

I narrow my lids, try to guess what they'll be.

"First—how was Vane Wick as a kisser? On a scale of one to ten. One being the worst ever—and ten being—"

"Ten being Dace!" Xotichl cuts in.

"Ew." Lita makes a face of distaste. "Sorry, I don't mean to be rude, but I can't get over him being Cade's twin."

Join the club.

"Seriously, though—was it dreamy? I mean, it must've been superexotic since you were in Morocco and all—but details are desperately needed. Nothing but full disclosure will do."

I glance at Xotichl, surprised to find her leaning toward me, just as hungry for the details as Lita. Then I slide my eyes shut and allow myself to remember. Allow myself to travel to a time before Dace. Though it seems like there was never really a time before Dace. It feels like he's always been with me.

"You know, originally I was so angry about that tabloid story and the way he betrayed me, I promised myself if anyone asked, I'd claim that he was totally overrated. But the truth is, he was a really good kisser." I slide my feet across the duvet, bringing my knees to my chest and wrapping my arms loosely around them. "But then, he should be. He's had a lot of practice, both in real life and movies."

Lita presses one hand over her heart while fanning herself with the other. Swooning onto my chair so dramatically, I can't help but laugh in a way I haven't indulged in for a while. And it feels so good to have this moment with my friends, I go on to say, "But—you know who's a *terrible* kisser?"

Xotichl perks up as Lita slides to the edge of her seat, lips parted in anticipation.

"Will Harner."

"No!" Lita cries, face lit with the kind of delight only the juiciest scandal can bring. "But didn't he win an MTV award for Best Kiss?"

"Trust me, he's the absolute worst—all spit, teeth, and crazy/ floppy tongue. It's like sitting in the splash zone at Sea World or going through a car wash with the top down—you end up drenched. The actress who played opposite him is truly gifted." I cringe at the saliva-filled memory.

"*So* disappointing." Lita sighs. "Still, I totally envy you. Even if it was a sucky, sloppy kiss, the fact is you still got to kiss him, while I've been stuck with the same group of boys my entire life. How can you stand it here? I mean, yeah, granted, I used to think this place was the greatest. Heck, I used to think *I* was the greatest—like Cade and I were the king and queen of Milagro High."

"Um, that's because you were Milagro royalty," Xotichl says, causing Lita to roll her eyes and groan at the not-so-distant memory.

"I guess so," she admits. "Still, it's so weird how I no longer care about that stuff. It's like I spent my whole life working to maintain my position as top dog—or top *bitch* as most people would say— but now all I can think about is ditching this place as soon as high school is over. I can't get out of here soon enough."

Her gaze drifts, as though searching for the exact moment when her opinion of Enchantment changed. Having no idea it happened on the Day of the Dead. The night a chunk of her soul was restored—released from those undead Richters and returned to her.

She's no longer under their spell. No longer seeing this place the way they once manipulated her to see it. For the time being, they're unable to touch her, unable to tweak her perception. And if it's up to me, they'll never be able to reach her again.

"This town is the epitome of dull," she says. "Truly. I don't know how you guys stand it."

"It's really not that boring." A smile plays at the corners of

Xotichl's lips as she tilts her head toward mine. "It just seems that way at first."

Lita quirks her brow, not at all in agreement. But then, she doesn't know about the hotbed of supernatural activity brewing just under the surface. And with any luck, it'll stay that way.

"Up until now, I've never had a place to call home. And while it may not be the kind of place I dreamed about, still, it's not all bad," I say, my mood turning serious again as the full truth of my words descends upon me. As bleak as this town undoubtedly is, there's no denying the fact that some of my most treasured moments have taken place here. I'll do whatever I can to defend it. I just hope I'm successful. I pull a pillow onto my lap and hug it tightly to my chest.

"You say that because you're in love." Lita glances between me and Xotichl. "Everything looks better when you've fallen hard for someone. It's only when the magic wears off—and trust me, it *always* does—when you can finally look back and say: *What the heck was I thinking?*" She picks at a loose string on the hem of her tight V-neck sweater. "Or maybe that's just me." She sighs, allowing her hands to fall to her lap. "Maybe I'm just jaded after wasting my entire youth on Cade Richter."

"I'm pretty sure you've got a whole lot of youth left in you." Xotichl laughs. "You're not officially old until you're twenty-five, right?" She leans toward me, seeking confirmation.

"Actually, I hear that forty is the new twenty-five. So, if that's the case, Lita's got loads of youthful years to look forward to."

"Great." Lita groans. "Decades of bad dates unfolding before me—oh, joy." She fills her palm with a chunk of her hair and hunts for split ends. "It's easy for you guys to laugh since obviously you'll never have to worry about that. Have you *seen* the way Auden looks at Xotichl?" She releases the strands, slumps low in her seat. "It's pretty much the epitome of what every girl dreams of. And clearly there must be more to Dace than meets the eye." She shoots me a guilty look and quickly corrects herself.

"Well, obviously there is. Objectively speaking, if I'd never met his creep of a twin, I might be willing to admit that he's cute. Maybe even hot. Heck, everyone else seems to think so, so there must be something to it. Still, the evil specter of Cade trumps everything. So, in the end, I'll just have to take your word for it."

"Anyway—" Xotichl prods, wisely steering the topic away from all things Cade. "What was the second question?"

"Oh, I don't know." Lita shrugs, still mired in deep disappointment over the lack of cute boys in this town. "I was going to ask what other famous people Daire might've kissed, but after hearing about Will Harner, I think it can wait . . ." Her gaze veers toward my dresser, and a moment later, she's jumping to her feet, retrieving the picture of Django in the silver frame. "Who's this hottie?" she asks.

"That's my dad," I say, breaking into laughter when I see the appalled look on her face.

"Clearly I'm in need of a boyfriend." She replaces the photo, shuddering with shame over her mistake. "Or at the very least, a date. Lusting after people's dads is really a bad sign, isn't it?"

"He was sixteen in the picture. So it's entirely age appropriate," I tell her. "Besides, I think he'd be flattered."

She makes a gagging face, reluctant to even contemplate such a thing. Then she grabs hold of my sleeve and drags me off the bed. "C'mon," she says. "Get dressed, we're going out."

"Where?"

"The Rabbit Hole." Xotichl grins. "Where else?"

"That's why we're here." Lita leads me to stand before my closet. "It's an Enchantment tradition to go there on Christmas Eve and stay until just after midnight."

"Does every holiday revolve around the Rabbit Hole?" My gaze shifts between them, failing to share what I really think: That this is all working out perfectly, as though it's meant to be. First I'll go to the Rabbit Hole, then I'll find a way to slip free from my friends and get to the vortex, and finally I'll deal with Cade once and for all.

"Pretty much." Xotichl shrugs, as Lita starts riffling through my clothes. Choosing one of the new tops Jennika gave me that I haven't yet worn.

"Wear this." She tosses it to me. "And do your hair curly like you did at my party. You looked really pretty that night."

"I can never replicate that look. My mom's the one with mad makeover skills, not me."

"Maybe so," Lita says. "But what you forget is that your mom taught me a few tricks. And after a lot of practice, I'm getting pretty good. So go on, get changed, and then meet me in your bathroom. You have an appointment with a curling iron and some serious eyeliner."

thirty-nine

Dace

After stopping by my apartment and changing into jeans and a sweater, I head for the Rabbit Hole. Intending to collect the paycheck they owe me before I head into the Lowerworld for a final round with Cade.

Or at least that's the lie I tell myself.

Truth is, I'm also hoping to see Daire.

Hoping Lita and Xotichl will invite her to take part in the Enchantment Christmas Eve tradition.

The brief time we spent together via the raven left me longing for more. And while I tell myself I'll be satisfied with a glimpse, just a quick look before I go on my way—the second I see her heading for the entrance with her hair shiny and curled, her eyes bright and happy as she walks alongside Lita and Xotichl, it's clear a mere glance will never suffice.

I want to share the space where she stands—breathe the same air.

I want to feel her in my arms—surrender to the very sweetness of her.

She enters the club with her friends while I force myself to stay put—ensuring my entrance lapses well behind hers.

As sweet as it was, her visit via the raven was not without risk. Until I make good on my plan, there's no point in chasing her. No point in strengthening Cade any more than we have.

Still, that doesn't stop my eyes from greedily devouring every square inch, the whispered mantra of *soon* playing at the edge of my lips.

Soon we'll be together.

Soon she'll stand alongside me.

When enough time has passed, I breeze past the bouncer, refusing that ridiculous red coyote stamp he tries to mark on my flesh, and head into the club. Bypassing the bar where everyone gathers, I make for the offices in back where I stand before Leandro's closed door. Fist raised and ready to knock, when I hear a pair of angry voices seeping through the wood.

I press my ear to the jamb, in order to better eavesdrop on Leandro berating Cade in a way I've never heard.

"I get back in town to find *this*?"

A hand strikes hard on a desk.

Leandro's hand.

Leandro's desk.

"What the hell are you doing? Are you out of your freaking mind?"

"If you'll just let me explain—" Cade's voice pitches high, but Leandro's unmoved by his tone.

"Explain what? That you're single-handedly destroying our wealth? Risking everything I've worked my entire life to accumulate?"

"But that's the thing—this tourmaline . . ." Cade starts, not getting very far before Leandro cuts in.

"You think I don't know about the tourmaline? What the hell is wrong with you? We've been hoarding it for years—how do you think those mines got there? Every time we breach the Lowerworld, we take what we can and stash it away for future sale. Its rarity is what drives its price. It's the philosophy behind any nonessential luxury item. You overprice it well beyond its value—release it in very limited supply—and before you know it, everyone is clamoring for a piece. Believing they can exalt themselves merely by owning the very thing everyone wants but few can claim. But now you come along and ignorantly flood the tourmaline market—effectively driving down the price and nearly gutting our wealth! Do you have any idea the kind of damage you've done?"

"You're wrong." Cade's voice is smug and sure. "The cash is pouring in. And there's absolutely no overhead—the labor is free! I'm surprised you can't see the brilliance of my plan. It's all good, Dad. The Lowerworld is corrupted, and soon the Middle- and the Upperworlds will follow. And with the money pouring in, and the people left without guidance, it won't be long before we rule all. Just give it time—you'll see."

"The labor is *free*? Is that what you think?" Leandro makes a sound of extreme exasperation. "The Rabbit Hole is a bar, Cade! And the success of this bar depends on the number of drinkers who show up each day. Drinkers, who, I come to find out, you've kidnapped for your own ridiculous uses. So, not only are you destroying the tourmaline business, but you're taking the bar along with it."

"But, Dad—"

"You listen to me—you will stop this nonsense immediately. Not only have you destroyed the value of the stone in a way that will take years to recover, but, if you don't put an end to this right now, you will destroy the very value of this town. Do you have any idea how hard I work to keep us off the radar? Do you have any idea why I do that? You kid yourself that you're so far ahead of me because your ambitions reach further—when, in fact, you are burning a path of destruction I may never be able to fix. The last thing we need is for the eyes of the world to turn to Enchantment. But with the population declining, how long do you think we can keep those disappearances out of the news? There are pictures of the missing plastered all over the alleyway. And this is all because of you and your ridiculous, immature, ill-conceived plan!"

"But, Dad, if you'll just—"

"Go!"

"What?" Cade's voice falls somewhere between a whimper and a whine.

"Now! Go! Get out of my office—out of my sight. And don't come back until you've cleaned up this mess."

A low growl erupts. The eerily, familiar sound cut short by Leandro's voice. "Don't you even think about shifting in front of me or anyone else, for that matter. You've caused enough grief for one night. Get a grip on yourself."

The door slams open but not before I've slipped into the shadows and pressed myself hard against the wall. Going unnoticed as Cade storms out of the office, so consumed by his rage, his entire body trembles with fury.

He struggles against it. Tries hard to stop it. Contain it. If for no other reason than to placate Leandro.

But he's too far gone. The shifting's become so ingrained, it's no longer his to control.

Barely making it halfway down the hall before he turns into the beast I know well.

The beast I was hoping to see.

I stare hard at his back, narrowing my focus until I've projected myself into his skin. Making the soul jump in the way Leftfoot taught me. Delving into his depths and exploring every dark facet, every shadow-drenched corner. Until I'm left gaping in wonder at the the bleak and wretched state of his soul.

Guided by his most primal, unbridled desires to slay and screw, conquer and consume—at first glance he appears animalistic—

just your everyday beast. Though a deeper look reveals a mad quest for personal exaltation and ego gratification that makes him dangerously human.

I drag out the visit—lingering, stretching, making myself at home in his skin. Exploring the rawness of his anger, the very core of his malevolence, the naked brutality that drives all his actions. And despite my initial revulsion, despite my complete abhorrence for all that I see, I waste no time in claiming a sizeable chunk of that darkness for me. Needing to examine it—understand it—in order to conquer it.

My body strains against it, struggles to reject it, to sever our connection for good. But my resolve to possess my brother's power, to feel his evil flowing inside me, prevails. And the longer I stay, the more I'm able to claim, until the surge of his strength reveals a truth I could only guess at before.

Just as he's able to tap into my love for Daire that drives me, I can tap into the unadulterated evil that drives him. And that's just what I do. Absorbing all that I can, well aware that the power I steal is power my brother can't use against Daire.

My body convulses. My blood boils violently through my veins, scorching and burning and cooking my insides, leaving a horrible pock on my skin. The pain so excruciating, I stagger forward, grasp myself low at the waist. Left gasping and shivering, unable to stop my breath from coming too hectic and fast, I slide my eyes shut and wait for it to pass. Committed to enduring this for however long it takes. Having no plans to surrender. With my brother's power now roiling within me, my original plan has changed. Instead of stealing his power to weaken him, I will use what I've taken to destroy him.

Leftfoot's warning a faint echo in my head: *You must never abuse the gift. Ever. I can't stress this enough. You use this gift if, and only if, you find that you must. You must first exhaust all other options. It is meant to be a last resort.*

This *is* a last resort. The only real option left.

The only way to conquer Cade is to claim a piece of Cade—become Cade—albeit temporarily.

It's like the lesson Leftfoot unwittingly shared with me: *Sometimes you must venture into the darkness to bring forth the light.*

Which is exactly what I'm doing. It's the finishing touch on the choice I made in the sweat lodge. Hazarding the darkness to save Daire—the light of my life.

It's a risk.

One that puts my very soul as stake.

Still, there's no price too high to save Daire.

Besides, I have no intention of losing.

As soon as it's done, I'll cast out my brother's shadow and return to myself.

Only better.

Purer.

For I will have confronted the very worst of men and lived to tell the tale.

I lift my head, watching as my brother ambles toward the vortex. The sight causing my blood to cool, my pulse to regulate, and when he bursts through the wall, our connection is severed.

All except for the piece of him lodged deep within me.

I stand before Leandro's door, stealing a few moments to center myself. And when I'm back to being the Dace everyone knows and expects, or at least on the surface anyway, I push inside and take my brother's place before Leandro's desk.

forty

Daire

"What's this?" I pause just shy of the entrance. Peering down the alleyway at a throng of people standing before a wall plastered with pictures, flickering tapered candles clutched in their hands.

"Candlelight vigil for the missing." Lita chases the words with a groan. "As if this town isn't depressing enough."

I glance among the photos, recognizing many of the faces from Cade's bogus job fair, as Lita steers Xotichl and me away from the crowd and inside the club. Easing into her usual smiling, waving, air-kissing routine, she turns to us and in a mocking voice says, "Hello-hello! Kiss-kiss! Wave-wave!" She frowns and shakes her head. "What am I—the freaking welcome wagon?" Spying Jacy and Crickett waiting in the usual place, she purposely veers the opposite way. "I can't do this anymore. I can't keep it going. I'm so freaking sick of this scene that for the first time ever, I'm actually considering early retirement. If Phyre's so eager to replace me, let her. She can be the new queen, for all I care."

"You sure you want to give up the crown?" Xotichl teases. "Without so much as a fight?"

"Being this popular is a total energy suck." Lita sighs. "You have no idea. I have literally known these people all of my life, yet I'm still expected to act overjoyed whenever I see them. If we could just get some more new students at Milagro—ones that *aren't* girls—I might reconsider. But look at them . . ." She motions toward a group of boys sharing the same table as Crickett and Jacy. "I've kissed every one of those dorks, and trust me when I say they got way more out of it than I did." She makes a face, turning to me as she adds, "If you go to LA to visit Jennika, you have to promise to take me with you. Seriously. I'll curl up in your carry-on—I'm so not joking. Think of it as a rescue mission. Only you'll be rescuing me from the very real risk of dying of boredom."

I try to picture Lita in LA, deciding she'd probably like it so much I'd end up returning to Enchantment without her.

"We can spend our days shopping and going to the beach, and at night you can take me to all the celebrity hot spots. How does that sound?"

"Better in your head than in reality," I say, my gaze drifting, on the lookout for Cade but catching a glimpse of Dace instead. And while I'm happy to see him up and about, the fact that he's here doesn't bode well for my plans. Now more than ever, I need to get to Cade before Dace can make good on the scheme he hinted at.

I force myself to turn away and focus on my friends, knowing better than to keep my attention on Dace. Though it's only a moment later when Lita taps my shoulder and says, "Uh, maybe you should go break up that party. I trust that girl about as far as I can fling her."

She gestures toward the place where Dace stood by himself just a few seconds earlier, only now Phyre is with him. Inching toward him. Crowding his space. Not seeming to notice or care how he leans away, purposely sways from her reach. And while part of me longs to march right over and demand to know what she's up to, the other part, the smarter part, stays rooted in place.

"Seriously." Lita nudges me, a little harder this time. "Aren't you going to do something to stop her from stealing your man?" She shoots me a look of outrage. "Why are you acting so passive? I don't get it. It seems so unlike you."

I'm just about to respond, when Xotichl speaks for me. "You can't *steal* another person, Lita. They either go willingly or they don't. And if they do go willingly, then good riddance—you're better off without them."

Lita's eyes narrow, weighing Xotichl's words as she fiddles with her Marilyn piercing, while I force myself to look anywhere but at Dace. Whatever he and Phyre are discussing is none of my business.

"Okay," Lita says. "Even if Xotichl's right—and I fully and reluctantly admit that she is—there's no doubt Phyre is poaching. And I think she needs to know that you're totally on to her and that it's neither appreciated nor cool. It's a tough world out there, and us girls need to stick together. We've got to quit with the backstabbing, bitching, and competing for boys as though they're some kind of grand freaking prize."

"You've come a long way," I quip, remembering how poorly she treated me on my first day of school.

"Yes, I have." She shoots me a tight-lipped grin. "And just so you know, if you don't march yourself over to Ms. Phyre Youngblood and repeat everything I just said—I'll happily do it for you."

I shake my head, allow my gaze to settle on Dace for a moment. Long enough to glean a bit of his warmth, before I look away and say, "Things are complicated with Dace . . ."

"They're taking a little break," Xotichl cuts in, supplying a truth that's too painful for me to admit.

"What? Exactly when did this happen? Are you saying we're both single now? Does that mean I'm competing against *you*?" Lita squints, trying to decide how she feels about that.

"Competing for *what*?" Xotichl says. "You just said girls have to stop competing for boys. You also said there's not a single interesting boy in this town."

"True." Lita turns to face Xotichl. "And I meant every word of it. What can I say? Sometimes there's a bit of a delay in putting my words into practice. Besides, the whole thing's moot. You snagged the only good guy to be had in these parts. Where is Auden, by the way?"

Xotichl tilts her head to the side. "He just arrived."

Lita and I look toward the door, where, sure enough, Auden stands, scoping the room, searching for Xotichl.

"How do you do that? How does she do that?" Lita glances between us, but I just shrug in response. I'm too busy forcing myself not to obsess over Dace.

"I'm here to collect," Auden says, working his way toward Xotichl. "Unless something drastic happens in the next few hours, the most we can hope for is a *wet* Christmas, not a *white* Christmas."

"Oh, ye of little faith." Xotichl grins. "Don't you know it ain't over 'til the fat lady sings and the white stuff drifts from the sky?"

I look at them. Hardly able to believe I'd been so busy trying to find answers in the codex, trying to rearrange the prophecy in my head and come up with some kind of plan, that I forgot about the snow.

Forgot about the one thing that's still—maybe—within my realm of control.

"I'll be back!" I turn away from my friends.

"Where you going?" Lita calls, as Xotichl's face creases with worry.

"I'm going to give Xotichl her white Christmas." I speed toward the exit, leaving Lita, Xotichl, and Auden staring after me.

forty-one

Dace

I barely make it halfway down the hall before Phyre finds me.
Like she's brandishing some sort of invisible radar that's programmed to track only me.

She steps free of the shadows, stands right before me, and
says, "Hey, Dace." Her voice soft, her smile pretty.

But it's the wrong pretty.

Not the pretty I seek.

I nod in acknowledgment. Start to move away. Stopped by her
fingers circling my wrist as she pulls me back to her.

"Can we talk?"

I slide my eyes closed. Search for a kind way to tell her to
quit thinking of me. Quit stalking me. To leave the past where
it belongs—dead and buried.

Opening my eyes again to find myself staring at Daire on the
other side of the room, unwilling to break the gaze now that I've
found her.

"You're always in such a hurry. You never have any time for
me." Phyre tugs on my arm. Using the tip of her fingernail to
trace light circles over my skin in a desperate bid to claim my
attention.

I drag my gaze from Daire and focus on Phyre. "There's nothing to talk about." I twist free of her grip.

"You say that—but how can you be sure?" She cocks her head to the side, allowing a spray of curls to slide across her cheek. It's a well-rehearsed, overplayed move. "For starters, aren't you curious as to why I came back?"

I just shoot her a patient look, hoping it'll help speed things along.

"It's no accident, you know."

"If memory serves—nothing you do is an accident," I say, remembering all the random times she seemed to just happen to be in the same place as me. How it took a while to realize there was nothing random about it. Though it's not like I cared. I was just happy to be noticed by a female who wasn't my mom. The fact that Phyre was so pretty was an added boon.

"You were always so quiet, so introspective. It wasn't easy to get your attention."

"You managed though, didn't you?" My gaze meets hers, and when I see her flinch, I'm surprised to find I enjoy it, which is not at all like me. Must be that piece of Cade asserting its influence. Reminding me I'm no longer the same guy I used to be.

"True," she admits, shoulders lifting. "What can I say? When I set my sights on something or someone, I usually—no, scratch that—I *always* get what I want."

Her gaze is open. Direct. A challenge I'm meant to either deflect or accept. But, instead, I meet it with a face so impassive it gives nothing away.

"After all, I got you, didn't I?"

My eyes graze over her, allowing myself to indulge in a few clips from the memory reel.

Sneaking away from our parents' prying eyes in pursuit of a few heady moments under a blanket of stars . . . a first kiss—her lips determined and sure, mine overeager and inexperienced . . . a first feel—my

awkwardness trumped by her surprising proficiency . . . another first—
the one she insisted upon—though that's not to say I wasn't willing . . .
and right after that, they were gone . . .

Cutting the movie that plays in my head, I meet her gaze and say, "Temporarily. For a short while, I would've followed you anywhere."

"It may have been brief, but for me it was totally worth it. Then again, I was all too willing to settle for whatever crumb you tossed my way."

"You sure about that?" I fetch a whole different memory—one where she manipulated me into wanting her, needing her, having her—and then, *bam*—next thing I knew, her family packed up and left, never to be seen or heard from again. The only thing that surprised me is how quickly I recovered. I thought it would hurt more than it did. It's because of her that I learned to differentiate lust from love. Shortly after, I made a deal with myself to never settle for less.

"It's not my fault we moved." She wages a playful defense. "But just so you know, now that I'm back, I'm unwilling to settle again. While it's kind of embarrassing to admit, truth is, I never stopped missing you. I never stopped thinking about you." She pauses, allows her tongue to cross her lips, leaving them shiny and wet. "I never gave up on you."

I swipe a hand over my chin, deciding brutal honesty is the only way to derail this. "Phyre. You were young and sad. You'd just lost your mom, and you were looking for a way to feel better—a way to feel alive—and I just happened to be there. That's all it ever was. Don't romanticize it into meaning something it didn't."

"Funny, that's not at all how I remember it."

I shake my head, try to look away. But the next thing I know, she's grabbed my wrist again. Her lips softly parting, hovering mere inches from mine. Her determination so steady, she barely reacts when I say, "Don't do this."

"Do what?" Her fingers form circles, her mouth angles toward mine.

"Don't force me to say the kind of things you don't want to hear."

She loosens her grip, casts a glance toward the far side of the room, the place where Daire stands. "Like what? That you're in love with the Seeker?"

I frown, not liking the sound of that coming from her.

"What? You think I don't know who she is? You think I don't see all the signs?" She gazes up at me from under a thick row of lashes, speaking in a voice gone throaty and low. "You're not the only one who grew up surrounded by mysticism. Unlike the rest of these people, my eyes have never been closed to the truth of this town."

"What do you want?" My tone is impatient, tired of playing this game. It's definitely not just me that she's after. There's always a deeper motive where Phyre's concerned.

"I want the same thing you want." Her shoulders rise and fall, abandoning all attempts at flirtation and pretense.

"Doubtful," I mutter, already turning away. Having tolerated more than enough of her manipulative game.

"Does that mean you *don't* want Cade dead?" She cocks her head, buries the tip of her tongue in the corner of her lip, challenging me with her gaze.

It's a gaze I hold for too long.

While the words are right—the energy's wrong.

I consider a soul jump. Promising myself I'll be brief. But nix it just as quickly. I can't afford to do anything that might compromise the work I've already done. Besides, I'm pretty sure there won't be much to see. It's obvious she's been listening to gossip. Thinks that claiming to share my newfound hatred for Cade is a sure way to get with me.

"I have no idea what you're talking about," I tell her, and this time I succeed in walking away.

My eyes briefly meet Daire's as I make for the door. A mistake I shouldn't have made. Knowing I can't cross the room to be with her leaves me feeling more isolated than ever.

I shove my hands in my pockets and exit the club. Ducking against the constant veil of drizzle as I make my way to the old chain-link fence, seeking assurance from that little gold lock.

Needing to see if the symbol of our love is still right where we left it—stronger than the forces bent on destroying it.

Wanting one last reminder before I find Cade.

forty-two

Daire

I slip down the alleyway, sneak around the crowd of people taking part in the candlelight vigil, and move toward a place in back where no one can watch as I clasp my pouch tightly and call upon the elements. Summoning Air, Fire, Water, and Earth, I sing their individual songs under my breath and beg for their favor. Pleading with them to do me this one small bidding. Bestow the gift of a Christmas snowfall for a beleaguered town and its people, who because of my failings—my failure to sacrifice Paloma's soul, my failure to evict all the Richters from the Lowerworld—have suffered far more than anyone rightfully should.

A rustle of wind lashes my hair. A surge of flame licks a path near my feet, leaving a trail of freshly scorched earth.

Though the promise of snow is soon dashed when the light steady drizzle increases to a hard sheet of rain.

I sigh in frustration. Bury my face in mitten-covered hands. Unwilling to reenter the club and face my friends, I head for the chain-link fence. Hoping to lift my spirits by confirming the lock is right where I left it, I round the corner only to find Dace there instead. One hand gripping the lock, the other fidgeting with the key that hangs from his neck.

My knees go feeble and weak, buckling beneath me.

My hand instinctively flies to my chest, as though to keep my heart caged, keep it from leaping free of my flesh.

While my eyes remain riveted on the very thing I'd hoped to never see.

Dace—holding the lock—wielding the key.

Dace giving up on us—giving up on me.

He turns, sensing my presence as his eyes light on mine. One look at my grief-stricken face enough to prompt him to drop the key, abandon the lock, and call out my name—but I'm already gone.

Already turning away.

Catching a glimpse of Phyre watching from the shadows, her eyes strange and glittering as they stare into mine.

I veer toward her. Deciding Lita's right, it's time I confront her, demand to know what she's up to—what it is that she wants. Having just reached her when the rain ceases and becomes something else.

Something lighter.

Drier.

Something that lands in small white squares at my feet.

I lift my chin, close my eyes, and allow it to drift softly onto my cheeks.

Heart soaring in triumph—knowing I did this—I'm responsible—it's because of me that it's snowing!

Excited shouts reverberate all around me, as the club empties into the alleyway, crowding the street. Throngs of people pushing and shoving, eager to get to it first—to take part in the miracle, my miracle, the one that I wrought. Voices overlapping, they call, "Snow! It's snowing—you've *got* to come see it!"

I turn, searching for Dace, needing to see his reaction. Finding him still beside the fence with his hands splayed before him, welcoming the bright white squares that fall onto his flesh.

His chin lifting, gaze darkening, as he motions to me—urges me to see what he sees.

It's not at all what we think.

Snow is crisp. Pure. Wet.

It doesn't smudge.

Doesn't leave a trail of charcoal when rubbed.

Only ash can do that.

We gaze at each other, separated by a shroud of white ash falling steadily between us, and a surge of people eager to witness a miracle that's really a curse. Dancing and twirling under the deluge, not realizing they've got it all wrong.

Not realizing they're in the grip of something far darker, far more sinister than they could ever conceive.

The earth beginning to tremble as those same squares of ash become a torrent of flames that fall from the sky.

It's the prophecy come to life, just like the codex foretold:

> *The other side of midnight's hour strikes a herald thrice rung*
> *Seer, Shadow, Sun—together they come*
> *Sixteen winters hence—the light shall be eclipsed*
> *Leaving darkness to ascend beneath a sky bleeding fire*

All around me shouts of excitement quickly turn to fear, as a crowd of people fight to take cover, push their way back inside. Forcing me to shove my way through them, my need to confront Phyre all but forgotten, as I go in search of my friends. Warning Xotichl, Lita, and Auden to run, to find a way out of here—to get as far from this place as they possibly can.

"What about you?" Xotichl's face pales as her fingers push into my sleeve, understanding all to well just what this means.

"I'm going to stop this. Fix this. If it's the last thing I do."

I jerk free of her grip, aware of her voice calling after me but unable to distinguish the words as I race toward the vortex.

forty-three

Dace

"What have you done with her?" I grip Phyre by the shoulders, demanding an answer. Last I saw, Daire was standing before her, and now she's as good as disappeared.

Phyre smiles, her gaze heavy and glazed. "Wasn't me. I swear it," she says, her voice adopting a tone so strange I have no idea how to interpret the words.

"Where'd she go?" My own voice is frantic, determined. Sure she's playing some sinister part in this, no matter how crazy it seems. But she just remains propped between my hands, staring dreamily at a night wrought with flames.

"It's starting." She speaks in a whisper. "The Last Days are here. This is one of the signs."

I roll my eyes. Dig my fingers deeper into her flesh, hoping to awaken her from her trance. "It's no such thing. Your father is crazy." Though my words go unheard, she's transfixed by a sky bleeding fire.

"I tried to warn you. Tried to talk to you. Remind you of what we once shared—if only so you could see what I see— know what I know." Her gaze is unreachable, voice weary, defeated. "But you didn't want to listen, and now this . . ." She gestures to the chaos occurring all around us. "Now it's too late for any of us."

I grip her shoulders tighter, searching for some hint of the girl I once knew. A sad, beautiful, complicated girl with a crazy doomsday prophet of a father. A girl who lost her mother too young—vanishing without a trace, her body never found. A girl I once cared about, however briefly.

"Come with me, Dace." She trains her focus on me. "My father will help us. Save us. He'll know exactly how to survive this."

"Your father can't help anyone," I remind her, but one look in her eyes tells me my words fail to penetrate. Still, I can't help but add, "Get yourself out of here. Go to Leftfoot's—he'll look after you."

When she fails to move, when she fails to react in any way, I give up and go in search of Daire. Figuring there's only one place she would ever think to go under the circumstances, and cursing myself for not heading there first. It's what I came here to do.

I race through the club. Ignoring Leandro's cries for help as he fights to break free of the fallen bookcase he's trapped underneath. All too aware of the earth violently shaking as bursts of fire erupt all around.

All too aware that the prophecy has started without me—forcing me to catch up.

I breeze through the vortex—noting there are no demons in sight—make my way through the cave house—now completely trashed, surely the result of Cade's rampage—then onto the valley of sand—all the while looking for Daire.

She's out there.

Somewhere.

Hunting for Cade.

I pray I will get to him first.

forty-four

Daire

I roll to a stop, spring to my feet, and take a quick look around. Pleased to find I've landed not far from the mine.

It's the first time I've been able to nail it like that.

The first time I've been able to declare a point of entry and actually find myself there.

A good omen, no doubt.

I hope more will follow.

I stay crouched and low, knees slightly bent, hands flexed and ready. Stealing a moment to adjust to the rhythm of the ground rumbling precariously beneath me—a long string of aftershocks coming in quick succession. Though, thankfully, their intensity lessens a little each time.

Good omen number two?

I'll take what I can get.

A crescendo of shouts drifts from the mine. The captives, apparently no longer enthralled by the Richters, are crowding the mouth of the shaft in an attempt to break free. Their bodies surging against the army of undead guards who push hard against them and shove them back in.

My gaze darts among them, searching for Cade but not seeing him anywhere. I slip my athame into my fist and advance.

Despite the odds stacked against me—despite there being
only one of me and loads of them—I find I'm bathed in a strange
sense of calm with not a trace of fear to be found.

This is the moment when theory and practice finally consum-
mate after months of chastely dating.

This is my chance to use all the skills Paloma has taught me.

This is when I fulfill my destiny—do what I was born to do
or die trying.

I creep toward the Richters, keeping my movements so silent,
so stealthy, they remain completely unaware of my presence. Remembering what Paloma told me, that the only way to rid the
world of them, send them back to their afterlives, is to either remove their heads or cut them cleanly in half.

Sounds simple in theory, but judging by the sheer number of
them, my only hope of seeing it through is to focus less on the
act and more on the end. Envision them lying in headless heaps
all around me. See it as though it's already done.

With the image fixed in my head, I rub my lips together,
tighten my grip on the knife, and spring toward the first one.
Amazed at how easily I catch him.

Then again, he didn't see me coming. Failed to sense me
sneaking up from behind him, blade at the ready.

Doesn't even realize what's happening, until the razor-sharp
tip jams all the way to the hilt. And though he puts up a bit of a
protest, it's too little, too late. My knuckles are already dragging
clear across his neck as I go about the business of severing his head.

He crumples to my feet, his pathetic gurgle lost among the
noise and the chaos, leaving no one the wiser.

As far as gore goes, there's surprisingly little. One of the older
ones I would guess—judging by the pile of bones and dust he
leaves in his wake. Though the small chunk of soul that once

served to revive him, hovers briefly, as though testing the limits of its freedom, before zooming through the sky.

It's a sight to behold. Though I don't watch for long. I'm quick to move on to the next one. Once again, imagining the deed as if it's already done, I shove my blade deep into his spine and saw a deep and steady line. While it proves to be an effective method of slaying, what Paloma failed to mention is it also gives them a chance to shout and scream and warn all the others.

It's a mistake I won't make again.

Clearly, decapitation is the better way.

With the eyes of countless undead Richters upon me, I take a moment to smile and wave.

While I would've preferred to have slain a few more before it got to this point, I've still managed to get them exactly where I want them: focused on *me*, instead of the mine. Which in turn allows some of those poor trapped workers to start sneaking out.

The Richters' first reaction is to erupt into an angry chorus of menacing shouts and growls. Though despite the show of bravado, it takes them a while to organize and adjust to the sudden change of plans. They're so used to following orders from Cade, acting on their own is pretty much a foreign concept to them.

No matter. I just cool my heels and wait where I am. Willing to hang for however long it takes for them to regroup, knowing that every second of delay allows more people to escape. Besides, there's no need to charge them when, soon enough, they'll be coming to me.

With one hand holding the athame, I rub the blade across the front of my jeans, staring impassively at the thick layer of sludge that falls away, while my other hand grabs hold of my pouch. Calling upon the elements, my ancestors, and whatever intrinsic bit of goodness is left inside our spirit animals and paying homage to the ancestral knowledge that lives deep inside me, that courses straight through my veins.

The blood of Valentina, Esperanto, Piann, Mayra, Diego, Gabriella, Paloma, Alejandro, and Django—all of the Seekers who've made great sacrifices so I could be here. Having braved the face of evil so that others could live their lives in relative peace.

With so many counting on me, I can't let them down.

When the largest among them comes at me, it's clear he's fueled on nothing more than anger and rage—reminding me of the way I used to operate until Chay drew my attention to the absolute foolishness of it. Warning me that raw emotion without the strength to back it is a sure way to find yourself dead.

Luckily for me, I listened. I'm no longer that girl.

Unluckily for the undead Richter, he never had a chance to know Chay.

He comes at me with gleaming eyes and a warrior's cry—his hands curled to fists that swing about wildly. And though it's an impressive display at first glance, it's only a second later when I grab hold of his arm and twist until it snaps. Barely allowing a second to pass, before I rend my athame clean across his neck, watching as his body falls separate from his head.

I gaze down at my feet, waiting for him to deteriorate. But when he bleeds out in a thick, black, viscous crud that seeps from his stump of a neck, I figure he must've been dead a much shorter time than the last one.

I kick him aside, wait for the next wave to come. Sure there will be one. Surrender is the last thing on their minds.

This group is smarter, taking a moment to gather axes and picks to use against me. Not getting very far before I relieve them of their weapons. Using my talent for telekinesis, with a little help from my element Wind, to disarm them—I take them down one by one. Indulging the occasional glimpse at the mine, relieved to see it still untended. The captives continuing to escape, as I continue slaying Richters.

As soon as that group is eliminated, the remaining Richters fall on me in a swarm of undead stench, fetid breath, gnashing teeth, and kicking feet. And, to their surprise, I refuse to fight back.

I refuse to deflect.

I stand loosely before them, head raised, arms held out to either side, accepting whatever they give me.

Allowing them to push me to my knees. Shove my face into the dirt. My nose jammed with bits of scorched earth as they bite me, punch me, savagely assault me—while I tell myself I deserve it.

That it's what I get for the long list of failures that resulted in so much misery and destruction.

That fist in my gut is for all those who needlessly died in the mine.

Those claws piercing my scalp is for those who suffered because of my inability to sacrifice Paloma's soul.

While the foot that repeatedly slams into my back is for my failure to stop loving Dace.

My skin splits, allowing rivers of blood to seep from my wounds, as my insides rattle and crunch, and my eyes stream with tears—though the tears aren't for me. They're for everyone I failed by allowing love to rule me.

Problem is—the pain and punishment I seek never comes.

The relief I expected to feel with each blow eludes me as well.

Despite the barrage of fists raining on me, I don't feel much of anything.

You can never be sick enough, poor enough, or beaten enough to help those less fortunate than you. The only way to empower others is by empowering yourself. Never apologize for the gifts that were bestowed upon you. Never punish yourself for your ability to love. Love is never a mistake—it is the epitome of grace—the highest power of all. It is the only thing that will lead us out of the darkness and into the light . . .

The voice belongs to Valentina. And though I'd planned to let them beat me just a little bit longer before I got back to the business of removing their heads and ripping them to shreds, I realize she's right.

Redemption can never be won in this way.

The best way to atone for my failures is by ridding the world of these foul-smelling, hate-filled, malevolent Richters.

I'm up like a shot.

My athame swaying before me as though conducting a glorious symphony heard only by me. Removing one head after another, knuckles repeatedly pounding into dead rancid flesh, as bodies fall all around me. So caught up in the melody, I hardly notice when the music has stopped and there's not a single dance partner left.

I just keep pounding bodies, snapping skeletons into small useless bits. Rendering them incapable of ever resurrecting again—ensuring the remains return to a place they never should've left.

When it's over, I still my athame, wipe a hand across my brow, and lift my gaze skyward. Dazzled by the constellation of brightly shining souls glittering overhead. Twinkling, circling, blinking, and spinning in a flurry of movement—unbounded and free. They float briefly, allowing me to see them, appreciate them, before winking out of sight, and soaring toward home.

Then I lower my gaze to the heap of remains at my feet, marveling at how it looks exactly as I envisioned it. And as I continue to pick my way through, I'm amazed to find I've wrought more change than I ever would've thought.

With each Richter felled, with each soul released, the Lowerworld has taken one giant leap toward healing itself. Patches of once-dead grass now sprawl into a lush and velvety lawn. While the hollowed-out trees, once bent like old crones, begin to straighten and stretch, as though encouraging their branches to shake off a long arthritic winter.

And it's not long after when the animals begin to venture out of hiding. Raccoon, Red Fox, White Wolf, Wildcat, Monkey, Squirrel, Jaguar, Bear, Lion, Bat, Opossum, Hummingbird, Eagle—even Horse and Raven come out to greet me.

Their bright and happy eyes providing all the proof I need to know that with the Richters finally evicted, the curse has been lifted.

The Lowerworld thrives once again.

I head for the mine, ensure that it's cleared, then make a quick assessment of the wounded, and discover that while it's not nearly as bad as I feared, that's not to say that it's good.

With no way to attend to them all, I turn to the animals for help. Pairing those who can't walk with the bigger, stronger ones like Horse, Bear, and Jaguar, while the rest follow the path set by Eagle and Bat, who fly overhead.

Trusting the elders are doing their part, working their magick, and remaining alert to the signals that will lead them to the crowd soon to be arriving at the vortex of twisted juniper trees, I take leave. Guided by Raven soaring ahead of me and the whisper of wind that swirls featherlike over my skin, I go searching for Cade.

forty-five

Dace

I check all my pockets. Hands obsessively patting my jacket, my pants, assured by the solid weight and heft that I find there.

This time I'm ready.

This time I'm armed.

With my blowgun loaded with darts dipped in poison no beast can survive, I make my way across a dry and scorched land, which, although it seems crazy, appears to be improving with each passing step.

Leaves are forming on trees. Buds are sprouting from the tips of once-barren flower stems.

Even the spirit animals, having spent the last month in hiding, are now out and about. Though, strangely, once they spy me they beat a fast retreat, eager to keep their distance and steer clear of my path.

Probably still suffering their version of post-traumatic stress disorder after all the hell Cade put them through.

Or at least that's what I tell myself, until I pass the reflective surface of a pond and see an image of Cade staring back.

I run a hand through my hair, ensure it's still long, unlike his.

Then I press a hand to my cheek, relieved to see the image reflects the same thing.

Still, there's no doubt that it's Cade's eyes staring back. The very reason the animals fled—they've mistaken me for him.

I'd be lying if I said it didn't bother me. Still, there's no time for regret, so I return my focus to finding him.

Needing to settle this before Daire can arrive.

I can't bear for her to see me this way.

forty-six

Daire

When Raven and Wind lead me to the Enchanted Spring—and it truly is enchanted again, no bloated fish, no rat-infested vines—I can't say I'm surprised. Allowing the Richters to pummel me has left me in a pretty sore state. A quick dip in its healing waters can only help to revive me.

Still, I take a moment to glance all around, needing to make sure I'm alone, that Cade isn't lurking in the shadows, waiting for the perfect opportunity to pounce. Finding the assurance I seek when Raven lands on my shoulder and nudges his beak to my shoulder, and Wind curls around me, prodding me toward the glistening pool.

"It's good to have you back," I say, watching as Raven flits toward a nearby rock. "I missed your company. It wasn't the same without you."

His purple eyes glimmer and dart, keeping careful watch as I strip off my clothes, kick off my boots, and place my knife within reach should I find that I need it. Then I slip into the warm bubbling spring, sinking under the water until it covers my head and goes about healing my wounds and restoring my energy, allowing me to emerge as though I'm reborn.

"We should bottle that." I laugh, picking my way out of the water and over the bed of rocks lining the edge. My grin fading when I notice the way Wind begins to kick, ruffling Raven's feathers as he fidgets, shifting from foot to foot as his eyes roll in their sockets.

"*Shhh! He's coming—he's coming!*" Raven croaks, imitating an unfamiliar female voice I can only assume belonged to one of Cade's unfortunate captives. Cringing at the number of times Raven must've listened to their cries of pain and fear in order to nail the fearful tone so perfectly.

The sudden shaking of the earth accompanied by a spine-chilling shriek that echoes through the land, prompting me to duck into my filthy, torn clothes, grasp the athame, and follow Raven and Wind to the place where it originates. Cade's personal epicenter just outside the spring.

"What the hell have you done?" Cade shrieks, greeting me with a gaping, fanged, snake-mouthed glare, though thankfully he's retained his normal size.

I glance at his feet, noting how the immediate area surrounding him remains corrupted while the rest continues to heal.

"If you wanted to see me, you could've called or sent a text," I tell him, my voice strong and sure. "You didn't have to create all this drama for me."

He lowers his clawed hands with a flourish, summoning the earth to still as the surrounding ring of fire smolders and dims, and I can only hope the Middleworld bears the same effect.

"Your sense of reasoning is beyond me." I sneer, allowing my gaze to drag over him as my lip curls with distaste. "You're like one of those crazy looters you see on the news. You live in Enchantment, your family practically owns Enchantment, and yet you choose to destroy it by virtually firebombing it with that fiery rain that you made. Do you have any idea how crazy that makes you?"

He swipes a hand at me, his long, razor-sharp talons veering uncomfortably close. "It's the prophecy, Daire. I figured you'd know that. It just needed a little push to get started. Now answer my question. Where are my ancestors—my employees? What the hell have you done, Seeker?" His voice booms loudly as the snakes thrash all about. Making the transformation from his demon self to his more normal self, he whistles for his creepy coyote, who obediently trots up beside him and heels at his feet with a bloodied, mangled rabbit hanging halfway out of his snout.

"That's someone's *spirit animal!*" I gasp, reaching toward Coyote, intent on wrenching it free.

But Cade steps between us, face enraged as he shouts, "Answer my question, Seeker!" His voice pitched so high it prompts Coyote to lift his snout and howl, allowing the dead bunny to topple to the ground.

I stare at the mess of a carcass, consoling myself that it was dead on arrival; there was nothing I could've done to save it. Returning my attention to Cade, I say, "Those weren't workers; those were *slaves*. And in case you didn't know, slavery is illegal, so I took matters into my own hands and freed them. Oh, and as for your ancestors—I killed them. Every last one." I pause, tapping a finger against my chin, needing to emend that last bit. "Or perhaps *killed* isn't quite the right word, considering they were already dead. Fact is, you're on your own, Cade. Your undead playmates have gone bye-bye. Forever this time. Which means that at this very moment, all those souls you stole are returning to their rightful homes. And the people you enslaved are now back in the Middleworld, where they'll not only be healed but also protected with the kind of magick you'll never be able to penetrate. You'll never be able to harm them or mess with their perception again. Which, in turn, means your business is dead. You've no slaves, no guards, no one willing to partake in your madness."

"You'll pay for this." He storms toward me, hands clenched by his sides.

"Maybe," I say. "But more likely not." I take a careful step backward for his every advance.

Not because he scares me—he doesn't.

Not because I'm intimidated—I'm not.

But because I want to lure him into my territory. Noting how the grass beneath his feet dies a quick death, only to revive once again when he's past. But now that the magick of the Enchanted Spring is restored—now that the Richters are gone, their shroud of negative energy rapidly dissipating—I'm confident there's nothing he can do to corrupt it. And with Wind calm and no protest from Raven, I'm free to proceed.

"You have no idea what you've done." He glares. His icy-blue eyes turned dark and stormy. "No idea how you'll pay for your foolish transgressions. You're so mundane in your thinking. So stupid and conventional. Every time I thought there just might be hope for you yet, you do something ridiculous like saving your *abuela*'s soul or killing my ancestors. I'm beginning to think I misjudged you, Santos. Fooled myself into thinking you were a person of substance."

"Oh, there's no doubt you've misjudged me." At the sound of the bubbling spring just a few feet away, I slip the athame into my hand.

His rolls his eyes, takes another step closer, and says, "Really? This again? Another performance of the Wiccan Warrior Dance?"

"The last one was such a success, I figured it was worth a repeat."

He looks at me, confused by my words and I'm all too eager to enlighten him.

"This is the same blade I used to wreak some pretty awesome devastation on your ancestors. Sent their heads rolling with very little effort. It's over, Cade. For real. And, if you don't believe me, take a good look around and tell me what you see."

He stares at me for a very long time, but ultimately curiosity gets the better of him and he allows his gaze to drift. Allows himself to see what I see—the Lowerworld slowly healing, reaching toward its former beauty and glory.

All except for the space just under his feet, which leaves me to worry.

I take another step back, this one a little hurried, uncertain. And like the beast that he is, he wastes no time exploiting my moment of weakness.

In an instant, he's on me, closing the gap between us. Standing so near, his hot breath pelts hard against my cheek, as Coyote growls and nips at my hand.

The move causing Raven to croak loudly in protest, as Wind picks up, fiercely lashing at Cade. Though it's only a second later when I've regained my footing along with my magick. I arrow my fingers at Coyote's glowing red eyes and watch as he falls into whining submission.

"Impressive," Cade says, sidling closer, seemingly unaffected by the gale at his back. "But if you so much as go near Coyote again, I'll kill you."

"I'd like to see you try." I wiggle the athame by my side, take another step back. Gazing covertly at his feet as I continue my retreat, pausing only when the ground stops changing and remains solid and green beneath him.

He stares hard at me, searching for access, attempting to siphon my energy, yank on my soul, but it no longer works. He has no idea the power I hold. No idea who he's dealing with now. I'm finally the Seeker I was born to be.

"Got you just where I want you." His gaze darkens on mine. "You and me at the Enchanted Spring. Just like the dream. The only thing missing is Dace."

I rub my lips together, stilled by the eerie sensation of icy-cold fingers traipsing my spine.

He's right.

It really is the dream come to life.

Only this time, it gets a new ending.

If it's the last thing I do, I'll make sure of that.

"So it is." I keep steady before him. "But you know what they say about dreams—there are so many ways to interpret them. Same thing with prophecies. It's only after the dust has settled when you can pin it down, put real solid meaning to the words and pretend that's what it meant all along."

Cade grins. Presenting a face that, from a distance, is objectively handsome. Though an up-close look reveals eyes that are empty and dull, devoid of compassion—bearing not one single trace of basic human emotion.

"If I remember right, this is the part where you get all hot and steamy with my twin. Shall we reenact it?" His tongue darts over his lips. "Seeing as he isn't here, I'm willing to volunteer as his stand-in. I think you'll enjoy it. You can finally see what you've been missing—the difference between an amateur and a pro."

"Sure." I shrug, my gaze posing a direct challenge to his. "Go ahead. Let's see what you got." I grip the hilt tighter, inch my fingers higher.

"Ladies first." He arcs an arm toward the spring.

Without hesitation, I leap away from the water and toward him. Enjoying Coyote's fierce but ultimately ineffective growl, he's still under my spell, but disappointed by Cade's failure to even so much as flinch when I press the edge of my blade hard against his cheek. Removing a broad sheen of stubble as I slowly drag it across, taunting, "Dream on, Richter. I'll never be that desperate."

I yank the blade down along the curve of his jaw, jerk it all the way to the hollow of his neck. Fascinated by the vein that throbs and pulses as I ready my hand. Anticipating the rush of seeing it forever stilled when his head drops to my feet.

I jab the tip in, just enough to draw a small speck of blood. Eager to see it replaced by a solid, arcing gush, I press my lips together and push the blade harder. My gaze narrowed to this one single point on Cade's flesh—mesmerized by the way the skin parts so easily—the blood flowing immediately. Caught between the thrill of the kill and the true horror of what I'm about to do next.

It was different with his ancestors.

The undead don't bleed.

When the body is pulsing with life, it feels much more like murder.

I clear my mind of the thought. Replacing it with reminders of all the horrible things that he's done . . . the fact that he's not entirely human . . . that his soul is pure evil . . .

His fingers catch at my wrist, clutching hard as he pulls the knife free of his neck, leaving behind a wound that's superficial at best. His touch surprisingly cool as he forces my hand to my side.

"Don't toy with me, Seeker." He shoves his face against mine, allowing his blood to trickle onto my chest as he inhales my scent slowly, deeply, as though wanting to savor it. "No one likes a tease. Besides, it's not like you haven't done it before. Though I promise, you will learn some new tricks."

His fingers tug at the waistband of my jeans, determined to rid me of them. While the other hand ensures the athame stays far from his flesh.

He's freakishly strong.

Stronger than I remember him being.

But that doesn't stop me from curling my leg around his.

Doesn't stop me from clutching him hard at the crook of his knee, as I drag his thigh forward, bringing it to rest between mine.

Equally sickened and spurred by his small groan of pleasure, the way he grinds his hips against me, I summon every ounce of my strength to butt my chest hard against his while I continue to tug on his leg. Watching as he slips out from under me, plummeting backward, face filled with shock and rage when his head smacks hard against the dirt.

I'm quick to pounce, not wasting a second before I plant my foot on his chest and return my blade to his neck.

"*What the—*" He bucks wildly, furious at finding himself beneath me. His eyes morphing from their usual icy-blue to a deep glowing red, as he fights to shake free, rid himself of my hold. Then, forfeiting that, he begins creeping backward, purposely edging toward the spring.

But I can't let him get there.

Can't run the risk that the water will empower him, strengthen him, in the way it did me.

I drop to my knees and grab hold of his jeans, tugging hard on his legs, jerking him the opposite way, as he continues to wrestle against me. Fighting and kicking, he snarls and bites like the beast that he is. Grinning in triumph when he swings a knee up and shoves it into my gut with such force, my body collapses in pain.

Vaguely aware of Raven's frantic croaks—the way Wind whips all around me—I gasp and wheeze in an effort to draw some air back into my lungs. All the while trying to veer out of Cade's reach, though it's too late for that.

He's already taken me by the waist.

Already locked his arms around me.

Already heaved me down until I'm clinched prone against him.

Leaving me with no other choice but to fight to break free. Fight to keep hold of the athame by swinging it wildly—stabbing at anything within reach. But Cade's too limber. Too quick. Easily dodging the blade, until I'm left gouging at air.

And before I can stop it, he's rolling me over until I'm trapped underneath him. His body pressed flush against mine, his face mere inches away, gazing upon me with a malevolent gleam in his eye.

His fingers inch toward the knife, as I frantically arc my arms overhead. Tendons strained beyond reason, I switch the knife from hand to hand, desperate to stay one step ahead. Still, I'm no match for him.

Cade's taller.

His arms longer.

Leaving me with no choice but to sacrifice the knife by tossing it to a place neither of us can reach. And it's only a second later when he clamps my hands in his fist, pinning them high above my head, leaving his free hand to explore. Pretending to misread my resistance—the way I squirm beneath him in a fight to free myself—as consent.

I shutter my eyes in revulsion. Steeling myself against the pinch of his fingers roaming my body, his hips thrusting and circling, seeking rhythm with my frantic attempts to relieve myself of his weight. A low groan building deep in his throat, as he reaches for the soft buckskin pouch that lies between my breasts.

He's trying to strip me of my power in every conceivable way.

Trying to demoralize me by rendering me defenseless and weak.

Knowing the moment he peeks inside, the magick of the talismans will be lost.

Knowing the moment he violates me, he will have won.

I turn my head to the side, press my cheek to the dirt, as I desperately search for Raven. Relieved to find he's still with me, perched only a few feet away. His mad squawking suddenly silenced, though his eyes glimmer in a way I've never seen. Their glint growing in intensity as Cade loops a finger around the strap and the pouch begins to tremble and heat.

I continue to buck hard against him, but with the way he lies astride me, his legs hooked on either side of mine, I can't get much traction.

"I've always been curious just what it is you people keep in these pouches," he says. "Guess I'm about to find out."

He drags on the drawstring, as I continue to squirm and resist with everything I have in me. Trying to summon my magick—summon the Wind. Summon the athame back into my hand, so I can jam it into Cade's eyes and ensure he never gets to leer at me again. But somehow, with his body covering mine, he's blocking my magick.

That's the only explanation for the way it suddenly fails me.

The only explanation for why the Wind slows, Raven falls into silence, and Coyote, now released of my spell, butts his snout against my forehead, emitting a low, menacing growl.

With no other options, I wet my tongue and take aim. Biting back a grin when the glob of spit lands smack between Coyote's creepy red eyes. The act causing the distraction I'd hoped for when he yelps in outrage, and Cade momentarily loses his grip. Enough for me to free a hand and crash it down hard on his head.

But it's only a second before he's regrouped and pinned me again. His face enraged when he says, "Don't mess with me, Seeker. Like it or not, you're soon to be mine . . ."

His hand slips to his jeans, loosening them, urging them down past his hips. Then when he's got them where he wants them, bunched around his knees, he reaches for the pouch once again. "First things first," he sings, yanking roughly on the draw-string, once, twice—

The next thing I know Coyote is yelping in pain and Cade's eyes are rolling back in his head as he's lifted by an unseen force and hurled into the air.

I leap to my feet, looking to Raven, sure he's somehow re-sponsible. But then I hear my name and whirl around to find Dace standing behind me, his brother a discarded heap in the very far distance.

I rush into his arms. My relief at seeing him trumping any fears I might've had about his coming here. Though it may play into the prophecy, clearly the prophecy's changed. Dace and I are together. It's the only thing that matters.

"You were just in time! If you'd been just one second later . . ." My voice fades as I shudder to think what nearly became of me. I burrow into his chest, seeking the comfort and warmth of his flesh.

"There's no reason to worry." His lips find my forehead, my cheeks. "I'm here. I'll always be here. There's nothing to fear. He'll never come near you again. I'll make sure of it." His whispered promise accompanied by the soothing hand that drifts down my back, before curling around and pulling me close.

I press my cheek to the small golden key at his chest, my voice thick with emotion as I say, "I saw you at the fence. I thought you'd—"

"Shhh . . ." He presses a finger to my lips and tilts my face toward his. "It's not what you thought. I'd never give up on our love. Never."

My hand finds his cheek, needing to see the words reflected in his eyes, only to notice how different he is.

He's darker.

Harder.

His energy odd and frenetic—offering only a fraction of the usual swarm of unconditional love I've come to expect.

And when my eyes meet his, it's like looking at Cade. His gaze is dark, fathomless, fails to reflect.

"Dace—what happened?" I ask, unable to stifle my panic. Watching in dismay as he quickly turns away, as though too ashamed to be seen.

"Don't. Don't look at me. Please. I'll explain later. As soon as it's over, I'll tell you everything. Just—trust that I did what I had to. I did it for us. For you. And it's nothing that can't be undone. But please, I can't bear for you to see me like this."

He moves away, but I grasp hold of his arm and pull him back to me. "Who did this to you?" I reach for his cheek, needing to look into his eyes once again, to determine it truly is as bad as I think, only to have him jerk free.

"Daire—*please!*" he cries, the words spoken with untold anguish. "What you see isn't me. I'm still in here, I swear. I just—"

I stand before him, too shaken to move.

Barely able to focus when he says, "It's temporary. It's what I have to do in order to save you. It'll all be okay in the end, you'll see."

My eyes search his, looking for clues to what that might mean.

"I know how the prophecy ends," he says, the words causing an ominous chill to creep over my flesh. "It's the same as the dream, and I won't let you die."

I shake my head, needing him to understand it's not what he thinks. "You've got it all wrong—that's not how it ends—that's not what it means!" But my words fall on deaf ears.

"This is it, Daire. This is how it goes down. I've dreamed it too many times. Seen the writing on the wall—literally. And while I can't do anything about the sky bleeding fire—I will do whatever it takes to keep the darkness from eclipsing your light."

"But I'm not the light—that's not how the dream ends! You're—"

The words interrupted by the sight of Cade sauntering toward us, casually plucking debris from his clothing and hair, with his faithful coyote trotting alongside him.

"Well, isn't this a touching scene?" He stops just before us, grinning at Dace as though he's the special guest he's long been expecting. "You've got quite an arm there, brother—who knew?" He laughs. Cricks his neck from side to side. But aside from the dirt on his clothing, he's no worse for wear.

Dace shoves before me, in an effort to shield me. Fingers snaking covertly into his pocket, he says, "Figured I'd find you down here, throwing a temper tantrum and sulking like the child you are. How many people need to suffer for your failure to impress Leandro?" He shakes his head. "We're all aware of your pathetic need for his approval. Must make you feel pretty awful when he yells at you like he did."

Dace glowers before him, as my gaze switches between them. And all it takes is the almost imperceptible flinch of Cade's shoulders to know Dace nailed the sore spot.

Reminding me of what I once said to Paloma, when I referred

to Cade as a: *psychopathic demonic freak driven by a pathetic need to impress Leandro by achieving world domination.*

It's the single seed of humanity that lives deep inside him.

The mine—his presence in the Lowerworld—it's only partly about amassing a fortune and controlling the Middleworld. At its very core, it's a bid to wow his dad. Willing to destroy countless lives in an effort to gain his father's approval. And, according to Dace, he's failed on every level.

Xotichl and Paloma were right—he's definitely human.

Though that doesn't mean I won't kill him.

"I stood right outside the door and listened to him verbally rip you to shreds," Dace continues. "Heard the way you begged— your voice high-pitched and whiny when he shot you down, re-fused to listen. See the smile I wear?" He stands before him, finger arrowed toward a wide empty grin. "It's nothing like the way I smiled then." He pauses, pretending that it's merely an af-terthought when he adds, "Oh, and by the way, you so much as go near my girlfriend again—you're dead." His fingers slip free of his pocket, revealing the blowgun that didn't work so well the last time. Though one look at his face tells me he has complete faith he won't fail again. "Actually, you're dead either way. So say good-bye, brother."

Raven squawks.

Wind swirls at my feet.

Coyote crouches, head lowered, teeth bared.

As I take a few backward steps, drop to the ground, and sum-mon the knife to my hand.

Unmoved by the threat on his life, Cade rushes Dace until only a whisper of space lies between them. Gaze probing with interest, he asks, "What've you done?"

He leans forward, attempts to grab hold of Dace's shirt if only to get a better look. But Dace veers from his reach, lifting the blowgun to his lips, as I grasp the hilt in my hand. Confident that from this vantage point, I can nail this particular bull's-eye.

Cade whirls on me, eyes blazing and red. "Sure you want to attempt that, Santos?"

I glance between them. Noting how aside from the hair, there's no discernible difference between them. Dace's eyes are as bleak and empty as his brother's.

"Daire, leave it. I've got this," Dace says, one eye closed, the other on Cade, taking aim.

And while I've no idea what's happened to make him this way, for now my only goal is to stop the prophecy from claiming his life—his light. So I inhale a sharp breath and hurl the athame at the same time Dace releases the dart.

Mesmerized by the way it glints—arcing in a quick flash of silver—as it slices through the air. Ultimately overtaking the dart to lodge deep in Cade's neck, just as I'd envisioned.

Only it's no longer Cade.

The demon has taken his place.

He hooks a sharp talon around the handle, drags the blade free, and tosses it to the ground, where it falls to a thud at his enormous clawed feet.

The sight so astounding, so unfathomable, I'm left blinking in confusion. Unable to make sense of why Cade stands monstrous and grinning before me, the knife and dart abandoned at his feet, as Dace collapses to his knees, blood gushing from the wound his brother should bear.

Cade glances between us, his face impassive, his voice toneless as he says, "Told you we were connected. Though I guess I failed to tell you how deeply. So let me enlighten you now. In order to kill me, you need to catch me in human form. But be warned, I will not go alone. I'll take my brother right along with me. And believe it or not, I prefer to keep him around." He turns toward me with glowing red eyes that fix right on mine. "Oh, I may rely on Coyote to keep him in line from time to time—the wounds he inflicts on Dace bear no effect on me. Which is something you both need to consider the next time either one of you gets another homicidal urge."

His words leave me speechless, numbed. I stare between the two of them, horrified by a truth made suddenly real.

Killing Cade means killing Dace.

It's an incomprehensible choice I could never, ever make.

Yet I have to.

It's what I was born to do.

Is this what Paloma meant when she warned me that a Seeker's life requires great sacrifice?

Did she suspect all along we were doomed from the start?

Cade looms before me, his monstrous face taunting as though this is his idea of big fun. While Dace ignores the rush of blood now streaming from his neck and grabs at Cade's ankles, his knees, trying to stop him from getting to me.

But in full demon mode, Cade wields incredible force. He won't go down easily. He kicks Dace away, barely sparing him a backward glance as he says, "Don't worry about him. He's hurting, no thanks to you. But your aim's not that good. You missed the main artery. Thing is, that's twice you've tried to kill me. Leading me to believe I can no longer trust you. You've run your course, Seeker. You're the end of the line. It's been interesting, but don't think for a moment I'll miss you."

Behind him, Dace leaps for the knife, willing to sacrifice himself in order to save me.

A selfless act that assures me he's still in there.

Somewhere.

I haven't lost him entirely.

But he's no match for Cade.

With a quick flick of his wrist, Cade's already snatched it.

Already coming at me in a blur of gleaming red eyes and two-headed snakes that shoot from his mouth.

Already shoving that two-sided knife straight into my chest, the blade making an awful scraping sound when it shoves past the key.

I stagger backward. My gaze swimming with the sight of his ghastly demon face bearing down on mine, as my hands fumble at the gash in my flesh. Watching in dismay when they come away drenched in red.

"Hurts, don't it?" Cade grins. Allowing those two-headed, soul-stealing snakes to leap from his mouth, going straight for the gaping hole he's left in my breast.

This is just like the dream. Just like the prophecy. Only I've managed to change the ending. Instead of Dace dying, I've taken his place.

I cling to the thought as I watch it unfold. Watch it as though it's happening to somebody other than me.

My hands flopping before me, useless and weak. Wanting so badly to tell Dace that I love him—that I'm sorry to leave him like this.

But the words are soon drowned by a torrent of something metallic and bitter that clogs up my throat.

Blood.

My blood.

And it won't stop. There's just so damn much of it.

Raven shrieks.

Coyote yips in unbridled excitement.

Cade shouts in unrestrained victory edged with frustration.

As Dace calls after me, shouting my name over and over again, his voice hoarse, mangled. Though it's not long before the sound begins to fade, as though it's being filtered through too many layers to be properly heard—drifting from a place that grows increasingly distant.

My body shivers.

My breath comes in desperate, ragged spasms—and sometimes it doesn't come at all.

If it wasn't for these strong arms that hold me, I'd be falling—tumbling to a place from which I'd never return.

If it wasn't for these strong arms that protect me, Cade would've succeeded in stealing my soul.

I want to tell Dace not to worry. Want to tell him about the golden one looking after me—the glowing hands that support me—but the words just won't come.

Hush, coos the being as he sweeps a long golden finger over my lips.

But I haven't spoken. I tried, but I can't.

Hush your thoughts.

I do. For a while. But then they pipe up again.

Where are we going? Where are you taking me?

Up.

My eyes drift shut. Aware of the light still shining behind them but too tired to keep looking at things I don't understand. Preferring to immerse myself in this warm, buoyant feeling of comfort and love that he brings.

You must be the sun! The thought rushes through me—my eyes snap open again. Trying to make out his form, but all I can see is a radiant blur of gold. *I told Dace he was wrong, said there is no sun in the Lowerworld. It's just some fable Leftfoot told him when he was a kid. But I was wrong, wasn't I?*

Do I look like the sun?

I squint, straining to see that which has so far remained hidden. Gasping in delight when the glow begins to fade just enough to allow the features to sharpen and a face to take shape.

The skin is fair, as though carved from beams of light. The hair so blond and pale, it's almost as white as the skin. Though the eyes stand in sharp contrast, the irises are an unusual yet beautiful shade of lavender that gaze down at me.

And before I can respond, I *feel* it.

The long slender fingers of death curling around me.

Heralded by the soft whir and hum of my life force quickly draining.

The corporeal flesh and blood part of me swiftly subsiding.

Surrendering. Allowing the soul to take over. To carry me ever higher—soar as high as I dare.

The sensation similar to how I felt when I was drowning at the falls. The glowing person similar as well. The same glowing person I once accused of haunting me back in that Moroccan square.

But now I know better.

So you remember? He tightens his grip when I nod that I do.

Only this time is different.

This is the prophecy come true.

The other side of midnight's hour strikes a herald thrice rung

Seer, Shadow, Sun—together they come

Sixteen winters hence—the light shall be eclipsed

Leaving darkness to ascend beneath a sky bleeding fire

Only instead of the light being eclipsed, it was me. But at least Dace is safe.

Right?

Right?

You ask too many questions. You must rest. We'll be there soon.

I close my eyes again, using my last burst of strength for one final request: *Can you please make it snow? Will you do that for them?*

Don't have to, he tells me. *You've already seen to it.*

My lips curl at the sides, my cheeks fall wet with tears, as I fumble for the blood-covered key at my chest and fold my fingers around it. *At least I'll leave them with that . . .*

My focus narrowing to a point so tiny—no bigger than a molecule. Surprised to find that the molecule is *me*—and that I'm connected to everything.

A cry of anguish sounds in the distance, though I'm sure the cry is not meant for me.

Why would it be?

I'm safe.

Loved.

Surrounded by light as warm and glowing as a kiss.

My heart flutters.

My lungs bubble with breath.

And the next thing I know, I'm crashing through a glorious silken spun web—bursting into a world of bright golden light.

season
of
miracles

epilogue

Axel

The girl lies bleeding in my arms.

Her brown shiny hair spilling over my shoulder—the pink of her cheeks fading as quickly as the life force within her.

Still, she is beautiful.

Far more beautiful up close.

Inquisitive too.

And though I long to reassure her, it serves no purpose to lie to her.

She teeters on the edge of the abyss. Stands a very good chance of tumbling in.

I press a finger to her lips and urge her toward silence. She can't afford the luxury of speaking and thinking—can't afford to expend the much-needed energy.

When her eyes flutter closed, I tighten my hold.

Every inhalation a prayer: *Save her! Spare her!*

Every exhalation indulging a long-dormant rage—cursing the lot of them.

She didn't deserve this.

Never stood a chance against them. And, as it turns out, neither did I. Having failed in my bid to help her—look after her—guide her.

Though it's not over yet.

I gaze upward, our destination still so far away. And though her heart continues to beat, it seems only to do so in order to pump more blood from her wound.

She's fading.

There's no way she'll make it.

Yet she still summons the strength to ask if it's snowing—hoping to leave a gift for her friends.

Ready to surrender to death just as soon as I confirm it. A trace of a smile lifting her cheeks as she rolls toward the edge.

And though I know it's wrong—though I've been warned many times before—it doesn't stop me from cupping her face in my hands and molding my lips tightly to hers.

My silent plea for forgiveness, chased by a single life-restoring breath.

Paloma

"Come to the window, *cariño*. It's snowing. Looks like Daire has done it after all."

Chay looks at me, waiting patiently. But when I fail to join him, he crosses the room to the battered old table where I hunch over a book that's been part of my life for so long, I can no longer remember a time before it.

"What are you looking at?" He rubs a comforting hand over my back.

I nod toward the codex. Robbed of my words along with my breath. Unsure if what I'm seeing is real, or if I'm merely a tired old woman gone suddenly mad. Needing him to confirm either way, and secretly hoping for the latter.

His whispered "My God" providing all the proof that I need to know it's not me.

His strong arms fold around me, though it's not enough to buffer me from the truth.

It really is happening.

A long-foretold future has gone into limbo.

The two of us huddle together, gazing upon the ancient tome.

Watching as words that have remained there for centuries, slowly lift from the page.

Leaving a large blank space where the prophecy stood.

"What does it mean?" Chay's haunted eyes search mine.

I pull my red cardigan tightly around me and look toward a window framing a flurry of snow that falls from the sky.

Reluctant to admit I don't know what it means.

I haven't a clue.

For the first time in a long time, the answers elude me.

Phyre

We're more than halfway home when the snow begins to fall.

More than halfway home before my dad decides to acknowledge my presence in his car.

"Is it safe to assume you failed?" he asks in a voice as stern as his face—as stern as the harsh black suit that he wears.

I press my forehead to the window, stare into a wide expanse of night now glinting with white.

"Answer me!" He slams hard on the brakes. Stops the car right in the middle of the road, as though we're the only ones on it. We are.

I press hard against the door, shoulders cringing inward. *I'm in for it now.*

I sneak a hand to my face, erasing the few tears I've indulged in before he can see them, knowing that'll just make it worse.

This is my role. It's not like I don't know the part. I've been rehearsing since I was a child, since the day he pointed his finger at me, declaring that between me and my sisters, I was his Chosen One.

"Well?" he demands, refusing to move on until I provide the answer he seeks.

"It's not as easy as you think," I say, regretting it the instant it's out. It's too defensive. Puts the blame more on him than me. I should know better. That sort of tactic never goes over well.

"Is that so?" He shifts in his seat, tugging hard on the cuff of his sleeves in the same way he does every Sunday, right before taking his pulpit. "Then maybe I should bring one of your sisters down here to take care of it for you. Ember or Ashe—which would you prefer?"

"Neither." The answer comes quickly, without hesitation. Swiveling in my seat until I'm fully facing him, I plead, "Leave them be. I can do it. I *will* do it. I just—"

He stares at me—his eyes dark and merciless.

"I just need a little more time. Two years is a long time to be gone. It's like starting over. I have to build his trust again. It's not so easy anymore. He has a girlfriend. Thinks he's in love. And he is. I've seen the way he looks at her." The truth leaves a bitter taste on my tongue.

"Well then, I guess you'll just have to find a way to distract him, won't you?"

I swallow hard. Nod in the way he expects. Focusing my attention on the other side of the windshield, watching the snow collect in small scattered mounds on the car's dirty white hood.

"Time's running out." He eases off the brake, allowing for a slow roll down the dirt road.

Time's always running out. Has been since I was a child.

"It's already started. The signs are everywhere."

Everything's a sign. A piece of toast weirdly burned—a cloud formation that resembles something unholy—a six-toed cat—he sees proclamations of doom wherever he looks.

"And you know what that means. You know what's expected of you."

I nod again. *I've spent my entire life training for the Last Days, if only to spare my sisters the task.*

"Your sacrifice is a serious one, though it is for the greater good of all. You'll be hailed as a savior—a saint!" He sings, eyes shining, lost in the false glories of his own weary diatribe. Never stopping to question why I would possibly care how I'm remembered when I'm dead. He turns, focusing hard on my eyes when he says, "Why is your makeup smeared? Were you *crying?*" His voice rises in outrage, prompting me to bring a hand to my face, wiping furiously at my eyelids, my cheeks. "You stop that at once! Do you hear me?"

He shoots me a look of warning, returning his focus to driving only when he's sure I'm resigned to obedience. Falling into a welcomed silence for the rest of the ride, until he parks before the small, abandoned trailer he's claimed as our home.

"I want the boy dead by New Year's Eve," he says. "Long before the clock strikes twelve. Dace—Cade—doesn't matter which. For all I can see, they're one and the same. Ruled by darkness. The absolute manifestation of evil. You do your job right, make the sacrifice you were put on this earth for, and the Last Days will be followed by the Shining Days of Glory I've long since prophesized." He looks in the rearview mirror, adjusts the lapels of his suit—the one he saves for holidays, Sundays, and his most favored apocalyptical occasions.

"Would you look at that?" His voice turns bright and cheery as he glances at his crappy watch with the cheap leather band. "It's the other side of midnight. Merry Christmas," he says.

"Merry Christmas," I repeat, dully.

Slipping free of the car and tipping my face toward the sky. Anointed by the snow left to melt on my cheeks, obscuring the tears I'm forbidden to cry.

Xotichl

"Stop the car!"

Auden slams hard on the brakes, arcs his arm toward me, try-ing to protect me from crashing into the dashboard, but I'm al-ready out the door.

Already seeking purchase with the slick, wet road, before moving to the center of the street where I turn my face skyward, allowing fat drops of snow to fall onto my cheeks.

"What are you doing? What is she doing?" Lita cries, throwing open her door and racing to catch up with me. Her tone instantly switching from reproach to delight when she says, "No. Freaking. Way!" She runs up beside me, as Auden joins me on my other side. "Time to pay up, Auden!" she cries, voice jubilant as she wraps her arms around me and does a little dance as she carefully spins me. "Looks like Xotichl was right—it really is the season of miracles!" She returns me to Auden, freeing herself to skip up and down the street. Or at least I think that's what she's doing judging by the surge in her energy, the swish of her feet.

"Hey, flower, looks like you got your Christmas wish after all. I promise I'll never doubt you again." Auden's lips find mine, his kiss reverent and sweet. Breaking away when he says, "So, why are you crying?"

I burrow deep into his arms, bury my head in the hollow of his neck. Seeking comfort in his strength, his scent—unwilling to speak the words aloud, make them any more real than they are in my head.

Unwilling to speak the horrible truth that lives deep inside me.

This is no ordinary snow flurry.

This is no meteorological inevitability.

Not when it sings like the wind—yet warms like the sun.

Falling from the sky in a rainbow of hues—accompanied by the most pure and glorious swell of symphony I've ever heard.

It's the sound of angels.

It's the sound of Daire saying good-bye.

Leaving us this one final gift—the snow as her elegy.

Dace

"Where is she?"

I cast about wildly. The words hardly more than a wet gurgled rasp, but I know that he heard me. Know he understood exactly what I asked.

I can feel him beside me.

Inside me.

All around me.

The boundaries between us now blurred.

We're connected like never before.

I gaze upon my freak of a twin, now returned to human form, bearing not a single mark—unlike me and the fountain of blood that continuously sprays from my neck.

Pressing a hand to my wound, hoping to stanch the flow, I gather the strength to say, "What the hell have you done with her?"

While the question doesn't sound quite like it did in my head, the smile that greets me is nothing shy of hideous, telling me he understood every word.

"Little glowing man took her," he says. "My guess is they're headed for the Upperworld. A world you'll never be able to crack.

Or at least not now, anyway. They're a snooty, elitist group. The ultimate country club. They don't welcome our kind. Still, it's not like that stops us from trying. I'm desperate to breach it, and I've no doubt I will. I hear everything sparkles and glows in those parts—that they have a perfect view of everyone else. I'd really love to see that. Maybe someday, *we* can." He shoots me a sardonic look.

I hate his use of *we*.

Hate that it's true.

Hate that I was led by my hate.

Hate is the reason I'm here.

The reason I willfully blackened my soul in an effort to save her—only to watch the whole thing backfire—unable to do anything but watch as the dream played out before me.

And just like the dream—I was too late to save her.

"I love a good irony, don't you?" Cade cocks his head, leans down to pet his ghastly coyote. "Did you see the way she looked at you? Did you see that delicious mixture of shock, revulsion, and grief when she realized what you'd done, what you allowed yourself to become, in an effort to defeat me?"

I stagger forward, my head growing increasingly dizzy, my vision fuzzy and blurry. Fighting like hell to steady myself—to erase the scene he paints in my mind, refusing to remember Daire in that way.

"Not to be rude, but I'm pretty sure it's quick to become my most favorite memory reel. Such tragedy! Such folly!" He throws his head back and laughs, emitting a sound as sick and monstrous as he is. Encouraging Coyote to point his snout in the air and let loose a long, plaintive howl, the racket they make an unwelcome disruption in a land returning to peace. He quiets himself, returning to me when he says, "To watch you purposely become the very thing that you hate, in an utterly foolish, and completely misguided effort to kill me—only to have that same transformation serve as the very thing that keeps you from her . . . It's priceless. Made to order. Too good to be true. I couldn't have dreamed it any better!" He indulges himself in a fit of amusement, before he turns to me and says, "Don't you know—you don't attract what you *want*, brother? You attract what you *are*. Figured someone like you would've known that."

I press my hand to my neck, my fingers coming away slick and red. "You'll pay for this!" I gasp. "I'll make sure of it."

"Doubtful," Cade says. "After all, you're the one bleeding, not me. You're the one who lost his fated one. Time to face reality, brother. Even if she was alive when she left here, she's most likely *dropped her robe* by now. Isn't that how your pal Leftfoot would describe it—a disrobing of the body?" He pauses long enough to smirk and roll his eyes. "Anyway, bro, I've no doubt she's dead on arrival. Next time we'll see her is on the Day of the Dead, when she's forced to pay her respects to the Bone Keeper. And I think we both know Leandro will forgive me well before then. He's always favored me. Has plenty to learn from me, whether he wants to admit it or not. In the end, this is no more than a speed bump—my life remains right on course. While yours, on the other hand, is anything but." He gestures toward my bleeding, wounded neck. "You know that's going to leave a scar, right? Yet another way they'll be able to tell us apart. When you think about it, it's really quite funny—the more you tried to become like me, the more you set yourself apart. If anyone failed tonight, brother, it's *you*."

I allow my eyes to drift closed, relishing the reprieve. But it's only a second later when they're open again, and I'm wiping my bloodied hands over my jeans. Gazing around a world returning to its former beauty, knowing it's Daire's doing.

The legacy she left us.

The least I can do is make sure it continues.

Cade's right.

He's not suffering. Has never known a single moment of it.

I'm the one who lost everything.

Took a risk by gambling my soul—only to lose it along with everything else that meant something to me.

But that doesn't mean I can't turn it around—make things right once again.

That doesn't mean I can't make one last bid at redemption.

I heave a shallow, ragged breath, hoping it'll fortify enough to sustain me. Allow me to do what's most needed.

Then I stare at the spot near Cade's feet—willing it to me, but it seems my magick has abandoned me.

Left with no choice, I make the leap and dive toward him. Watching as he dances out of my reach. Wrongly assuming I'm diving after him.

But I'm not.

Not by a long shot.

There's only one way to make up for what I've done.

Only one way to remedy all the wretchedness and ruin the Richters have wrought.

I reach for Daire's athame—the one Cade used against her, still wet with her blood—and grasp hold of the hilt.

Only one way to end this—and I'm the only one willing to do it.

I raise the blade high, my gaze never once leaving Cade's as I say, "Turns out, you were right all along. We're connected in ways I never would've imagined."

Reveling in the mix of horror and understanding that crosses his face.

Frantically lunging, though the move comes too late.

I've already swung the knife down.

Already jammed it straight into my gut.

The act scored by the sound of Cade screaming—Coyote yelping as though I struck him.

My vision blurred by a great spray of blood.

My blood. Cade's blood. It's one and the same.

Watching as my brother—my twin—the one I entered the

world with, crumples to the ground, as I collapse right beside him.

They say when you die your whole life flashes before you— but all I can see are visions of Daire.

Daire laughing.

Smiling.

Daire lying beside me—cheeks flushed, looking at me with a gaze filled with love.

My fingers curl around the small golden key, as my eyes slide shut, determined to take the images with me.

Cade and I exiting same as we entered—together, yet alone.

The Soul Seeker Series Continues with

mystic

Coming May 2013

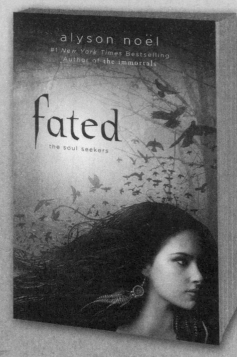

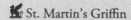